SECRET LOVERS

SECRET LOVERS

Patricia Anne Phillips
Maxine Thompson
Michelle McGriff

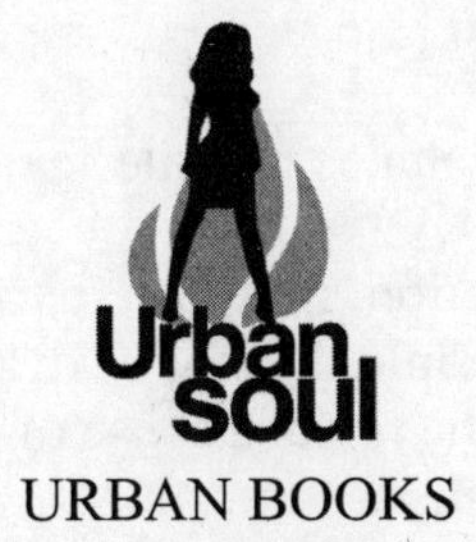

URBAN BOOKS

URBAN SOUL is published by

Urban Books
10 Brennan PL.
Deer Park, NY 11729

ISBN: 978-0-7394-7033-6

Printed in the United States of America

Contents

IRRESISTIBLE FLAMES

Patricia Anne Phillips

1

He was suffocating her.

Kelley lay in bed beside him, listening to the ticking of the small clock and Byron's heavy breathing. From the bed she watched the view of the blue sky and stars that seemed to light up the sky.

She was too hyped to sleep and the insomnia had taken over body and mind.

Kelley gently moved his hand from her bare stomach and tiptoed into the bathroom.

Kelley looked in the middle drawer where Byron kept a supply of shower caps for her. He kept everything she needed, right down to her Dove soap and Victoria's Secret scented lotions. Peach was his favorite.

In spite of all these nice gestures, Kelley was having second thoughts and her mixed feelings about marrying Byron caused her insomnia. She had to be sure that she wasn't making the wrong decision by marrying a man who constantly checked on her every chance he got. He called her as soon as she got to her office and home every evening. He had to know where she ate lunch, and with whom. He didn't want her to do anything without him. Could she really live with him?

Kelley pushed her black, silky mane underneath the shower cap and stepped inside the shower. The hot water began relaxing the muscles down her neck, splashing against her back, and tinkling down her curvy, sable-brown body. She closed her eyes; her body felt free, and the stress was fading.

Kelley opened her eyes. He was standing there waiting. She hadn't meant to wake him, but he was such a light sleeper. She sighed heavily. Now she had to explain why she was leaving so early.

Kelly stepped out of the shower where Byron held a large white towel waiting to dry her back.

"You couldn't sleep, sweetheart?" He took her by the hand as she turned her back to him. "What's on your mind?" he asked. He kissed the back of her neck, the middle of her back, then guided her around to face him. Every time she was nude, her beautiful well-proportioned body stunned him and summoned his sexual desires. He kissed the mole on her right breast, breathing in the scent of the soap.

"This is how I love to look at you, Kelley." His voice had taken on a lustful tone. He took her hand and guided her back to his bed.

Byron laid Kelley on her back and made love to her again. He could never get enough of her. He started slowly, wishing he could keep her there forever. And as always, she was driving him out of his mind. The feel of her soft flesh against him made him lose control.

Kelley felt his body stifen, then relax. As always, she knew that it was over before Byron wanted it to end as he collapsed on top of her.

Bryon looked at the clock on the nightstand, then the window. It was barely daybreak. "Why are you leaving so early, Kelley?" he whispered against her ear, then rolled off her.

Kelley sat up and pushed her hair from her face. Playfully, Byron pushed a lock of her hair against her face and forehead.

"I'm going to look at the apartment complex that Angie and I may buy as investment property. We can't beat the price, and I can't sleep until I see it. We can submit a bid on it today."

"So, it's you and Angie again? Why not the two of us, Kelley? I'm your man and soon to be your husband. A man wants his woman with him."

She whirled around to face him. "You're not my husband yet, Byron."

"I know that. But why would you go with Angie, but not include me?" he snapped back at her and sat up in bed. "A real man wants to do everything with the woman he loves. I include you in every corner of my life. But you include that cousin of yours."

"Yes, she is my cousin, and my business partner. And remember, Byron, we were cousins and partners before I met you. Why do you expect me to change my entire life because we're engaged?" Now she was getting angry and her voice was rising. He always demanded so much of her. She was beginning to think that maybe she couldn't give all he would need in a marriage. And she was tired of reporting her whereabouts every minute of the damn day.

Kelley rose from the bed and slipped into her jeans and sweatshirt, then grabbed her blue flat shoes.

"All I'm saying is why can't we invest together? After all, we're both workmen 'comp attorneys and we are getting married. I do expect for us to become partners. You'll have to learn how to handle a real man, Kelley."

She looked at him in disbelief. Did he really believe that she would terminate her partnership with Angie because she was getting married?

"I can't believe what I just heard, Byron." She ran her fingers through her hair and marched out of his bedroom, grabbing her purse off the dresser on her way out. "I've got to get out of here," she said over her shoulder.

He followed her. "Are you telling me that you have never even considered us going into business together? We're going to be a team, Kelley. That's what marriage is all about."

"No, Byron. Rearranging my life is what you seem to think marriage is all about. I would rather not lose my temper this early. But hear me clearly, I'm not the woman that you should marry. You need someone that you can order around, and know where she is twenty-four-seven. I'm not that woman, Byron, and I don't need to hear you preach about your being a man either. I know what a man is."

As far as Kelley was concerned the conversation was over, and with an outraged toss of her head she stormed toward the front door and slammed it.

Kelley could imagine Byron running behind her, but he was still undressed; the most he'd be able to do was stick his head out the door. If they were married he would realize that she had a mind of her own. She knew that he loved her with all his heart, and she was the only woman he wanted. He had bought her diamonds, expensive clothes, anything she wanted, and he had told her more than once that he loved giving her the best of everything.

She felt a chill when she heard him yell behind her, "Don't forget to call me as soon as you get home, Kelley."

Kelley made a left turn on Lincoln Boulevard onto the Marina Freeway. Once she got to Prairie Boulevard, she made a right on Regent Street, and her car came to a crawl so she wouldn't miss the building. It wasn't daylight yet so she kept her lights on.

The neighborhood was vacant and quiet. As she cruised down each street, she thought of Byron again. He had been good to her, but she wondered, how could she marry him? She wasn't even sure if he would be completely happy with her. Call me when you get to the office, Kelley, or call me when you get home. Who did you have lunch with today? And if she had lunch with a male client, he wanted to know if he flirted with her. It was getting to be overwhelmingly stressful. Would it get worse if she married him? she wondered.

She suddenly hit the brakes. The flutter of movement, and the small thump against her car happened so fast that Kelley blinked hard to see if anything was in front of her car. She was afraid to get out, so she peered out the window, appalled to see an old, brown shoe on a man's foot.

"Oh no," she screamed, hearing her voice reverberate inside her head.

Kelley jumped out of the car and raced around the hood. She saw what appeared to be a bum stretched out on the asphalt. He was unconscious, and his face was bloody. Did she hit him? Because she had been thinking of Byron, she'd hit a man. She wanted to feel for a pulse, but he was so dirty, and she was afraid to touch him. She reached inside her car for her cell and dialed 911.

"Please get the paramedics, and fast. I . . . I think . . . I've killed a man, I mean I don't know if he's dead. Just hurry, he's bleeding, and I'm alone. I don't know what to do," she blurted into the phone.

"Oh God, what a morning," she said to herself. Kelley looked at her watch several times while she paced back and forth in front of her car. She knelt down and took a closer look at the man's face, but couldn't tell what age he was. All she knew was that he could possibly die and she was responsible for it.

Finally, Kelley heard sirens approaching closer; the closer they got the more her adrenaline pumped. She had no inkling of how this had happened. The thump against her car was so slight that she barely felt it. But he was there, and she had hit him.

When Kelley saw the paramedics and the blue and white

Inglewood police squad car, she burst into tears. She ran to the officers before they could get out of the car. The two paramedics went to the injured man.

The paramedics searched the injured man's pants and shirt pockets, but both were empty.

"He has no identification on him," one paramedic said to the officer who stood nearby.

"I didn't see him, Officers. I though that I saw a slight movement and when I got out of the car he was there. I swear I didn't see him," she said loudly, and pointed nervously at the man.

"Miss, have you been drinking any alcohol?" one of the officers asked.

Kelley looked ahead to the other officer, who was speaking to the paramedic about the man's condition.

"No, I haven't had anything to drink. Certainly not this early and I'm insulted that you would ask such a question." Her bottom lip pushed out into a pout.

"Sorry you're insulted so early in the morning. Now, you being insulted or not, I need your driver's license," he demanded, flipping open his pad.

"It's inside my car."

"Okay, then get it, miss."

Kelley sighed heavily and grabbed her purse from the front seat and pulled her license from her wallet. She gave it to the officer, then started moving toward the injured man.

"Please come back here. I'm not finished with you yet. Are you always out before daylight?" he asked. He got inside the car to call and check for outstanding warrants, or unpaid tickets, but Kelley didn't have any.

She took a step back. "No, not this early. I wanted to take a look at an apartment complex to buy as investment property. As a matter of fact, it's only a couple of buildings down. Is he dead? Will he be all right? I've got to know if he's going to live. He hasn't moved since I hit him."

"He's alive, miss. But I don't know for how long," the

paramedic answered. And between you and me, you don't look intoxicated." He gave her a warm smile.

"Thank you."

"Miss, miss, we're not finished. Just tell me what happened," Officer Reid said impatiently. "First, how fast were you driving?"

"Slowly. I don't understand how he could be injured so badly, because I was driving slowly," she repeated. I was trying to see the numbers on the buildings, so I had to drive slowly."

"If you were driving as slow as you claimed, certainly you wouldn't have hurt him so badly."

Kelley started to sob. "I don't know what happened. I just don't understand it."

"We're trying to figure out what happened here. It seems to be a freak accident."

"Well, I'm not under the influence, Officer." Anyone could see by her reflexes that she wasn't inebriated with alcohol, she thought as she tossed her head and looked at the injured man.

"May I ride with the paramedics?" she asked.

"Why, are you hurt?"

"Officer Reid, he has no one else, and I did hit him. Now, why wouldn't I want to go along with him?" The tears were still coming, and she stomped her foot in frustration.

"You're not a relative, but in this case I guess it's okay. But we'll be in touch with you. Miss Wilson, it's not over yet."

He had gotten brusque with her as he looked at his watch. She overheard him tell the other officer that he should have been off duty an hour ago and she had gotten on his nerves.

The other officer helped Kelley into the truck. And she was sturdy and on her feet. It was one of those freak accidents that were inexplicable. Besides, the man was probably hurt before she had hit him.

Both officers watched the paramedics as they drove off.

"You know what I think happened here?" Officer Reid speculated.

"I sure as hell can't figure it out. So tell me what you think," Officer Marshall said.

"Well, she pointed out the building that she wanted to check out, so she probably was driving slowly to see the numbers clearly, which she stated."

Officer Marshall nodded in agreement. "I knew when I first saw him that he was already unconscious, and it wasn't because she had hit him."

"I'm beginning to agree. But we'll have to speak with the doctor tomorrow to see when we can speak to the man. She's a good looker too."

"This may be a good street to buy investment property on. It's past seven and it's still pretty quiet."

2

The ride to Centinela Hospital was fast, wild. Kelley couldn't seem to draw her eyes from the injured man. She watched the paramedic insert an intravenous into his vein and work on him vigorously. He hadn't moved an inch and they were now driving into the emergency parking lot. "Is he still alive?" she asked. But she was nervous and was afraid of what answer she might hear. Had she killed this man?

They jumped out; Kelley was right behind them as they carried the stretcher inside the emergency room. She stood back and watched the lifeless body, his eyes closed, and lips slightly parted. Kelley noticed for the first time that he was wearing only one shoe.

"You'll have to wait in the waiting room, miss. I know you are concerned, but you're not a relative. No one will tell you anything," the paramedic said in a rush.

A nurse came from behind the double doors. "Right this way, gentlemen." She winked her eye and smiled at Kelley. She didn't hear the paramedic tell Kelley that she wasn't a relative, and assumed that Kelley was since she rode with the paramedics.

"Here, take this card. Go home and call me later. I'll check on him and let you know if his condition has changed."

"Thank you so much," Kelley said. She watched as they rushed behind the double doors. The breeze from the forcing doors swept across her face. Kelley sighed and took a seat. It was almost eight; she pulled out her cellular phone to call for a taxi. Then she saw Byron's phone number where he had called. She would return his call later.

She stood in front of the apartment building that she and Angie had decided to buy. The building was painted white and appeared well kept. As she walked to the right side of the building she could see the parking spaces in back. Good, she thought. As soon as she got to the office she and Angie would call the Realtor and submit an offer.

Now standing in front of her car, Kelley looked down the street where the accident took place, and felt the same lump in her throat that was there earlier. She could still see his battered face, his closed eyes, could still hear his labored breathing. "God," she said out loud to herself.

3

Kelley strutted fast inside her two-story town house in the Fox Gate Complex in Culver City. She rushed upstairs to her bedroom and switched on the answering machine, hoping she had gotten word regarding the injured man. As she listened, there was another message from Byron. "Kelley, you should be home by now. You're not at the office, so where are you?" he asked with anger ringing in his voice.

Kelley could picture his face as he spoke. He was probably in his office sitting behind his desk. He had a habit of playing with his thick, black mustache. She was certain that he had slammed the phone down like she had seen him do when he was annoyed or fighting to win a complicated case. Then he would get up and stare out the window, his wide back straight, one hand pushed down into his pocket. He'd hold the phone and pace in front of his desk, giving an occasional glance at the flower shop across the street.

She listened for the message, but there wasn't one regarding the man. Instead of returning Byron's call, Kelley went to the kitchen, got a cup of tea, and sat at the table. She would purposely make him wait, she thought with an angry glint in her eyes and a faint frown across her forehead.

Kelley sipped her tea as she tried to rationalize what had happened that morning. She knew that her own life needed to be thought out as well, but it could wait till later. At the moment the injured man was more urgent.

She was tired of Byron treating her as though she were his own personal property. The doubt she had about marrying him was maturing into a reality. She didn't feel the excitement of a woman about to be married. Instead, all she felt was that marrying Byron would be a life sentence. Sure, he bought her exquisite gifts and flowers. But the novelty had worn off and had been replaced with an overwhelming feeling of imprisonment. She only wanted a man who loved her. She didn't need the expensive gifts, or the trips.

"Shit! Was he dead? I would die if it were me," Angie said, giving Kelley a cup of coffee. "Don't cry, honey." She sat next to Kelley on the brown leather sofa in their office. "Byron called twice after he couldn't get you at home, and now I know why. You had better call him."

Angie started to tease Kelley about calling Byron, but it wasn't the time. Kelley was too upset.

Kelley sipped her coffee and closed her eyes for a few seconds. She had too much work and a time limit on a report that was due in two days; plus she had to leave the office. She was in no position to be too upset with so much work to do.

Kelley and Angie had gone to UCLA, and gone on to be partners as workmen's compensation attorneys. Their small law office was in a brick building located on the corner of Pico and Fairfax Boulevard in Los Angeles.

"Today I have to leave early, Angie, so I can stop by the hospital on my way home. Tomorrow I'll be in Santa Monica all day. Oh, and I agree with the offer on the apartment building."

Angie nodded. "Good. I'll give the Realtor a call." She stood up and went to her desk to answer the phone. She had glowing, ginger-colored skin, high cheekbones, and large dark eyes. "It's time I meet Pamela Hollingsworth in court today. Try and take it easy, Kelley. I'll call you tonight." Angie strolled out the door with her brown briefcase in hand.

Kelley was glad to have this time alone, and pulled out a file from her filing cabinet. The phone rang; knowing it was Byron, Kelley sighed before she answered. "Kelley Wilson."

"Kelley, I called you at home. What took you so long to get to your office? I was worried about you. Are you all right?"

"No, not really. When I went to see the building this morning, I hit a man. I rode with the paramedics to the hospital. This must be the worst day of my life. And he's hurt real bad, Byron," she said hastily.

"See what happened, Kelley? You never listen to me. But no, you had to buy some place with Angie instead of me." Silence fell between them. "Kelley, did you hear me?" he asked impatiently.

Unable to speak, she shuddered angrily, then hissed into the phone, "Yes, and I'm damn sorry to say I did hear you. All I've heard has been about you. A man might die and you're worried about why I didn't drop everything and call you, or why I decided to buy property with Angie. I have work to do and then I'm going back to the hospital. I don't want to talk to you anymore today, Byron." Pissed, she hung up, but as she opened the file, he called back.

"Kelley Wilson," she snapped angrily.

"Why do you feel like you have to go back to the hospital, Kelley? I'm sure he has family for that."

"Because I hit the man," she answered and rolled her eyes up at the ceiling.

"You are still upset, Kelley. I can hear it in your voice. Now, you need to go home and relax before going to the hospital. I'll pick you up by six and drive you. Baby, you've been through enough already."

"No. This is something I have to do. I'll call you when I get home from the hospital."

"A real man helps his woman at a time like this. I'll be

there at six." He hung up before she could protest any further.

Kelley sighed. She finally agreed to go home and wait for Byron to drive her to the hospital.

At precisely six, Byron was ringing Kelley's doorbell. By habit he was always punctual.

Kelley answered on the third ring. "Sorry it took so long. I was on the phone speaking with a client."

"That's why I should have a key to your house. Then I wouldn't have to wait, would I?"

"No, not if you had my door key. But we've gone over this before, right? I'll get my purse." She flounced off to her bedroom and took a red blazer from the closet. She had already changed into a pair of jeans. As she checked herself in the mirror one last time, she looked at her trembling hands. Every time she thought of the injured man she felt a queasiness in her stomach, her hands trembled, and she hadn't been able to eat anything for fear it would all come up. She grabbed her purse and went back to the living room where Byron was wating.

"Come on, honey, don't look so grim," Byron said, and rested his hand on her shoulder as they walked out the door.

"I can't help it, Byron."

Kelley and Byron rode the elevator to the floor that the man was on, and trays of food left over from dinner were still in the hall.

"Why don't you wait in the waiting room until I come back?" Kelley said.

"No, honey. You're much too nervous to go in alone. Now, come on. I'm with you because you need me. You really shouldn't be alone, Kelley." Byron had no intentions of allowing his woman to visit another man without him.

"Okay." She took his hand and started inside the man's room. But they ran into the nurse on duty.

"Miss, he's asleep. Are you a relative?" the nurse asked.

"No, but I was driving the car that hit him this morning. I only wanted to know if there was anything I could do for him. Do you know if the police have found any family members yet?" Kelley asked with concern.

"Miss, the bruises on him weren't caused by a car. As a matter of fact, he was hurt before you found him. So don't worry, he's in good hands now."

"Will he be all right?" Kelley asked.

"I really can't say any more than I already have. When any relatives are contacted they can take care of him." The nurse left Kelley and Byron standing and went back to the nurses' station.

Kelley and Byron looked at each other and walked outside. Once they were at Byron's car he held the door open as Kelley got inside.

"See, baby? You've been through hell for nothing."

Kelley turned to face him. "I wouldn't call inquiring about a man's health nothing, Byron."

"You're just edgy right now, Kelley. You need a good meal and sleep."

Byron stopped at a Mexican restaurant. They ate, but he noticed that Kelley was very quiet and only picked at her food. He reached across the table and touched her hand.

"Kelley, it's all over now. You can relax. The man is alive, and you didn't hurt him. After a good night's sleep, tomorrow you'll feel differently." Byron leaned over and kissed her on the cheek.

"I know. But I just wished that I could have seen him. Now I'm remembering more than I did earlier. If only you would have seen him this morning lying flat on his back, blood dried on his face. I almost collapsed when I jumped out of my car and saw him. And you'd think one of the police officers would have called to tell me that it wasn't my fault.

They're really not handling the case very professionally. Well, like you said, it's over now."

Kelley ate half her food and asked the waitress for a doggy bag. Once they were outside, she closed her eyes and inhaled the fresh air as a soft breeze blew against her face. The day was like she had stepped inside the twilight zone, and was coming back to the real world again. It was an experience that made her want to reassess her own life.

"Now, I'll stay at your place tonight. We can shower together, and I'll rub your back. Baby, you'll be relaxed in no time at all."

All of a sudden she felt her body stiffen. He had already taken her for granted. He hadn't asked if he could stay with her tonight, but had already made plans without consulting her. She listened as he drove.

Kelley sighed. "Not tonight, Byron. I need to be alone."

"Alone? It's over, Kelley. You didn't hurt the bum. I said that I would stay at your place till morning. A beautiful woman like you should be well pampered by her man."

"Byron, I appreciate you, I really do. But tonight, I need to be alone. My fingernails need polishing, my hair needs shampooing. I have all kinds of female chores to do."

In front of the complex, Byron drove to the curb and proceeded to park his car. "No, don't park. I can get out here. You can watch me go inside."

"But, Kelley—"

"I'll call you tomorrow. Good night, Byron." She jumped out, not giving him enough time to answer.

Kelley showered, washed her hair and called Angie. She needed someone to lift the melancholy mood off her shoulders.

"Byron loves you, Kelley. If only I was so lucky. Jeff calls me when he gets good and ready to, and that's only when he wants sex. I'm telling you, Kelley. When the right man comes along, I'm dumping the jerk. But with Byron, you can't go wrong. And that man looks at you with those sexy, brown eyes as though he could eat you."

"I know he's good to me. But he's just so overwhelming and controlling. Does he really look at me that way?" she asked, and smiled with gleaming eyes.

Angie laughed out loud. "Hell yes, he does. Now, go to bed and be in the office early. You can help me with this problem client I have. And he's cute, too, makes a lot of money, and he's single."

"Then I'll be in early. We'll have to find a way for you to get him."

"Good, now you're talking. Get some sleep, Kelley."

Kelley did go to bed and slept for two hours before she woke up screaming from a terrible nightmare. She wiped moisture off her forehead with the back of her hand. Kelley got out of bed and stood on the balcony. She looked off into the night, and then went back to bed again, but the injured man was still too fresh inside her mind. In her dream she hit him so hard that he flew up into the air and landed on top of her car. Blood gushed out on the windshield, but his eyes were still open. He called out her name as though he knew her. And he was conscious when the paramedics arrived. She held him in her arms during the ride to the hospital, and he snuggled closely against her.

Finally at five, Kelley got up and took a hot shower. She had too much to do in her office to try to sleep any later. And even if she did fall asleep, that terrible dream might reoccur.

Kelley walked into the office at precisely seven o' clock. Good, she thought, Angie wasn't there yet. Before she could place her purse inside her desk drawer, the phone rang. "Kelley Wilson," she answered. But before she heard his voice she knew it was Byron. No one else called so early.

"Hi, baby. Why are you in so early this morning?"

Kelley sat behind her desk. "Good morning, Byron. I had too much work along with a nightmare I had of the accident. What time are you going in today?"

"I have to be in court at nine this morning. Why don't you come to my place tonight and I'll throw a couple of steaks on the grill?"

"I can't refuse an offer like that. I'll be there around seven."

"No need to go home, Kelley. I have everything you need at my place."

"Yes, you do. Then I'll see you at six." She hung up, went to the coffeemaker, and brought a filled cup back to her desk.

She had worked vigorously for two hours. At nine, Angie arrived.

"The coffee is strong and from the looks of your red eyes, I think you can use a cup."

With her purse still hanging on her shoulder, Angie filled a tall mug, no cream or sugar. "Want a slice of toast? I don't think my stomach could digest anything else," Angie said.

"Just one slice, thank you. Girl, what did you do last night?" Kelley asked and laughed out loud while she watched Angie place both hands against her temples and ease carefully into the chair behind her desk.

Kelley admired Angie's short boyish haircut that accentuated her high cheekbones. She was five feet six, and weighed 190 pounds, but her curvy hips, full breasts, and lovely face made any man do a double take when she passed. Her weight was distributed evenly in all the right places.

"I went out with Greg last night. He was so nice, Kelley. We had champagne, a nice dinner, and more champagne. That cheap jerk that I've been dating for the past year and a half is getting to be a waste of my time. I want a man like Byron, a man who loves the ground I walk on. If only he had a brother. I bet because you had gotten upset, he's going to buy you a piece of jewelry that will make a woman's mouth water. And, girl, if I were you, I would flaunt it everywhere."

"Expensive gifts are not the only reason I'm with Byron. I love him, and that's what's important to me, Angie. We can accomplish the material things later, together. Don't you want a man who loves you?" Kelley asked, and closed the file she was working on.

"Yes, I want a man who loves me *and* can give me gifts—expensive gifts. Our fathers gave us everything we needed, and we're both used to nice things. I don't want a man who is broke, no decent job, and a measly paycheck. I mean, look at Byron. He has his law office, makes a lot of money. He's going to buy you a big beautiful home when you two get married. By the way, what's keeping you from giving him a date, why are you holding back, Kelley?" she inquired.

"I'm not exactly holding back, as you call it. I'm just trying to think of the right time, and our workload is heavy right now."

"It's been heavy before. And Brenda knows what to do. She's too damn dumb to pass the bar examination, but she knows her job. So don't use workload as an excuse. I think you're afraid to give him a date," Angie challenged.

"What?" Kelley's mouth dropped open. "That is so not true."

"You think about it, Kelley. Byron is a good-looking, dark-skinned man, and other women admire him. But it's you he loves. Now, I better turn this chair around and do some work."

A week ago Kelly had delivered a report to a doctor's office in west Los Angeles and the doctor was six months pregnant. She seemed so happy about starting a family. Kelley knew that Byron wanted a child, and so did she.

Angie turned around and looked at her. "What are you thinking of, Kelley? You were smiling."

"I was thinking about having babies. Angie, are you going to have a baby when you get married? You know that one of us could have twins since our fathers are twins."

"Is that what you're afraid of? So that's why you haven't

given poor Byron an answer? Sure, I'll have a child right away, but my husband will have to have some money. If he leaves me, honey, I'll still have money coming in. But I only want one child."

"What about Greg?" Kelley asked. "Is he the man you want to marry?"

"Yes. He has everything I want in a man. A nice house, money, and he's good looking and smart. I do want to marry him, Kelly."

"And what if you have twins?"

"I'll have a baby, or twins, what's meant to be will be."

That day Kelley and Angie had lunch delivered. They went over their files together, discussing the different cases and court dates. At six, they were wiped out and called it a day.

Angie planned to go home and have Greg over for dinner and make love till morning. If she was lucky, she would get pregnant.

"I've been waiting for you, baby," Byron said softly against her ear. He kissed her hard and circled his arms around her waist.

"I stopped at the post office to drop off some mail," she whispered between kisses. "That's why I'm late." She smiled and kissed his square chin.

Byron led Kelley to the sofa and pulled her down to his lap. He cupped her face with both hands. "Your skin is so soft, and your lips are sweet. I love you so much, Kelley. I can't keep my mind off you."

Kelley felt a familiar tremor deep in her heart. She responded with a low moan as she felt one hand leave her face and ease into her blouse, gently touching and bringing her right nipple alive. In a matter of seconds his warm mouth had covered it and aroused her even more.

Byron had to have her. "Dinner now or later?" he whispered, his voice smothered with passion.

"Later." The stress that Kelley had felt disappeared as though it were never there. The passion she was feeling had overpowered all the doubts she had about marrying Byron.

They had made it to Byron's bedroom and undressed in a matter of seconds. In the center of his bed, his long, hard body on top of hers, and her legs circled around him, she lifted herself as he pushed deeply inside her.

Kelley climbed on top of him so she could see his face while lifting her hips. The rolling sensations were pushing her, making her twist and arch her back.

She moved faster, her elbows resting above his head, and her body lowered so he could stay deep inside her.

It was a beautiful picture, and a beautiful moment that neither of them would ever forget, or get enough of. She moaned loudly as her head jerked back, her eyes were dazed, and as she relaxed on top of him she gave him a lazy smile and rested her head on his chest.

"You were wonderful, baby. I feel as though I have so much more than any other man does. With you I have it all."

Kelley rolled over beside him, her breathing labored. She closed her eyes and felt him kiss her lips and face; she felt his warm, full lips nibbling at her neck.

An hour had passed before they got out of bed and showered together.

In the kitchen, Kelley tossed the salad while Byron placed the steaks on the grill. She was dressed in her blue bathrobe that Byron had bought for her the week before. In his closet, she had a red one, a white one, and now a blue one with slippers to match, but Kelley preferred walking without shoes to feel the soft, plush carpet beneath her feet. Byron was a good man. If only he were able to compromise and understand that she wasn't his mother. He needed to realize that being a man didn't mean being exceedingly possessive.

Kelley started to think back to the conversation she and Byron had had on their first date. He had appreciated the women he'd dated in his life. And all he expected in return was to know where his woman was every minute of the day, and wanted her to be at his apartment when he needed her, make love when he needed it, and forget the life she had before him. Kelley was too smart and independent to agree with him.

There were times when he wanted to be with her and she had other plans. Several times, she reminded him that she had her life, and he had his. Which was not acceptable from the woman he was going to marry.

As far as Kelley was concerned, to tame her would be a challenge and possibly the hardest of all for Byron. She was certain that if she married him, there would be no compromises. She would have to leave Angie and go into business with him. They would buy out Kelley's share in the properties that she and Angie had purchased together, and he and Kelley would buy new ones. Byron was dictatorial enough to plan their lives from year to year. He was joking with her one day and said the first year of their marriage, she would get pregnant and stay home with their child for two years before going back to the office. They would represent the same clients. Representing male clients on her own would be over. And in return, he would give Kelley whatever she wanted, and needed.

There would be no more use of condoms when they made love. If she got pregnant more than once, that was good, too. After all, his mother had eight children and abided by his father's wishes. Was Byron really joking? Lately she wondered. There were times when Kelley wasn't so sure he was. But she had better find out before she agreed on a date to marry him.

"The salad is ready, honey," Kelley said. "You looked as though you were thinking of something deep."

"I was, Kelley. When are we getting married?"

The knife in her hand fell to the counter. "What?" she sputtered.

Walking to the refrigerator, Byron brushed past her and

gave her a quick kiss on the cheek. He took the champagne out and reached into the cabinet for two glasses.

"Why do you act so shocked? We are getting married, you know? All we need is a date, a month, year, give me something, Kelley."

She inhaled; the grilling steaks permeated the air. She frowned and shot him a dubious glance. "You're pushing me against the wall, Byron. And we're together practically all the time now. What's the hurry?"

"I don't mean to push you, Kelley. But we've been dating for one year and two months. We know everything there is to know about each other. Why not get married?"

She loved him, she really did, and she knew that he loved her. No man had ever loved her so much. Maybe she should consider a date to marry him. But she and Angie had too many cases for her to leave the office for a honeymoon. She needed more time. Neither Brenda no anyone else could step in and pick up where she would leave off until some of her cases were closed. Workmen's compensation was cutting back and she had to close some of her cases before the end of the year.

"Okay, just give me a little more time, Byron. It's September, and I need to wait at least three months before we can set a date. That will give me time to close my cases."

He gave Kelley a quick kiss on her forehead as she filled their glasses. "We have so much to do, sweetheart. But I can wait three more months." He had never shared such closeness with any woman before he met Kelley. They had made love and now were preparing dinner together as though they were already man and wife. He looked at her standing in her short bathrobe and wondered if she was wearing anything underneath. "Now, the steaks are ready and I'm starving."

After dinner, Kelley helped Byron clean the kitchen. By ten-thirty they were in bed.

Kelley fell asleep as soon as her head hit the pillow.

4

The next day Kelley left Santa Monica workmen's compensation court at five. She had a splitting headache and went straight home.

Once home, as usual, she played her messages. The first was from Angie. The next was from the nurse at the hospital where the injured man was admitted. He had been moved to a room and could receive visitors. His name was Jonus Tate, which had a nice ring to it. Kelley's day wasn't so bad after all, she thought.

She changed into a white bathrobe and went into the kitchen to grab a bag of potato chips on her way to her home office. She took a seat behind the desk and dialed Angie's home phone number.

"Did you get an appeal for the Richardson case?" Angie asked.

"I sure did, and I had to fight for it. I'm tired and my head was pounding when I first got home." She paused momentarily. "Angie, on my way to the office tomorrow I'm going to see him, so I'll be a little late."

"See who, Kelley?"

"Jonus Tate," Kelley said. She liked saying his name. A name like Jonus Tate went with a professional man who came from a well-to-do family. His name was a classic. But she was certain that Jonus was a blue-collar worker if he had a job at all.

"Why are you going, Kelley? You didn't hurt him and besides, you're never going to see him again, and, honey, I know you're not going to tell Byron. That fool would explode through the rooftop if he knew."

"No. He doesn't need to know. But I have to, Angie. I guess once I see that he's all right, I'll feel the entire bloodcurdling ordeal is over. But it's been hell for the last few days and I think of him constantly."

"Well, maybe you need to see him if it'll help you move on."

"It will. It would help if I could close my eyes and not see him on the ground in front of me." Kelley held her head back against the tall high-back chair and closed her eyes, but because she was talking to Angie he wasn't there like when she was alone.

"Will Brenda be in tomorrow?" Angie asked.

"Yes. Today was the last day of her vacation. Do you have a date tonight with Greg?"

"No. I have another date with him tomorrow night. We'll be going to dinner and a movie. He wants to get to know me. And I can't wait. Girl, I'm going to show him what it's like to handle a real woman in bed. I'm doing all I can to get the man to marry me."

"Good. I hope he's the one for you. Now I have to work on the Miller case tonight."

"Okay. I brought some work home, too. See you tomorrow."

After Kelley hung up she went to the kitchen and grabbed a can of apple juice from the refrigerator. She worked until ten that night. Looking at the clock on her desk, she knew that Byron would be calling her to say good night. And before she got to her bedroom, the phone rang. She answered. It was Byron.

He was suffocating her.

As Kelley walked down the long hospital halls, she wondered what Jonus would say to her. She sniffed, and frowned. All hospitals had the same smell, medications.

She made a right turn into room 301. Kelley stopped abruptly when she saw a long, muscular leg hanging high in a swing, pillows propped underneath a head of curly brown hair, and light brown eyes that focused on her face. His sandy brown skin looked healthy, but his cheeks were gaunt. And as she took a step closer, she saw that his hospital gown was open at the top, revealing a hairy chest that beckoned her to come forward, pulling at her like a magnet.

Kelley stood at his bedside as he stared up at her. He raised one hand and motioned for her to sit in the chair next to the bed.

"I'm Kelley Wilson, the woman who hit you . . . I mean found you. It's good to see your eyes open." She wanted to say more, but those eyes were cold and unyielding.

"It's nice to open them again. And it's nice of you to come and see me, Miss Wilson." The large diamond on her finger, the Gucci purse on her lap, and the $350 dollar navy blue suit did not go unnoticed. Mesmerized, he couldn't take his eyes off her.

"You left the nurse your name. Is it Miss Wilson, or Mrs.?"

"It's Miss Wilson, for now," she answered.

"Oh, well, in that case I should say congratulations. When is the big day?"

She just looked at him. Then she saw him frown as he moved.

"Are you in very much pain, Jonus?"

"Yes, you can say that. I've got four broken ribs that hurt like hell when I move, not to mention the blow in back of my head and the kicks against my spine."

Kelley grimaced at the thought of the pain he must be experiencing.

"Now, what was it that you wanted, Miss Wilson? You haven't anything to do with harming me. And if it's your auto insurance you're worried about, don't be. It was never reported as an accident on your part." He moved again, and again he frowned and cursed under his breath.

Kelley was astounded, and appalled by his dry tone of voice. And she had been so concerned about him. "I'm sorry to have bothered you, Mr. Tate. But rest assured I won't worry about you any longer," she said and stood up.

"And rest assured, Miss Wilson, that you have no reason to." He turned his back to her and the pain in his ribs penetrated through his body.

Kelley stormed out of his room and ran into the nurse who had called her house.

"I take it you've found out what a pretty disposition our patient has. But don't take it personally, because he's the same with all of us."

Kelley nodded. "Thanks for your help. I really needed to see that he was all right."

"And many thanks to you for the beautiful flower arrangement. It was nice of you to send me flowers."

"That was the least that I could do," Kelley said. She watched the tall, redheaded nurse walk away and disappear down the hall.

As Kelley walked out of the hospital she shook her head in dismay. "Egocentric, conceited fool," she whispered to herself, then got inside her car. She stared ahead. "What just happened back there?" she whispered and sped off.

Her cell phone rang. She knew that it was Byron but didn't bother to answer. He could wait until she got to the office.

"Hi, Kelley." Brenda beamed.

"Hi, girl. Good to see you back."

"How did it go and do you feel better?" Angie asked. She turned around in her chair to face Kelley.

"To tell you the truth, I don't know how it went. He was a complete jerk. And to think of the sleep I lost because of him. Do you know what he said to me?"

"No, but we're all ears," Angie said anxiously.

"He said if I'm concerned about my auto insurance, not to be since I didn't harm him. Then he turned his back on me as though I was excused. Can you believe that? I don't like him at all." Kelley stood with both hands on her hips.

"Well, you're rid of that problem and got another one. Brenda didn't know that you hadn't told Byron where you were going. So now he knows. He's called about three times already since he found out."

"You know what?"

"What?" Angie and Brenda asked in unison.

"I'm angry so he better not push the wrong button when he calls back," she said, and slammed the drawer at her desk. "Stupid, stupid," she bellowed.

"Well. I guess that went well," Angie said, and turned her back to continue her work.

Brenda went to the coffeemaker and placed a cup of coffee in front of Kelley. "Drink this. It's a new flavor."

5

Kelley held the phone to her ear, and straightened the picture on the wall with her free hand. She could hear Byron tapping an ink pen against his desk as he talked.

"I can't believe you were late this morning because you had to see some deadbeat loser. And I guess you conveniently forgot to mention it when I called last night."

"No, Byron. I didn't forget. This was my decision and mine alone," Kelley answered, and unconsciously ran her fingers through her hair.

"You know what, Kelley?"

She sucked her teeth before answering. "What, Byron?"

"Maybe you're not ready for marriage. And now that I'm thinking of it, maybe you're not the woman I thought you were." He pushed his chair hard away from the desk and paced in front of the large bay window looking at the view directly across the street.

"And you know what, Byron? I agree with you. Maybe I'm not the woman you should marry. Maybe we need to spend some time apart. You expect too much of me and take too much for granted. Nothing is enough for you and you want more than I can give." She paced in the small kitchen as she waited for his response, but silence lingered in the air.

Byron felt his heart sinking. She did not give him the response he'd expected.

He sat slowly behind his desk, rubbed one hand across his forehead. "Hold on, Kelley. I didn't mean that, honey. We're both speaking out of anger." He held the phone and waited. "Kelley, are you there, baby? Maybe we should talk tonight. I just don't want you to feel obligated to a stranger you shouldn't even be around."

"Believe me, there is no chance of that." She had stopped pacing and took a seat at the table sipping the coffee that Brenda had given her.

"Well, why don't I come to your place tonight? I don't like it when we fight, even though fighting is good sometimes. Let me come over so we can kiss and make up."

"Okay, Byron," Kelley answered, trying to calm down. "I'll be home by four."

"See you at four." He placed the phone down. Of all the women he'd dated in the past, Kelley was the only one who aroused him over the phone. He had to have her every time they were together, and when they were apart, Byron could only wonder what she was doing. He would have to marry her soon. Byron had seen the way other men looked at Kelley with passion in their eyes. He would be her husband; she would depend on him for *everything*. . . .

He walked in with a bouquet of flowers. Byron gathered Kelley in his arms and kissed her passionately.

"They're beautiful, Byron." She left him standing and ambled to the kitchen for a vase and placed the flowers in water. When she went back to the living room, Byron had taken a seat on the sofa and was watching the four o'clock news.

Kelley took a seat next to him. "Any good news?"

"A gang member shot another young kid, another American was killed in Iran, and the prices of homes are increasing. There is no good news, baby."

"I have to agree." She moved closer to him and unbuttoned the top of his shirt.

Byron gently placed her hand against his lips. "I think that we should spend a weekend away together. We can take a Friday off and leave early that morning. How about Vegas, or Santa Barbara? Any place you want to go, baby."

Kelley was silent for a few moments. "It all sounds good, but Brenda just got back from her vacation. And I have court dates. You know how well you have to go through the cases to make sure that everything is up to date. Shouldn't we wait until our honeymoon? We'll be away for two to three weeks."

"So, you're still going to marry me?" he teased, his set features relaxing into a smile.

"So far I am."

Byron looked at the T-shirt that she was wearing. Kelley didn't wear a bra when she was home, and her protruding nipples were driving him crazy. They were never angry for very long. All he had to do was see her, touch her, and the anger would just seem to disappear to be replaced with an irresistible urge to have her nude, hot, and under him.

Her hand touched his thigh; she felt how much he wanted her and their desires were entirely mutual.

Jonus Tate hobbled to the window and stared out at the star-filled night. His broken ribs caused him to lean clumsily against the wall for support. His back was tired and stiff from lying in bed day and night. To make matters worse, he couldn't sleep, and it was all because of a woman who was engaged to be married to another man. *Kelley Wilson.*

Kelley Wilson, with all that beautiful, black hair that shone against the rays of the sun, the corners of her red lips turning up into a delicate smile. She was apprehensive when she walked into his room for the first time, and perched on the edge of the chair adjusting her skirt to her knees. Now she might never return again.

Remembering the suit she wore and the diamond on her finger, he thought she had expensive taste, what men called high-maintenance.

Back in his bed, Jonus held the white piece of paper with Kelley's phone number scribbled across it. He'd gotten it from the young redheaded nurse who had immediately developed a crush on him. She informed Kelley that he could have visitors. She graciously handed Kelley's phone number over to him. Maybe he should call and apologize for his rude behavior. Maybe she would even empathize with him and come back to visit again.

So what if she found him dressed in cheap, dirty clothing? And from the looks of her diamond ring and the delicate white pearls around that pretty neck of hers, her fiancé had money. Jonus looked straight ahead and smiled as he envisioned her freshly in his mind.

When Jonus wanted a woman as much as he wanted to get to know Kelley, extravagant or not, he'd at least try. He could charm the pants off women with or without money. He loved them all. But this one was special. This one he had to have. *Kelley Wilson.* Her name caressed his tongue as he said it out loud.

Kelley was driving on the freeway when the phone rang. "Shit, with the traffic and now the phone, will I ever get to the beauty salon?" she said and answered on the third ring.

For a moment Kelley was sure that her heart had stopped beating. It couldn't be him.

"Kelley Wilson, Jonus Tate here. I called to apologize for my contemptible disposition. You were concerned about me and there is no excuse for my behavior."

There was silence on the other end; he had totally surprised her.

"Mr. Tate. You didn't have to call me," she answered brusquely with an arch of a brow.

"Call me Jonus. I know that I didn't have to call you. But you cared enough to come. I thank you for that." He waited for her to speak.

Kelley hit the brakes to prevent banging the car in front of her. "Actually, I'm glad you called me, Jonus. And I accept your apology."

"Good. Now if we can meet again I promise I can be a nice guy. Would you please come to see me again?"

"Yes, sure. I can visit you Sunday evening." *Oh God, did I say that? Did I just agree to see him again? He's a complete stranger and Byron's temper will blow up in flames.* But she didn't have to tell him, and she couldn't take back what she'd already agreed to. So Sunday evening, she'd have to visit Jonus.

"It'll be nice to see you again, Kelley. Is it all right to call you Kelley?"

"Sure, please do. Kelley is fine. I'll see you Sunday evening, Jonus."

She hung up and sighed heavily. Why was she so compelled to see this stranger?

As she was driving, she tried to forget the conversation she'd just had with Jonus, but it kept creeping back into her mind. His voice was as smooth as the music she was listening to. She envisioned him in bed with bandages still wrapped around his ribs and the brown hair exposed across his chest.

Her cell phone rang and she grabbed it with one hand.

"Hi, baby, are you on your way home?" Byron asked.

"No, I'm on my way to the beauty salon."

"Maybe tomorrow evening we could go out for dinner. I saw a new jazz club in Manhattan Beach. We could go there and back to my place."

Kelley smiled. "Okay, but I'll be in Chino Hills at my book club meeting. I won't be home before six." She heard Byron sigh through the phone. What now? she wondered.

"Baby, can't you cancel so we can get an early start? Gee, Kelley, you can go to your book club meeting anytime."

"I missed last month because you wanted to see a movie. I can't miss this time, and I selected the book for this month, Byron," she said firmly. Nothing was ever enough for Byron, and it was weighing her down.

"Okay, okay, I'll be there at seven."

She hung up and placed the cell phone on the passenger seat.

And at precisely seven, Byron was there. But as he brushed past Kelley, she glanced up at him and saw the anger in his eyes. "If it's too late, Byron, we can go another time."

Byron took a seat on the sofa. "It's all right, Kelley. But book clubs don't make much sense to me."

"They do to me," she snapped. Before going to her bedroom to get her purse, Kelley held her breath and counted to ten.

6

It was a sunny Sunday evening. After her shower, she looked inside her closet and grabbed a pair of tan slacks and matching blouse. Kelley looked at her reflection in the mirror that hung on the closet door and pulled the pins from her hair.

"Why am I doing this?" she whispered. "Why do I even care? I didn't even hit the man, and yet I'm going for a second time to see him." And Jonus was so good looking, and sexy enough to get a woman in trouble. But she wasn't that woman, and she wasn't worried about his charm that probably worked on other women. No, she wasn't the woman who was looking for a man to hook up with. She was a strong, independent woman with a man who loved her. Now, the pertinent question was, did she love him enough to marry him?

Kelley applied her makeup flawlessly, shook her hair loose, and sashayed out of her apartment. She felt an airy chill and looked up at the sky. Rain hovered over her head despite the sunshine.

* * *

As Kelley walked down the hospital halls, she felt a jarring inside.

He was asleep when she walked inside his room. An open book in his hand, the hair exposed on his sable-brown chest and his lips slightly parted. She felt her heart hammering against her chest. He was still asleep. Maybe it was just as well; she didn't belong there anyway. As she took two steps backward, her body jerked from the sound of his rich, tantalizing voice.

"You're not leaving so soon, are you?"

"I didn't want to wake you so I thought it would be best to come another time." Kelley sat in the chair next to his bed and hung her purse on the back of it.

"Let's start over, we'll meet for the first time." He extended his hand. "My name is Jonus Tate."

Kelley smiled and extended her hand. "Kelley Wilson. Nice to meet you, Jonus."

"You too. And you have beautiful hands, Kelley."

"Thanks," she said, feeling foolish for blushing. "Are you in very much pain?"

"Yes. The doctors are concerned with the dizziness. When I try and walk I get dizzy enough to collapse. That can be dangerous. But I'm ready to go home and eat some real food."

Kelley nodded and crossed her legs. "Do you have family here in L.A?"

"Only an aunt. She was my mother's only sister. My mother and father are deceased, and my aunt raised me. She's a good woman." He moved around and groaned. "Broken ribs are painful."

"I can only imagine," Kelley answered. "You were out very early the morning I found you."

"Yes, but only because it's where I was attacked. I went to see an old school buddy of mine. Two men caught me outside late the night before, and you know the rest. My friend just left me an hour ago. And what were you doing out so early?" He watched her pearly white teeth as she smiled.

"My cousin and I are in business together. I was going to take a look at an apartment building that we're buying. I wouldn't have gotten out of the car, but I saw a slight movement in front of it. When I did get out to look, you were lying there. I thought that I had hit you. It was the worst day of my life."

"Well, thanks for getting out. I needed the medical attention badly."

Their eyes locked as they looked at each other in utter stillness.

When Kelley looked at her watch again, she saw they had laughed and talked for two hours. Kelley told him about her childhood and work, but to prevent herself from feeling guilty, she kept Byron's name out of their conversation.

Jonus told her about his childhood and his aunt. He managed a small factory downtown but didn't elaborate about his job, and it wasn't clear what he did. Even though he seemed to feel comfortable with her, it was as though he was ashamed to talk about what he did for a living, and didn't mention where he lived. And Kelley didn't push him.

Kelley loved his smile and sense of humor. She could relax with Jonus. There was no stress between them, no demands, and she realized that he made her laugh more than she had in a long time. She even felt giddy inside.

The time had passed faster than she wanted it to. "Well, I better let you get some rest," she said, standing up to leave.

"All I've been doing is resting. When are you coming back, Kelley?" He wasn't smiling as he looked straight into her eyes.

"Coming back?" she asked, as though coming back to see him had never occurred to her.

"We're friends, aren't we? Well, dear, friends see each other in their time of need," Jonus said, and smiled at the astonishment in Kelley's eyes.

She paused before answering, "Yes. I can come back. Can I bring you anything? Magazines, novels?"

"No. Just bring yourself. That's all I need."

All he needs? What does he mean? "You get some rest and take care until I get back." She turned around and started to walk away with the feeling that he was watching her back.

"When?"

Kelley swirled around on her heel. "When?"

"Yes. When are you coming back?" he asked with a teasing glint in his eyes.

"What about Tuesday?"

"Tuesday is good."

What was this man trying to prove? But as she looked at him he didn't look as though he was joking; instead he looked serious. With an air of confidence she ambled out before he could stop her again.

Once Kelley was in the hall, she exhaled. He was beyond handsome or good looking, or fine.

When Kelley got inside her car, she pulled her cell phone out and checked her messages; there weren't any. She headed home.

Unusually quiet, Kelley kept her head down in a file that she was having a problem with, and was still waiting for the AME doctor to send his report.

"Good morning," Brenda said. "How was you guys' weekend?"

"It was okay," Kelley answered. "But I was busy."

"So was I," Angie replied. "I went to a movie Friday evening and to brunch on Sunday."

Brenda nodded, and pushed her fallen French braid off her shoulder. "Kory and I took the girls ice-skating." Brenda watched as Kelley walked slowly across the office. She frowned when she saw Kelley kneel down to the lower drawer as though she was in pain.

"Does your leg hurt, Kelley?" Brenda asked with concern.

"Just a little. But I guess I'm lucky. Some can't walk as well after breaking a leg. Even though it's been a long time I still hate talking about falling out of that tree and breaking my leg. And by the way, it was Angie's idea to climb the tree." She looked at Angie.

Angie nodded in agreement. "Will I have to hear about that damn tree for the rest of my life?"

"That damn tree was high. It's going to hurt every once in a while, especially during the winter months. And you always came up with some spontaneous idea," Kelley argued.

"We were only kids. And you've been quiet all morning, Kelley. What's wrong besides your sore leg?" Angie asked. She got up and filled her cup to the brim with coffee.

Kelley went back to the filing cabinet and frowned again as she attempted to bend over.

"Here, honey, let me put it away for you," Brenda offered.

"I went to see Jonus again." Kelley looked at their faces to see what reaction she would get.

"Who's Jonus?" Brenda asked, pushing a French braid from her face.

"The injured man in the hospital, Brenda," Angie answered.

"I thought you had gone for the last time. Besides, he was rude to you," Angie commented. "Was he as nasty as the last time?"

"No. He was very nice. As a matter of fact, I enjoyed his company."

Kelley saw Brenda and Angie look at each other. "Look, it's not like I'm sleeping with the man. I went for one visit. I may go back on Tuesday, but I'm not completely sure yet. But it's what I told him."

"Are you crazy, Kelley? What will Byron say when he finds out?" Angie asked.

"She's not married to Byron yet, Angie, and he doesn't

have to know about everything she does," Brenda interjected.

Angie ignored Brenda. "Kelley, you better be careful. You're going to ruin a good thing is all I have to say."

"How can I do that, Angie, as long as Byron doesn't know?" She stared at Angie questionably.

"I guess you have a point there. But he isn't worth it. You said yourself that his clothes were cheap and dirty. Did he even say if he had a job?"

"His clothes were dirty because he was beaten, and yes, he did say that he had a job, but I'm not sure what he does. You seem to forget that I only went to see him, not ask the man to marry me. I didn't ask for his life story either, Angie. Don't I have a right to have a friend to just talk to or be concerned about?"

"You have all that in Byron. And the security he can give you is a bonus. Don't be stupid, Kelley." Angie turned around in her chair and went back to work.

Brenda decided that she didn't want to get in the middle of their disagreement, so she kept silent.

Kelley shook her head irritably at the shrill of the ringing phone. She grasped the receiver up fast. "Kelley Wilson."

"Hi, baby, what's up?" Byron asked. "You sound angry, Kelley. Are you okay?"

"Sure. I'm good. Just very busy, that's all."

"I'll be close to your office around one. Want to meet for lunch?"

"Yes. How about the Chinese restaurant?"

"Good choice. I'll see you at one."

"One it is." Kelley hung up and tapped her ink pen on the top of her desk.

"How was your date with Greg, Angie?" Kelley asked.

"I thought you would never ask." Angie turned her chair around. "Listen to this. We're doing great together. I spent the night at his house last night. It's so big and all it needs is a woman's touch. I want our relationship to work out so badly and I want a child, the whole works. Shit, I'm thirty-six already. He's all I think of."

"Sounds to me like you're already in love with the man," Brenda said.

"And so what if I am?" Angie answered.

"My, aren't we bitchy this morning? You guys say you've had a good weekend, but it sounds like your nerves are on edge." Brenda turned her back and they all worked quietly until it was time for lunch.

Knowing that Byron hated waiting, Kelley rushed inside the restaurant. As usual, he was already there waiting for her. Kelley blinked so she could see clearly. The sun was bright outside, and her eyes had to adjust to the dim lighting.

"Hi, baby," he said and kissed her on the cheek. "You look good enough to be my lunch." He motioned for the waiter to escort them to a table.

"How long have you been here?" Kelley asked.

"About five minutes. But do I complain about you never being on time?"

Kelley stopped as they followed the waiter. "No, because I'm never late enough." She continued walking ahead of him. She wasn't in any mood for his complaints or smart-ass remarks. She looked back at him again as he hunched his shoulders with a confused stare.

After the waiter pulled her chair out and gave them menus, Byron reached across the table to touch Kelley's hand. "I'm sorry, baby, but I was only kidding. Even if you are late the only thing that matters is that you don't stand me up."

"Of course I wouldn't stand you up. And I'm sorry, too. I had no right to jump all over you." She felt uptight. And she had to be perfect for Byron's approval. But it was eating at her nerves. She was tired of being what he wanted, and not being herself.

"Trouble at the office, Kelley?"

"No. Not really. I guess it's just the Monday morning blues."

"Did you miss me not calling you last night?" he asked.

"Yes, as a matter of fact. Where were you?" she asked.

"With my brother-in-law. We went over to his friend's house to watch the game. After we had a couple of beers, I didn't want to call you at ten-thirty. But I almost weakened and called anyway."

"You and your brother-in-law are getting pretty close." Waiting for Byron to respond, Kelley felt her mind floating back to Jonus. It was hard to get him out of her mind. All of a sudden she wanted to know more about him. He was evasive about his life, which made Kelley more inquisitive than ever. Where did he live? She'd forgotten to ask him that. She would make a mental note to ask the next time she saw him.

Byron pulled his hand away from Kelley and cleared his throat. "Warren is my sister's husband. What's wrong with us being close?"

As Kelley looked at Byron's face she could sense the aggravation because his jaw had tightened.

"You don't have to get so edgy about it. It's just that a couple of months ago you didn't mention him at all. Now you speak of him often."

Annoyed, Byron snatched the white cloth napkin off the table and placed it across his lap. "My sister loves seeing me and her husband getting closer. After all, we are family."

Kelley looked at him strangely. Why was he getting so uptight? she wondered. And what had she said? She shrugged unconsciously as he looked away from her.

"Hey, maybe we need to play hooky today. We haven't for some time now."

Kelley laughed. "We just played hooky a month ago, Byron."

"Well, at least I got you to smile for me. And a month ago seems like a long time. I thought we could start today and end it tomorrow." He winked at her.

"What a lovely thought. But today is not a good day for it. Plus it's only Monday. And I have a busy week at the office."

"Okay, okay. Are you coming over tonight?"

"Yes, I am." She looked up and saw the waiter approaching.

The waiter came with their orders of fried rice, egg rolls, chicken, and soup. They ate and Kelley asked his advice for a new client. Byron was a brilliant lawyer.

Holding hands, they walked outside. Byron walked Kelley to her car and stuck his head inside to kiss her. "I guess that will have to last until tonight," he teased.

"Yes. It will have to last." She drove off and watched him standing there until her white BMW was lost in traffic.

It was Tuesday evening, and as promised, Kelley decided to stop at the hospital on her way home. It surprised her how excited she was to see him. Seeing Jonus was like an irresistible force that drove her against her will. Kelley had to know what it was before she could walk away from it. She felt so free and young with him, as if she were on a first date.

Jonus was on the phone when she walked into his room. He beckoned for her to have a seat. But instead, she went to the window that overlooked the visitors' parking lot.

He watched her standing with her back to him. Her shoulders squared, she looked businesslike wearing a black skirt, white blouse, and black and white pumps. Her hair was pulled back tightly at the nape of her neck with a fringe of bangs lying across her forehead, and white pearl earrings dangling at her ears. Jonus could watch her all night. If she were his, he would keep her undressed and in his arms. He hung the phone up and she turned around to face him.

"You look very nice, Kelley. Do you have a jealous fiancé?" he asked teasingly.

"Yes, as a matter of fact." She took a seat in the chair that was always close to his bed. She felt somehow connected to him when she was close, and it felt strange.

"I don't blame the man. I would be jealous, too. And I haven't been jealous behind a woman for quite some time." He would have to be careful with her. He wasn't ready to reveal too much about his past and he didn't want to frighten her away.

"Why would you be jealous?" she asked as though she really didn't understand why. Or would she ever understand men?

He was amazed. She had no idea of the affect she had on him. "I would be jealous because you're so beautiful. Any man in his right mind would be."

Now she was embarrassed. It was odd to hear him say that. To avoid his eyes, Kelley looked over his head.

"Do you want children, Kelley?"

"I would like to have one, at least. And you?"

"One, at least."

"Why haven't you had one, Jonus?"

"Waiting for that special woman, I suppose. I don't want a kid unless I live in the same household. And I wouldn't want my kid to be another black kid without a father."

She saw Jonus trying to prop the pillow behind him, and got up to help. Kelley paused, realizing that she was so close to him, and for a moment their eyes locked. It was like time stopped. She held her breath and prayed for strength that her legs wouldn't buckle under her then and walked back to her chair.

"What do you really want from me, Jonus? I didn't hit you, so what exactly do you want?" Kelley sensed this man was playing some sort of game. But with her, he would never win. She was aware of the games men played.

"To be your friend," he finally answered.

"But you don't know me and surely you must have other friends." She eased her right foot out of her shoe. The shoes were new and her foot felt cramped inside.

I'm in love with you, was what he really wanted to say, but he knew it would frighten her away and he might never see her again. "You even had the nurse call you when I was well enough for visitors. Besides, who wouldn't want me as a friend?" he answered as best he could.

"What are you going to do when you leave the hospital? Who'll take care of you, Jonus?"

"Don't worry about me. I'm learning to get around better. I even walk more during the day and my aunt will be around. Did you want to help take care of me, Kelley?" He watched as she moved uncomfortably in her chair. Jonus smiled. "You don't have to answer right now."

Her expression remained impassive. "I couldn't help you even if I wanted to. You know that I'm engaged to be married."

"Yes, I know you are. I haven't forgotten for a minute. But ask yourself if you're in love with him."

She sat up straight and opened her mouth to speak. But Jonus put one hand up to stop her in midstream.

"Don't answer now. But think long and hard about it, Kelley. He's a man you'll have to spend the rest of your life with. Just make sure you don't make a mistake that you'll regret later. Maybe you do love him, but are you in love with him?"

As Kelley listened he talked logic like an older man, and looked seriously into her eyes. But she couldn't argue with him. He was right about everything. However, she didn't want to admit it. But it was time she did think long and hard before marrying Byron.

He watched the reluctant smile curve her generous mouth. "I'm not one to preach, but if not with me, I still wish you happiness."

Seconds passed, and they were quiet. She kissed him on his cheek and said good night.

She was relieved to walk outside, inhale the air, and think clearly.

He was confusing her.

* * *

The next morning Kelley was the first one in the office. She stopped at Starbucks on Fairfax and Venice Boulevard to buy coffee and muffins.

Kelly arrived at the office first, and sat behind her desk and read a report from her client's doctor, looked at her watch, and closed the file. She thought of the conversation that she'd had with Jonus the day before. Visiting him had given her a lot to think about. After she left she started to pick up the phone to call Byron. It was a time when she really needed him. She needed him to make love to her and make her realize that she was only confused about marrying him. But as it turned out it was the night of his African-American Male Attorneys monthly meeting. After their meeting, the men would eat and play cards. Of all the nights, Kelley needed to hear his voice and have him near. Then, finally, he would convince her to marry him. After all, he loved her. She sighed, and her breath expelled in a rush.

Kelley sipped her coffee as she prepared her workmen's comp case for the judge.

"Good morning," Angie said, and dropped her briefcase on her desk. "This thing is too heavy."

"I bought coffee and muffins. And good morning to you, too," Kelley said.

When Angie came back to her desk she saw Kelley gazing at the folder. "You have to open the folder to do the work, Kelley."

"I know that." But she made no effort to open it.

"Is it Jonus again?" Angie asked and sat behind her desk. She turned her chair around to face Kelley.

"If I was really in love with Byron, would I be seeing Jonus? We're not dating or anything. And he scares me, too, Angie. I don't know this man. He's so self-confident and acts as though he knows me so well when he doesn't."

"He doesn't have anything to offer you, Kelley. I've been thinking about this whole scenario, and maybe you shouldn't see him until you are completely sure about marrying Byron.

And Byron pushes hard. His mind is hell-bent on marrying you. But ask yourself, do you really want to marry him? Are you ready to marry anyone?"

"I do love Byron. Maybe it's cold feet. I don't know what to do about it. But I keep asking myself if I should marry him."

"Good morning," Brenda said. "I'm starving. The muffin looks good on your desk, are there any more?"

"Yes. They're in the kitchen," Kelley said.

"I've never met a man who has to account for every minute of his time. Do you get tired of it, Kelley? I'm not even dating the man and I get tired of his calling," Angie complained. "That overinflated ego of his would drive me crazy."

"I try to tell him but he just keeps on doing it. The only problem is that he expects the same from me."

"How is our sick friend, Kelley?" Brenda asked with interest, taking a large bite out of her blueberry muffin. A blueberry fell from the muffin onto her pink silk blouse, and she jumped.

"He's getting around now, and will go home soon."

"Will you visit him at his house?" Angie asked curiously.

"No. The visits stop when he leaves the hospital. I think going to his house will be carrying our friendship a little too far. I don't want to do anything to lead him on." But she wasn't entirely convinced that she wanted to stop seeing him. She sighed. Her expression flickered with indecision.

"Good idea," Brenda advised.

"Well, if it were me, I would go to his house if I really wanted to," Angie interjected and smiled wickedly. "That should tell you more about him as long as he doesn't live in a rough area," she said, smirking at the idea of Kelley walking into a dump. Kelley was so used to having the best of everything.

"Angie, you change your mind as fast as the weather. First Kelley was wrong for seeing the man at the hospital.

Now you're saying there isn't anything wrong if she went to his house." Brenda shook her head. "I have work to do. You two figure it out."

"But don't you even wonder where he lives?" Angie asked Kelley. "You know we can easily find out."

"I know, but I don't want to sneak around in his personal business. Like I said, the visits end once he leaves the hospital."

Kelley opened the file and read it out loud to Angie.

"Ladies, I have to leave at three today so I can get my hair French-braided," Brenda said.

"We have everything covered, don't we, Kelley?" Angie answered.

"Yes. Everything I need, I can do for myself."

They worked for another hour. Kelley took her cup to the kitchen and returned to her desk. "Angie, you haven't said anything about Greg today."

Angie adjusted her skirt. "He's all right, I suppose. But I can't say it's all good."

Brenda and Kelley looked up at the same time.

"All right? What kind of answer was that, Angie?" Brenda asked.

"Well, first he was all hot and ready for me. Suddenly he's acting distant. Today is Thursday and I haven't seen him since last Sunday night. It's quite obvious that he's not ready to make a commitment. I'm getting tired of dating. I mean, it's just too much pressure. Is he going to call, will he come over, is there someone else? It's just too much drama."

"I'm glad that I'm already married," Brenda said, and began entering a new case into the computer. "I couldn't tolerate the drama that exists in so many lives today. Dating is just too difficult, if you ask me. People lie, pretend, and play with other people's lives, oh, and not to mention selfish."

"You're right, Brenda. You know, maybe he's afraid that he might be falling in love. You two have been seeing a lot of each other lately," Kelley pointed out.

"I don't know what it is. I'm just so tired of men afraid to make commitments. You should get in touch with your feelings about Byron before you marry him. Maybe you should see Jonus more so you won't have any regrets later." She flipped on her computer and opened her file.

"Angie, I'm surprised to hear you say that," Kelley said.

"I agree with Angie," Brenda said. "See him a few more times. Then you won't have to wonder what could have been. I have a feeling that once you're married to Byron, he's going to change. Kelley, he's too controlling and he seems to like it that way. Also, he needs to have more trust in you. He calls so often because he doesn't trust you enough. If you are going to marry him, then you need to discuss his controlling issues, and there's something unsettling about him, too."

"Like what?" Kelley asked.

"Like what's he doing when he's not with you?"

"What are you saying, Brenda?" Kelley asked.

"I don't know yet, but if it were me, I would make excuses to stay away from him for at least two weeks. That will give you some time alone and a chance to sort out your life without Byron pressuring you to marry him. Make out a list of questions that you need answers to before you marry him, Kelley. Pin him down and get the answers you need."

"That's a good point, Brenda. Maybe you guys are right," Kelley said. "Just the idea of it takes a load off my shoulders. I don't know what I can tell Byron for two weeks. Guess I'll tell him that we need some time apart. I still love him, but we do need a break if we are going to make the right decision."

"If he loves you as much as he says, he can wait two weeks," Brenda said.

Angie sat back and smiled. This was getting good. The diamonds, expensive clothes, weekend trips, and vacations. Why Kelley would throw it all away for a man that didn't have anything, Angie didn't understand. She felt the envy seeping in as she looked at Kelley's lovely face, a face with such innocence. Did she even know what she was doing?

7

Byron slammed the phone down hard. What was Kelley doing to him? Hadn't he given her everything a woman wanted? Damn, damn, he loved her. Didn't she know that? All he wanted was to marry her, get her pregnant, and make her happy like a real man was supposed to do for his woman.

Byron went to the kitchen and took a seat at the counter, filled a glass with gin, and took long swallows, feeling the gin tugging at his throat. Tonight he would go to Kelley's apartment and make her change her mind. Moreover, he couldn't imagine not having her in his bed for two weeks.

The doorbell rang and he cursed angrily with clenched teeth and swung the door open.

She stood wearing a short, tight leather skirt with a red low-cut sweater and high-heeled shoes. As he looked at her luscious full lips, all sorts of sexual images rushed through his mind. It was like seeing her for the first time.

"Angie, what are you doing here?"

"First, aren't you going to ask me in? I thought that after what my cousin pulled today you might need some company," she answered and brushed past him. "What a nice place you have, Byron."

Byron sighed, threw both hands up in the air, and closed the door. "I'm drinking a glass of gin, would you like a drink?" He watched her as she perched on the sofa, her short skirt rising halfway up her beautiful brown thighs.

"I'll take whatever you're drinking, Byron." She sucked in her bottom lip, then ran her tongue over it. Her mouth was just as sexy as her body.

As Byron started to walk into the kitchen, he looked back at Angie again. This was weird, really weird, he thought. And it didn't feel right, but what the hell?

He came back to the living room and placed the glass in Angie's hand. "So, is Kelley at home tonight?" He sat next to her.

"Maybe, maybe not," she teased and sipped her gin.

"What does that mean, Angie? Is she at home or not?" Wrinkles creased his forehead as he tried to figure out why Angie was in his apartment.

"I really can't say, Byron. Now, between you and me, I think she's at the hospital. Why she feels such responsibility toward a stranger, I don't know." Over the rim of her glass, she saw Byron's jaw tighten. She smiled with pleasure as he took a long swallow of the gin.

"Oh, but you knew that already, didn't you, Byron?"

"What do you think?" He narrowed his eyes and made an inscrutable comment under his breath.

"Goodness me. I thought you knew already." She placed her glass on the coffee table in front of her.

Angie moved closer to Byron and held his hand. "I'm so sorry, Byron. Please don't mention any of this to Kelley. I was so sure that you two had no secrets."

Two weeks, and she had to work her magic fast. She had to convince him to dump Kelley. Once she got him in bed, it would be all over for Kelley, and then she would wear the diamonds, and go on expensive vacations. His apartment was nice, but once he married her she wanted a large house for their family. If plan A didn't work she always had plan B.

She would have his baby. And she didn't bring any protection to prevent her from getting pregnant. Safe sex was not included in her plan.

"No. Kelley didn't tell me anything. But I should have known." His blood was boiling inside, and he should never have agreed to this two-week bullshit separation.

"I tried to talk some sense into her, Byron, but once Kelley gets something in her head that's it." She looked at the empty glass in his hand.

"Why don't I give you a refill, honey? Looks like you could use one."

"Refill your glass too, Angie. No use getting wasted alone." He leaned forward and rested his elbows on his knees and placed his hands against his forehead. How could he have been so stupid? *This can't be happening to me*, he thought.

Angie was back; instead of going back to her side of the sofa, she slowly stepped over Byron and made sure she faced him.

Byron smiled with hunger in his eyes. Two more drinks, and Angie intended to have him in bed. And when she sat closer to him she saw his eyes linger at her thighs. Angie crossed her legs and her skirt rose even higher than before.

"Kelley is a lucky woman, Byron. You've always been so good to her. But I'm sure she knows it. She always speaks well of you."

He looked at Angie's face. "Does she really? Funny, I can't agree with that right now." Damn, why hadn't he pressured Kelley harder for a wedding date? His second mistake was allowing her to call the shots.

Angie turned to face Byron. She wanted to make sure that he had a full view of her. Whatever it took, she was going to get him. It didn't matter if he wasn't in love with her; she wasn't in love either. But in time he would be. With Byron, she could have her baby and all the luxuries that went along with it. Besides, Kelley had her chance and blew it. So it would be her loss.

She looked at him with admiration and smiled as she thought of herself as his wife. What a nice couple they would be.

"One more drink and I can sleep through the night." He went to refill his glass and talked to Angie from the kitchen. "Maybe you better go light on the gin, Angie. I wouldn't want to see you drink too much and drive."

That wasn't exactly what she wanted to hear, but it would do for now. This was only their first night together.

When Byron came back to the sofa, Angie was waiting. "I hope you're not ready for bed, Byron. I need to wait awhile before I can drive. It was stupid of me to drink so much."

"No problem. You can always sleep in the spare bedroom," he said and stretched his legs out in front of him.

She looked at his white T-shirt fitting tightly against his wide shoulders. His brown shorts stopped right above his knees. "Thanks, Byron. You're a nice man. I just thought you needed someone to talk to tonight. I was in the office when Kelley called you."

"You mean that you heard our conversation?"

"Yes, of course. How would I know that you needed company tonight? I'll tell you what, why don't you pretend that Kelley and I don't know each other very well? Just act as though I'm a good friend and I'm not dating either. I can't stand dating people who turn on and off. It's like going on a roller-coaster ride, dangerous and on the edge."

"We've never sat down alone and talked before, Angie. I think we could become friends, and that's exactly what I need." He smiled for the first time that night.

"Just sitting here talking to you, I've decided not to call Kelley. She can't have it all her way. She's got her two weeks. I'm a man, and I'll show her what a man really is." He held his glass up and Angie picked up hers. "To friendship," Byron said. Their glasses clicked, and both took a drink.

"You're very understanding, Angie. I appreciate it, too." His eyes settled on her breasts. He had never noticed her full breasts or beautiful, brown thighs. He used to think of her as just being overweight. But how did he overlook just how sexy she really was? Kelley was the only woman Byron had really looked at since the first day he met her. Other beautiful women were seen and quickly forgotten.

"Well, it's late, Byron. I don't want to wear my welcome out on my first visit." Angie stood up with her purse in hand. "While you and Kelley won't be seeing each other for a while, maybe we could go to dinner. I really think you need the company, and I know that I do. My boyfriend is thinking the same as Kelley. So we're going through a cold spell together."

They were standing and she moved closer to him. Her breasts was so close to his chest that he had to squeeze both hands into fists to prevent him from touching them and feeling the smooth, soft skin in his hands, then tasting them. He wanted her. She was Kelley's cousin yet he wanted her.

Byron wiped his hand across his forehead and Angie smiled with triumph. She had achieved what she wanted. One more night of consuming too much gin and she would have him.

Angie gave Byron a quick kiss on the cheek and brushed past him slowly to the door. She wanted him to get a full view of what could be his. All he had to do was make the move.

8

"Good morning, Brenda. What time did you get here?" Kelley asked as she walked inside the office and hung her black blazer on a hanger. It was only seven-thirty; Brenda's usual time was nine.

Brenda wrote letters and took care of medium legal aspects in the office since she hadn't passed the bar exam. She studied hard and had gone twice, but both times she had broken out in cold sweats, gotten nervous, and the queasiness in her stomach was unbearable. Now she wasn't entirely sure if she would try again. She lived a simple life. So why complicate it by sweating over a bar exam? Working with her two cousins was fine with Brenda. They paid her well and she did a great job.

"I've got letters to mail out and doctors and insurance companies to call. You know how you're placed on hold when you call the doctor offices. They all have too many workmen's comp patients."

"Yes, I know." Kelley checked her messages and had one from Jonus, but not from Byron. Maybe Byron was really trying to be considerate about giving her the time she needed to sort out her life.

"How's the sick patient?" Brenda asked.

"We had a long conversation over the phone last night. But he's still very evasive about his life. When I met Byron he told me everything on our second date. But of course I already knew that he was a lawyer because we met at the courthouse. But Jonus wants to know everything about me, but says very little about himself. I enjoy talking with him, and I'm impressed with his knowledge and intelligence. You wouldn't believe how much we have in common to talk about."

Brenda turned around to face Kelley. "Listen to him closely, Kelley. He could be setting you up by looking for a woman who can give him the lifestyle that he can't have on his own. You're too good for that. And if you two have so much in common, then he should have some of the same achievements in life. So far he hasn't shown you anything."

"I'm too smart. Believe me, I'm keeping score. And you know what I find peculiar? He's an educated man. I could tell when we were talking. I think there's more to him that I need to know. I need the time to myself."

Brenda gave Kelley a new perspective regarding Jonus's situation. It was possible that he could be looking for a woman to support him. Once he got it would he leave her for someone else?

Kelley knew in her heart that Byron loved her, and if she had a child he would support her. It wasn't Byron's love that she doubted, but what price she would pay for it was what concerned her.

"Byron wants me to give up my life just to marry him. He's always preaching about how he's the man," she said as she pushed her chest out.

"Please don't mention this to Angie. But after we're married, he even wants me to leave Angie and go into business with him. Well, that's if we do get married. He even got angry the day I left his apartment to see the building that Angie and I are buying together. It's as though I'll have to change my entire life if I marry Byron."

"He's a very selfish man, Kelley, and he's taking it too far. He'll take your independence away if you let him. That's precisely what he wants, you know."

"That's why I'm having doubts about marrying him. If I marry Byron he would take care of me. But he has issues. Serious issues.

"With Jonus, it's like, God, it's hard to explain or understand but I'll do my best." She placed one hand under her chin and bit her bottom lip. "It's like reading a romance novel, but you're playing the part in real life. And it's like feeling a delicious sort of fear. And inside you know it's going to happen, and you're anticipating what it is. You can't wait for it to come, but there is nothing that you can do but wait and imagine what it is. Your blood runs hot inside. And, Brenda, when I'm with him, I feel as though he could will me to please him in any way he wants me to. The excitement and waiting are killing me and ripping my insides apart."

Kelley looked at the perplexed expression on Brenda's face, then laughed. "I've never felt that way with Byron or any other man. I have to know what's driving me to him. I keep telling myself to run, but I can't. Mentally, he holds me there with him. And I don't know what it means. My blood is hot for it, and I feel as though my life is on the edge, and will tumble over any minute."

Brenda stared at Kelley with her mouth open, her interest on the brink of overflowing. "That's deep. I mean really deep. Be careful, Kelley. I think it's called lust and love at first sight. I've never heard anyone feel such force or urgency for someone. Girl, I don't know what to say, except, hell, to experience something like that, I wish that you could bottle and sell the stuff. I would buy it at any price. Maybe you should sleep with him. It might take the edge off, or drive you mad," she said, and laughed out loud. "Just teasing, I think."

Kelley laughed, too. "Now this is just between you and

me. I don't want Angie to know. She's too judgmental, and that's not what I need right now."

Brenda got up and peeked out the window. "Here she comes, so let's get to work."

"Good morning, ladies. I see your heads are in your work," Angie said, smiling. She placed her purse inside her desk.

"Boy, you're in a good mood this morning," Kelley said.

"And you are not usually a morning person," Brenda said as she looked over the rim of her new black-framed eyeglasses.

"I know, but I had a good night."

"Are you and Greg all right now?" Kelley asked.

"No. We didn't even talk last night. But I've decided to take it easy and not worry so much about him. If he calls me back soon, well, whatever. For a change I'm going to go after what's good for me. Life's too short to sit around and wait for people while putting your own life on hold. I'm taking my life into my own hands."

"I'm so glad to hear you say that, Angie. That's precisely how I feel," Kelley said. But as she watched Angie, she looked as though she had more to say, but didn't.

"Good, then you understand. Now we have to compare this file with the doctor's report." Angie pulled her chair over to Kelley's desk and opened the file.

"Have you ever thought of going into business on your own, Kelly?"

Kelley and Brenda looked at each other, then back at Angie.

"Why would you ask me that? Of course not, honey." Kelley placed the file flat on her desk. "Don't ever worry about that, Angie. Our relationship is as solid as a rock. Always will be," Kelley assured her. "You know that. We've always done everything together, even as children."

But they were no longer children, Angie was thinking. They were adults, each making a life for herself.

Kelley and Brenda looked at Angie peculiarly as she got up and ambled into the kitchen.

"What was that all about?" Kelley asked.

"Beats the hell out of me," Brenda answered.

"I'm going to my aunt's house tomorrow, and I'll go home in a few days. I wanted to go home tomorrow but she got too upset."

"You two are very close, aren't you?" Kelley asked.

"Yes, I owe her everything. She made me her life when my mom died. I have a lot to be thankful for."

"At least you're aware of it."

"I'm lucky to have met you, too, Kelley. You're like a breath of fresh air every time I lay my eyes on you. I hope we can really get to know each other."

Kelley took a deep breath. "But we do know each other."

"Not the way I want us to." The chair was close to his bed; he reached over and rubbed his hand against Kelley's arm. "I think of you all the time," he murmured, his voice taking on a sober tone. He looked deeply into her eyes, but had no idea what she was thinking.

"I think of you all the time, too, Jonus." Kelley couldn't believe she had just said that to him. Not only did she not know Jonus, she was beginning to think that she didn't know herself very well either. This was a stranger that she was giving her heart to. And day after day, she was blissfully and continuously falling in love.

"Having dinner tonight was a good idea, Byron."

"And having you join me was even better. I haven't spoken with Kelley for three days and it seems strange. I really miss her, Angie. If I hadn't had your company, I would have called her the next day. But you walked in as a friend." Byron placed his glass of wine on the table in front of him.

They were having dinner in a small Italian restaurant in Torrance. It was Kelley's favorite place and Byron took her there often.

Angie had suggested that she meet Byron at his apartment. She rode with him to the restaurant. After dinner, she would have to go back to his place to get her car. And tonight would be her first night with him, in his bed and into his heart.

"How's your love life, Angie? I hope it's better than mine."

"It could be better. We're like two peas in a pod. I guess that's what drifted us together, and I needed the company as much as you did," Angie answered.

"Before I met Kelley I dated a lot. But I stopped all that when I fell in love. We should have been married by now." He looked away and shook his head in dismay. Had he lost Kelley? he wondered, feeling his blood curdling.

"You're a good man, Byron, and you are indeed a man." She remembered Kelley's frequent complaints of how he'd repeat the fact that he was a man.

Byron looked at his watch. "It's getting late and I know that you have to get up early tomorrow morning."

"Yes, it's time we leave. But I've been so upset about Greg that I haven't had a good night's sleep in four days."

"Same here. I wake in the middle of the night thinking of Kelley."

Byron paid the bill and left a five-dollar tip on the table. They walked outside into the night.

"What a beautiful, romantic night it is," Angie said. "Look at how bright the stars are, Byron."

Byron inhaled the fresh air, but his mind was heavily on Kelley. A night like this he would make love to her and hold her in his arms till morning. Just thinking of her, he felt his heart tug inside. And he wasn't certain of what would happen after two weeks.

The ride back to Byron's apartment was quiet. Angie tried to make idle conversation, but since she had mentioned the night was romantic, Byron couldn't seem to block Kelley from his mind.

He drove into the garage. "Would you like to come inside for a glass of wine before you leave?"

"I was hoping you would ask." She followed Byron inside.

Once they were inside, Byron went to the bar and came back to the sofa with two glasses of white wine. He flipped a Baby Face CD into the CD player.

"Oh, so you love Baby Face, too," Angie said. "I never knew that we had so much in common, Byron."

He stood up and held his hand out to her. "Whip Appeal. That's my favorite."

Angie got up and followed him to the center of the living room. He placed his arm around her waist as she stood close and swayed into step with him. God, he felt good and strong, and the wine on his breath smelled sweet. This was what she needed, a good man to be close to and held by. It was time to make her move, and she was sure that he would welcome it happily.

Angie's face was against Byron's cheek. She gently turned her face to see if his eyes were closed. They were open. Seconds passed as their eyes were locked on each other. She felt Byron's hands move lower, circling her butt and drawing her closer. Their lips touched, and she felt his sweet tongue searching the inside of her mouth. Her body went limp against his and her arms circled around his neck.

Only moments passed before they were in Byron's bedroom and in his bed. They were hungry for love as flames ignited around them.

Angie never knew a man could be so sexy while making her feel as though she were the only woman alive. *Kelley,* she thought, *what a fool you are.* Angie was going to enjoy this night, and tomorrow, he would be hers. She would never let him go after tonight.

9

"How was your night?" Brenda asked.

"Jonus and I got a chance to talk more on a serious level and it scared me to death. I feel as though my life is upside down, Brenda. And it's been a week and Byron has really been considerate. I was sure that he would have called me by now." Kelley sipped her coffee and felt a drop on her white blouse. "Gee. Every time I wear white to work I spill something on it. And I have to be in Santa Monica at three today."

"Use cold water on it. Have you noticed how quiet Angie's been lately?" Brenda asked. "She comes in for a while, then leaves. And she's become clandestine with her comings and goings."

"Yes, now that you've mentioned it. Usually, she can't keep her mouth shut for five minutes." Kelley was wiping the coffee stain from her blouse with a wet paper towel. "Now that should do it," she said, and dropped the paper towel into the trash can.

Byron turned over in bed and watched Angie as she slept. He quietly got up and went to shower. As the warm water beat down his back, he thought of the night before. Angie was good, damn good, but what had they done? She would have to understand what they did the night before was caused by loneliness, and too much wine, anger, and confusion. Now look what he had done. He looked up and Angie was easing into the shower with him.

He watched as she stood in front of him. Her breasts were wet, and pushed against him, her hips were curvy, and again, he couldn't control himself. They hungrily made love in the shower. They stepped out and rushed to the bed still wet where they made hot, mind-blowing love for an hour before they came up for air.

Byron rolled off Angie and sat up on the edge of the bed. "What are we going to do about this, Angie? We both know I'm in love with Kelley. You're her cousin, for Pete's sake." He unconsciously rubbed his hand over his head.

Angie felt a stab in the pit of her stomach. Oh no, she thought. He couldn't be saying this to her, after they had just made love. She sat up and rubbed her hand across Byron's back. He moved aside as though he couldn't tolerate being close to her.

"Byron, if she loved you the way you deserve, then I wouldn't be here. But I am here and we're right for each other." She laid her head against his shoulder, circling her hand slowly across his hairy chest.

"You felt the same as I did, Byron. We're so together, baby. We can't even control ourselves around each other anymore. How are you going to be with Kelley again and see me?" Her hand moved slowly toward his thigh; she knew that he wanted her again, and again. They were totally out of control, this time more than before. Her passion catapulted as she felt him moving slowly inside her, making her want more of him.

An hour later they were both dressed. Byron was standing in the middle of the bedroom and turned to face Angie.

"I've got to drive downtown, Angie, I've got to clear my head, alone," he said with a distinct edge to his voice.

Angie went to the living room; he followed. She picked up her purse from the coffee table where it was left the night before. "You think long and hard about it, Byron. Every time you see me you are going to think of last night, and this morning. How can you look into Kelley's eyes knowing what we've done? You know you loved it," she said with a smirk across her face.

She started to the door and stopped. "Oh, one more thing. You didn't wear a condom last night or this morning, and you know why? You couldn't wait to have me. Face it, Byron. I could have your child in me right now." She smiled and stormed out the door.

Byron picked up his briefcase from the coffee table, then slammed it back down. He flopped down on the sofa, his elbows resting on his knees. "I'll be damned," he shouted. He had screwed up big time.

"Oh, so you decided to come to the office, huh?" Brenda asked. "Kelley had to be in Santa Monica."

"I had to take care of some business for my mother this morning," Angie answered and took a seat at her desk between Kelley's and Brenda's.

"Are you sure that you're all right? You women need to find yourselves a husband and settle down. Between you and Kelley's love lives I'm getting dizzy."

"Did Kelley say anything about Byron this morning?" Angie asked curiously.

"No, not a thing. What about you and Greg?"

"I got a message from him this morning, but I haven't returned the call. I don't think I will either."

Brenda looked surprised. Why haven't you, Angie? I'll bet he misses you."

"Yeah, sure. We'll go to bed, and a week later he'll be taking me through changes again. Like I said before, I don't need the drama." Angie sat at her desk. She had better things on her mind, like last night, and this morning. So what did she want with Greg?

Brenda closed the file she was working on. "So much for the Ashford case. Workmen's comp is settling tomorrow. This is the only file left that you and Kelley worked on together. Do you two have another joint case?"

"No. I think that we should start handling cases separately."

"Why separately, Angie?" Brenda turned around to face her again.

"I don't know what's going to happen between Kelley and Byron. But I think it's best they settle their differences before we bring in another case together."

"Okay. But it doesn't make much sense to me. Besides, even if Byron wanted Kelley to go into business with him she would never leave you." Brenda looked at Angie closely. She was up to something, but Brenda couldn't quite figure out what it was. Even as a child Angie was difficult to get along with.

Angie's cell phone rang and she answered. When she heard Byron on the other end she went into the kitchen for privacy.

"Look, Angie. I've been thinking of what happened between us."

"Wasn't it wonderful, Byron?" she asked and smiled at the silence between them. "I knew you would call."

He sighed impatiently. "Look, Angie. What happened was a mistake. We were just two lonely people who needed each other at the time. It was no big deal to me. It can't happen again," he said with honesty and bluntness. "And what was that talk about how I didn't wear a condom? Do you lie up with every man without using some kind of protection?"

He was insulting, and Angie got angry. How could he be so obdurate after they had made love?

"It all happened so fast. Do you sleep with everyone without a condom? Do you even practice safe sex, Byron? It was your responsibility as well as mine. I could be pregnant right now. And what if I am?" She could taste the tears that fell from her eyes, her spirits deflating immediately.

"Then I'll have to give you the money to get it taken care of. No way you can have my baby. I want to be married to the woman who carries my child. And you're not the woman, Angie. I hope I'm making myself clear."

"Crystal clear. But I will never take care of it, Byron. You're not thinking. What if it turns out that Kelley doesn't want you after all? You do want a child, don't you?"

"You just don't get it. You can't want a man who doesn't love you." He shook his head, and his sigh was the epitome of irritation.

"You loved what I did to you, Byron, and you know it. Are you willing to lose me while Kelley may not want you? What do you think she and that cripple are doing? They're not holding hands, Byron. Now, why don't I come over tonight and we can discuss it like two adults?"

"There is nothing to discuss."

"But there is, Byron. You are not thinking with a full deck."

"No, Angie. The first time I slept with you, I wasn't thinking with a full deck. Be there about seven so you can understand once and for all that it's over," he said, hanging up before she could answer. "Why am I seeing her at all?" he murmured out loud.

Angie's hands were trembling. She had been so sure that she had him, but she was wrong, and needed more time. Still, she had tonight to work on him. When she finished, he'd have to have her again, and again . . . he had to.

The woman was tall with a warm smile, and a short, fashionable haircut. The town house was located in Woodland

Hills. As Kelley stepped into the living room she noticed it was very neat and expensively furnished. It was like stepping into a beautiful home magazine.

"You must be Kelley Wilson because my nephew says you are beautiful, and I agree."

Kelley smiled and immediately relaxed. "Thank you. How is Jonus feeling today?"

"Oh, he gets better every day. Nothing can keep that man down. He's been busy ever since he was a boy." Gloria's face softened as she spoke of Jonus.

"Aunt Gloria, is someone at the door?" Jonus yelled from the spare bedroom.

"Yes, Jonus. Kelley is here. Let me take your jacket for you, honey. Would you like some dinner?"

"No, thank you. That's very gracious of you though."

"Well, just go down the hall and make a right at the first door."

Kelley walked into the bedroom. The décor was tan and white. Jonus was sitting up in bed. He looked stronger, and was fully dressed in a pair of khakis and a white T-shirt. He gave Kelley a wide smile as she waltzed in.

"Here, sit next to me, Kelley. The chair is too far."

"The chair is next to your bed, Jonus," Kelley said. But she smiled and gave in to him. As soon as she sat next to him he kissed her on the cheek, then held her right hand against his lips.

"You smell good," he said in a low, husky voice.

"Thank you." Her heart was racing. She was alone with him, and on his bed.

"What's a woman like you doing with someone like me?"

She cleared her throat. "You're a nice guy, Jonus, and you have a good sense of humor. And, and . . ."

She felt his finger against her chin, and then he cupped her face in both hands and kissed her deeply. "You were saying?" he whispered against her ear.

"I forgot." He kissed her again, and this time she placed

her arms around his neck and responded warmly. She felt weak and wanted more. But this was his aunt's home, not hers, or his.

They stopped kissing, but he kept her hand in his, and kept her close to him. Jonus wanted her, but she had to accept him as he was. So many women were deceitful, and greedy. But somehow, he thought Kelley was different. He had to find out soon before he went out of his mind with passion. She was simply irresistible.

"What are you doing the day after tomorrow?" Jonus asked.

"Why?" she asked with an arch of a brow.

"I was wondering if you could drive me home."

Kelley looked at him questionably. Where did he live? Was it a bad neighborhood? She wouldn't dare ask now. "Yes, what time?" she asked.

Jonus smiled as he looked into her eyes. He didn't want to frighten her, and it was better that she came before dark so she could find her way again. That's if she would see him after she took him home.

"What time is good before dark?"

"How about three?" Kelley answered.

"Three's good. Are you still engaged to be married, Kelley?"

Kelley was still sitting next to him with her hand in his. "Shouldn't you have asked me that before you kissed me?"

"No, I shouldn't have. Dear, you're not married yet. Who knows? You might change your mind. Not about being engaged, but being engaged to him."

She gently pulled her hand away. "You're so sure of yourself, aren't you?"

"No, not at all. But the fact is, you aren't married . . . yet." He kissed her again, and this time she sank miserably into his kiss.

Now she knew why she was afraid of him. It was because she was in love without even realizing it. She had never felt the same excitement for anyone.

Oh God, she thought. *What do I do about Byron?*

10

It was six-thirty that evening, and Angie was at Byron's door. She smooth her short, black skirt down and checked the low-cut red sweater. It had to fall off one shoulder to expose her skin. Tonight, she had to convince him that she was the woman for him.

Byron opened the door and stepped aside as Angie brushed past him. She gave him enough space to view her from head to toe.

"Can I get you something to drink? Are you hungry?" He looked at her beautiful legs, and his eyes lingered. He felt the same stirring inside as before. What was it about this woman? He didn't love her, he didn't even want her, except in his bed.

"I'm not hungry for food, Byron, and you're not either." She spoke low, and stepped closer to him. Angie took his hand and led him to his bed. She stood close enough to touch him as she undressed slowly, and seductively, never taking her eyes off his. She beckoned for him to come to her.

Byron knew it was wrong to make love to her again. And he knew that he should have slammed the door on her when she walked in dressed to lull him into bed. She was lying on her back, waiting. He had to have her, just once more; he had to have her.

The next morning Byron woke up first. Angie stirred and kissed him on his back as he perched on the edge of the bed.

"This has got to stop here and now, Angie. I mean no more." He felt guilty, unable to look into her eyes. "We won't see each other again."

Angie sat up quickly. "I can't believe what I'm hearing. We made love all night, and this morning your mind is still on Kelley? What kind of man are you . . .?"

Byron swiftly spun around. "Don't you ever question my manhood," he said as his jaw tightened. His eyes had gotten wide as he stared angrily at her.

For a fraction of a second Angie was sure that he would strike her. She moved aside to get more space between them, and jumped up quickly to begin dressing. "Look, I didn't mean it the way it slipped out of my mouth. But do you really think that Kelley would have you after you've cheated on her?"

"And how would she know?"

"She is not stupid, Byron. You can't marry her knowing what we've done. And she's my cousin, too. It wouldn't be right if I didn't tell her that she was marrying a man who slept with her cousin." She closed her eyes and willed herself to stay calm.

"Oh, so all of a sudden you're worried about what's right or wrong. Look, I gave you what you came for. I'm warning you, Angie. You better not tell Kelley anything. I've told you repeatedly that I love her."

Angie was standing in front of him and her strategy was falling into pieces. "Byron, when you made love to me a second time, I was sure that you wanted to marry me. How could you do such a terrible thing?" She placed both hands to her face and began crying.

"You are sick as hell. I should have known you were creeping up to more than just the sex. Surely you didn't think that I would marry you. I was under the impression that you knew it was only sex and fun, not a relationship." Angry and unable to look at her any longer, he turned his back and stormed out of the bedroom.

Angie followed, and stopped behind him. "While I still like you, don't say something that you will regret later, baby." She stepped in front of him and placed her arms around his neck, but Byron grabbed both hands and pushed her away.

"Not this time, it's over."

With long strides he went straight to the door. "I want you to leave now." He opened the door wide. "I'm going to call Kelley and tell her everything."

"She doesn't want you now and she won't want you after you tell her. Besides, you forgot to use a condom again, honey. Maybe you do want me to have a baby." She waltzed to the door, turned around to face him again, smiled, and flounced away.

11

Jonus limped to the door at the sound of the ringing doorbell. His face lit up; he grabbed Kelley and gathered her into his arms. "You look sensational, Kelley. I'd gotten used to seeing you in suits. He held her at arm's length to get a full view of her purple jeans, matching sweater, and white Reeboks.

"You're such a charmer, Jonus," Gloria said as she walked in and admired the young couple. "I wish you would stay here longer so I could keep an eye on you. I know you haven't everything that is needed at your place."

Kelley looked from Gloria and back at Jonus. Could the man afford to purchase what was needed while he was recovering? But she would not agonize over it now. She would wait until she took him home.

"One would think that my nephew would take care of himself as well—"

Jonus quickly intervened before Gloria could continue. "Don't worry about me." He kissed Gloria on her cheek as he limped past her.

Gloria stood in the door and watched as Kelley helped Jonus inside the car. "I think she is the woman that will tie

Jonus down and marry him," she whispered to herself while closing the door.

"Take the Hollywood Freeway to Burbank Boulevard and I'll give you directions from there," Jonus instructed, and fastened his seat belt. He wanted to laugh as he saw the perplexity on Kelley's face. She had to know about him today if they had any future at all. *Would she come this far and walk out on him once she saw where he lived?*

Jonus watched as the wind blew through Kelley's hair. Her hair had blown back and her brown skin was radiant. He wondered what it felt like to wrap her hair around his fingers and jerk her face close to his, lips to lips. But she was as delicate as a flower, and not to be treated roughly. With that thought in mind, Jonus smiled and looked straight ahead.

Kelley didn't know what to say, or where Jonus was instructing her to take him. After she took him home, and God only knew where that was, she was going home. Maybe seeing him wasn't such a good idea after all. As she saw him watching her, a reluctant smile curved her generous mouth.

"Make a right on Mulholland Drive, and a left at the first light."

"Does your boss live here?" They were in an exclusive neighborhood and Jonus hadn't revealed what he did for a living. As a matter of fact, he gave her the impression that it was possible that he didn't have a job. If this was where his boss lived, what kind of work did he do? she wondered, looking at the homes on both sides of the street.

"Yes, I should have a couple of paychecks waiting for me. You can come in. He's very nice and will welcome you into his home."

"Well, if it's okay, I guess." She got out and held the car door open for him.

Just as Jonus and Kelley got to the door, it opened widely.

"Dr. Tate, let me help you inside. Your aunt says I should stay here with you at nights, too. She doesn't want you left alone." The woman raised one brow as she took a quick glance at Kelley. "So I brought enough clothes for three days and nights." She glanced at Kelley again as she enunciated the word *night*. "Lunch is ready so I hope you're hungry."

Kelley's mouth dropped open as she stepped inside the foyer. She stood in the center of the room and stared, speechless. She looked at the exquisite oil paintings; the décor was similar to his aunt's town house. In the living room, she could see a piano and Colonial-style mantel over the fireplace.

Kelley sighed, blowing out a rush of wind, but no words emerged.

"You look tired, sweetheart. Would you like to have a seat before you pass out on my lovely carpet?" Jonus asked teasingly.

Kelley shut her mouth tight and threw her head up. She looked at the smirk on his face and had an urge to slap it off. "Your little charade was not funny, Jonus. Why did you pretend to be dirt poor? Not that it mattered, but why, Jonus?" she demanded, and stomped her foot.

"I said no such thing, darling, so I didn't lie. You just assumed that I was dirt poor. You never questioned me about how I made a living, or where I lived. So I didn't elaborate on it."

"And you didn't volunteer either. I can't believe the game you've played." She turned her back to him. "I hope you had fun at my expense."

The woman came back. "Doctor, I made some fresh lemonade if you would like a glass. Your favorite drink."

"Yes, Betty. Please bring two tall glasses to my study." He waited until she went back to the kitchen. "Now, where were we? Oh, I remember. Come inside my study. I have something to tell you." He turned around slowly while Kelley held his arm for the support he needed.

"More surprises?" she murmured.

They walked down a long hallway and into the study, which was larger than her living room and dining area combined. The oak desk shone, and the ceiling-to-floor bookshelves were fully supplied with books. Kelley walked around the two tall leather chairs and peeked out the bay windows at the green vines that had grown against one side of a brick wall.

"Here, sit next to me," Jonus said, and pulled her onto the sofa close to him. He held Kelley's hand in his. "I've dated women who want a doctor, lawyer, and anyone with money. Those are women who are looking for one thing, and I was hurt deeply by a woman a few years ago. After that episode in my life I've been very careful."

"What happened?" Kelley asked with interest and moved closer to him. For a moment she thought of Angie. She, too, was looking for a man with money.

"I met a woman and fell deeply in love. I overheard her telling her sister that if I weren't a doctor, she wouldn't have time to waste on me because I was younger than she was. And she didn't love me, but after all, I was a doctor and could give her everything she wanted." He reached over and grabbed Kelley's other hand. "I liked you the moment I laid eyes on you. And since then I've fallen in love with you, Kelley. I just had to be sure that you love me, too. I didn't want to be just the doctor. I wanted to be the man you're in love with.

"Kelley, if you were in love with the man you're engaged to, you wouldn't be here with me, and you know it. I just need the chance to show you how I feel about you. You won't be sorry, darling. I'm really a nice guy."

"I love you, too, Jonus."

"When are you going to tell him, Kelley?"

"As soon as possible." She laid her head on his shoulder.

"I don't want anything to keep us apart. Stay with me tonight."

She smiled and nodded in agreement. Her heart raced beyond its normal pace in anticipation of what would come next. "I'll stay with you . . . forever."

He kissed her again. "Okay, I'll show you the rest of the house."

It was a two-story house with three bedrooms. Jonus's room had a fireplace and balcony. The décor was black and white with two large bathrooms.

That day they watched TV in his bedroom. Jonus instructed the housekeeper to leave and return the next morning.

Jonus lay in bed and watched Kelley as she undressed and climbed in bed beside him.

That night was all that Kelley had anticipated and more. Bodies sweaty, rockets went off, and stars shot through the sky. It was as though they were making love in slow motion, reveling in every touch, and feeling the thrill that went off like fireworks. It was a dream come true. They didn't leave his bedroom till the next morning, and Kelley knew she would be back for more.

Kelley arrived at the office and walked in on Angie's and Brenda's disagreement. She stopped as she heard Brenda refer to Angie as a snake. Kelley raised one brow. *I should go to my desk and start working, keep my mouth shut,* she thought. She wanted to tell them about her and Jonus, but this wasn't the time. Besides, Angie was still too upset about Greg. Angie tried to conceal it, but Kelley sensed that she was deeply hurt. Kelley worked through the morning and was surprised at how fast the time had passed. From time to time she looked up at Angie, but she was just as busy.

It was noon, and the office was quiet, except for the constant ringing of the phones.

"I have to go downtown and file a petition. I'll be back tomorrow," Angie said.

"Is there something I can do on this file, Angie?" Kelley asked.

"No. And we don't have any more files together." Angie

turned on her heel and rushed out the door before Kelley could respond. She didn't want to stay in the office all day with Kelley and Brenda. Since she had slept with Byron, it was difficult to face Kelley.

"She's really been miserable over Greg lately. She doesn't want to talk about it, and we used to talk about everything together."

"Yeah, sure. Under the weather my ass," Brenda replied.

"Now, now, Brenda. We both know how moody Angie can be sometimes."

"Damn, Kelley. You can't see any further than your nose. She's . . . nothing, nothing. Anyway, what are you doing tonight?"

Kelley looked at Brenda strangely before she spoke again. "I was thinking about going to see Byron, but tonight is his meeting with the boys. He wouldn't miss it for anything. Not even for me." She had to break their engagement and give his ring back. It wouldn't be easy, she knew. If only there was a way of breaking the news without hurting him.

Kelley and Jonus talked on the phone before she packed an overnight bag to go to his house. She was humming through her apartment and started to the door when the phone rang; it was Brenda.

"Hi, I hope I'm not disturbing you, but I won't be in until ten tomorrow morning and the Franklin file is on my desk."

"Good. Have you talked to Angie tonight? I'm worried about her."

"No. And I don't want to," Brenda answered bitterly.

"Don't be like that, Brenda. She'll be in better spirits in a couple of days."

"Look, Kelley. I hate to be the one to tell you, but moody little Angie and Byron are sleeping together. I walked in on her in the kitchen. They were on the phone. I overheard everything, Kelley. And it didn't just happen once."

Kelley hadn't realized that she had dropped her overnight bag to the floor, then eased down on the sofa. "Are you sure, Brenda? How could they do that to me? I was going to break off our engagement tomorrow. But, Angie, she's my cousin." Tears were falling from her eyes. "I trusted her. Even as children I've always trusted her."

"Now we both know why she's been acting so peculiar lately. And another thing, I think she's going to do business alone, or maybe with someone else."

"I hope she does. I don't want to see her again. But thanks for telling me, Brenda. You've always been a friend. I'll see you tomorrow." But now that Kelley was thinking, maybe giving Byron two weeks threw him and Angie together. Maybe it was her fault by expecting Byron to wait for her. Had she asked too much of him? But Angie, how could she?

Kelley was driving in the direction of Jonus's house when she turned her car around in the middle of the street and decided to go speak with Byron first. She had to get the frustration off her chest before she could enjoy her night with Jonus. Byron's club members would be there, but he'd just have to step outside.

Kelley rang the doorbell, but there was no answer. She rang again, still no answer. She sighed, and waited.

Kelley rang one more time, and the door opened slowly. She stepped inside. The lights were dim, and looking around the room, she thought that she was in the wrong apartment. Her mouth fell open as she looked at the familiar surroundings of Byron's apartment. She was in the right one.

Kelley stared in shock at the man who opened the door wearing a white shirt and no underwear. He opened the door as though he was in a daze. He didn't even look at her, and stumbled back to the sofa. His partner, *another male*, lay on his back and waited. The sounds resonated against Kelley's ears, and the smell of sex clogged her nostrils. She backed away; her hand was reaching behind her, searching for the doorknob.

Kelley heard moaning and groaning from the bedroom. Her head jerked when she heard Byron's voice yell out with passion, "I'm the man." She reeled from the shock of hearing him.

One hand covered Kelley's mouth when Byron came out with his brown bathrobe open. He was stark-butt naked underneath, his brother-in-law by his side. Kelley sensed Byron's embarrassment by his wide eyes as they met hers. His brother-in-law left Byron's side and rushed back to the bedroom.

Kelley stumbled backward as Byron came closer to her. She watched as he wiped his hand across his face. The two men on the sofa frowned as though they were being interrupted.

Kelley felt ill and placed one hand against her stomach. Dear God, they were lovers. Byron was sleeping with his sister's husband. She felt beads of perspiration form across her forehead and soak into her blouse; trying to keep her lunch down, she swallowed hard, held her breath, and backed against the door.

As though her vision had blurred, she shook her head from side to side, and blinked, but when she opened her eyes, she knew it was real; Byron was standing in front of her. Naked, raw, but he was standing there. She saw tears rolling down his cheeks.

"What are you doing here, Kelley?" he yelled, and she jumped. "You know it's my meeting tonight."

"Is meeting what they're calling it these days, Byron?" she snapped with disgust. "Because I have a better name for it."

He could hear his own voice quiver, and looked around wondering which idiot had opened the door. Byron reached for her, but she jumped back. "Kelley, don't—"

"Don't what, you disgusting, low-down son of a bitch? You're gay," she screamed. "Gay."

He held both hands up to quiet her, but she still yelled.

"I'm not gay, you got it all wrong. Kelley, baby, please let me explain," he cried. "I've been so hurt. It was just for this one night. I swear to you just one night, one mistake. It never happened before." He clasped his hands together as though he were praying.

Kelley looked at him in disgust and felt sick as he tried to grab her, but she turned her back and fumbled for the doorknob. She managed to open the door. Kelley was too fast, and shook Byron's hand off her. She dashed out the door like she was running for her life.

"Don't touch me, Byron. You tell Angie it's for this one night." With a dismissive gesture, Kelley started to run. She looked back and Byron was behind her, but she was too fast. She turned to face him again. "I said don't touch me. Gee, you make me sick," she yelled from the top of her lungs and bolted out of the building like a flash of lightning.

Kelley watched Byron from her car. He was disrobed and had to stop, but kept calling after her. "Angie, damn, you did say tell Angie. So you know," he yelled after her.

After seeing him tonight she knew everything about him. Kelley watched him as he slumped against the building, and crying out loud he placed both hands to his face. *"I'm a man, a real man, the man,"* he shouted after her, and struck his fist against the cement wall. He yelled in pain, then crumpled to his knees.

Kelley touched her face when she felt tears escaping from her eyes. She got inside her car, inhaled deeply, taking long breaths and fighting for air. She reached inside her purse, pulled out her cell phone, and started pushing the numbers hard, her finger slipping with each push.

"Brenda, it's me. I need a favor."

"What, Kelley?"

"As soon as I hang up call Angie and tell her that since

you will be in late tomorrow, you stayed later today. Tell her that Byron called and wants her to go to his apartment as soon as possible for a surprise he has for her. He'll meet her there, but just get there."

"Kelley, what's going on?"

"I'll tell you all about it tomorrow. Call her on her cell phone, Brenda, now. Make it sound urgent so she'll hurry." Kelley hung up.

Thank God, she had insisted that Byron use condoms when they made love, she thought. He didn't want to, but she always insisted. She opened the door and hung her head out to vomit. Everything she'd eaten gushed out onto the ground. The image of the naked men assailed her and made her ill all over again. What an education Byron had given her.

Feeling like a bird that had escaped a gilded cage, Kelley looked one last time at the building that Byron lived in. She sighed, and drove off.

She was going home to her man.

"Where have you been all my life?" Jonus asked as he pulled Kelley into his arms.

"Waiting for you." She felt good in his arms. Without a doubt, she loved him.

He held her hand as she followed him to his bedroom. The fireplace was lit and a bottle of white wine and two glasses were on a small table. Kelley poured wine, as Jonus stood behind her looking at her tight-fitting jeans.

Over the rim of his glass Jonus watched Kelley sip her wine. He took the glass from her hand and held her in his arms. "I'm going to make love to you, Kelley," he said huskily. "Every time I see you I want to make love to you. I want you to know how much I love you."

Savoring every part of her body, he undressed her slowly, piece by piece.

Jonus tasted the sweet wine on her breath as his tongue searched the inside of her mouth.

Kelley was deliriously falling into the rhythm of his every movement. He was dexterous with his way of making love to her. At that very moment, she knew that she would never want another man inside her.

In unison, both bodies jerked, and then they held each other, floating into a world where they would always be together . . . forever.

12

The next morning, Kelley told Brenda about her visit to Byron's apartment. She packed all of Angie's personal property into a brown box. It was Kelley's name on the lease, and Angie had to go. There was no way she could work in the same office with Angie.

It was noon, and they hadn't heard anything from Angie. Two days had passed, and still no word from her. Kelley figured she was still getting over the shock of discovering Byron as a man on the down low. All she had sacrificed to get him, and now she was left alone. Not only cousins, but also their friendship, respect, trust, and she had lost it all.

As the months passed, Kelley and Jonus had fallen deeply in love, and Kelley moved into his home.

Jonus went back to his practice at Cedars Sinai Medical Center. He came home early with flowers and a diamond ring to propose marriage to Kelley. After dinner they retired to the bedroom and sat in front of the fireplace. Kelley was curled up close against Jonus.

"Baby, I've gotten used to having you here with me every evening. I want it permanently, Kelley."

"I've gotten pretty used to being here." She didn't want to ever leave him.

Jonus gently pulled loose. He kissed the back of Kelley's hand, then slid a diamond ring on her finger. "Will you marry me, Kelley?"

With a burst of happiness, an ocean of tears, Kelley circled her arms around Jonus's neck, then looked into his eyes. "Yes, yes, I will marry you, Jonus." They made love in front of the fireplace.

That next day, Kelley and Jonus went to her uncle's birthday party, the uncle who was Angie's father.

When Kelley and Jonus arrived, Brenda and Angie were already there, but they weren't together. Kelley and Jonus were having a conversation with her parents when Angie walked in behind them.

"Kelley?"

"Yes, what . . ." Kelley stopped in mid sentence as she noticed the protruding stomach. Brenda stepped next to Kelley; both wore shocked expressions.

"Hi, Brenda. You didn't say anything when you came in," Angie said.

"Hello, Angie. I wondered if you would be here," Brenda said.

"Of course I would. After all, it's my father's birthday."

Kelley took a step closer. "This is Jonus Tate, Angie. Dr. Jonus Tate," she said clearly with pride. "He practices at Cedars Sinai Medical Center." Kelley got such pleasure by seeing the disappointment on Angie's face.

Angie swallowed hard. "Did you say doctor? I certainly didn't expect that," Angie answered, feeling her blood boiling over. "So, the injured man turns out to be a doctor?" she whispered to herself, not realizing she had said it out loud.

"Yes, Angie, I did say doctor."

Jonus held his hand out to Angie. When she held it longer than necessary he gently pulled his hand from hers.

Kelley looked at Angie with a warning eye, and took a step between Angie and Jonus. "I didn't know you were pregnant, Angie. When do you have your baby?" But somehow Kelley already knew.

"I'm five months pregnant."

She had just confirmed what Kelley and Brenda thought. It was Byron's baby.

Brenda and Kelley looked at each other, then back at Angie.

They separated, and Kelley introduced Jonus to her friends and family. Jonus stepped away to fill his glass with punch, leaving Kelley and Brenda alone.

"He's a handsome man, Kelley. I'm so glad that he is the man you are going to marry. Angie was so busy trying to get a man who had a home and money that she forgot to look for love and commitment. Now she's pregnant and alone."

"Look at the way she's eyeing Jonus. Can you believe her?" Kelley asked, and sighed.

"Sure I can. Angie doesn't surprise me anymore."

Jonus came back with his punch in his hand. He had to be at the hospital early the next morning, so he and Kelley had to say good night to everyone.

"Sweetheart, I'll get your jacket," Jonus said, and walked away to the guest closet.

"Does Byron know?" Kelley asked.

"Yes, he knows and he wants nothing to do with me or the baby. He doesn't even want the baby to have his last name. I guess I should thank you for sending me to his apartment so I could see what he really was."

"Don't thank me, Angie. I didn't do it for you as a favor. I did it to you."

Jonus came back with Kelley's jacket and they strolled toward the door.

Brenda followed. "It's nice to finally meet you, Jonus." She touched Kelley's arm and ambled to the door.

Jonus turned around to say good-bye to Angie as she stood close to him. She ran her tongue over her bottom lip. "A doctor, huh?" she repeated under her breath, and gave him a long, dazzling smile.

Kelley looked at her, shook her head in disgust, and pranced out the door.

Two months later Kelley and Jonus were married. Brenda finally passed the bar examination and worked as a workmen's compensation attorney in the office with Kelley. They hired a man as their assistant to fill Brenda's old position.

So far, Angie was tested negative for HIV. And planned to raise her child alone.

SECOND CHANCES

Maxine Thompson

1

Capri
West Los Angeles, California
6:00 a.m., September 2003

"It's true what they say."

Out of the corner of my eye, I steal a glance at Marquise as he twists his mouth like someone who'd just swallowed castor oil, then, in what can only be described as a backward crab crawl, glides his body away from mine. As an afterthought, though, he reaches back and pecks my lips with this offhand, fake kiss. I peek out one eye so I can study his face as he kisses me. I swear I can see a cumulous cloud passing over his features. This is not exactly how a man should look after he's just made love to his wife.

"What'd you say?" Marquise turns away again and buffs up his muscular back to me. Although his voice is muffled, the tone is *cold. Well, I'll be a flying donkey,* as Aunt Mutt used to say. Just moments before, he'd acted if I were the last lifeboat thrown to him in a shark-infested sea. Now I'm a pan of dirty dishwater to be tossed aside.

Miffed, I snatch the ecru satin sheet from his side of the

bed, tighten it under my armpits, then lean on my elbow and study the freckles on Marquise's persimmon back. Goose bumps rise on my neck and an ice dagger lodges between my breasts as I recall my recurring dream from last night. I dreamed I was drowning.

I decide not to drop the subject. "It's true what they say about the seven-year itch."

Right eyebrow lifted, Marquise jackknifes straight up in the bed and cranes his neck around. "Come again?"

"You know what I'm talking about." I chew the inside of my left cheek, a habit I have when I'm annoyed; then I heave an exaggerated sigh, cross my arms across my chest, and wait. After a few moments of silence, I realize Marquise isn't going to respond. Instead, he takes a deep yawn, stretches out his body in a lotus position, then clambers his six-foot frame out of our king-sized bed. His feet hit the hardwood floor with a thump. Momentarily, he stumbles over the circular oriental rug in the middle of the bedroom.

"It's you. Something's going on." There, I'd said it.

Marquise pivots around and my eyes dive-bomb right into his light tiger-eyes. For a nanosecond, he holds my stare, then looks away.

"What are you talking about? Didn't I just take you to Solvang?"

"You acted like you didn't want to go."

Marquise's full lips curve upward in a slur. "What d'you expect? I work midnights and usually don't get three days off together."

Bingo. That's it. Something about our getaway, second anniversary, Labor Day weekend trip, which we'd just returned from the night before, just wasn't quite right. The memory of Solvang parades before my eyes in a blur, an array of terra-cotta, rustic shops and a splash of Danish culture away from the craziness of Los Angeles. Even the soothing sage and sable setting hasn't been able to hold at bay this gnawing evil at the pit of my stomach. Why did our trip feel more like a three-day game of charades than a romantic tryst? Something is wrong. Something I can't quite put my finger on, but . . .

"Who is she?" I blurt it out. I'm just fishing, but I want to see his reaction. I'm sure he will deny any indiscretions and assure me nothing is going on.

Marquise is silent for a moment, then surprises me. "Don't start that Jerry Springer drama again. Maybe you need to close that business of yours and get a real job." With that, Marquise reaches for the white terry cloth towel draped over the mahogany headboard, snaps it around his loins, and pivots on one foot as if he was doing a salute at roll call. Mmmm. Nice way of showing me which side of his behind I can kiss. I recall how at one time, the sight of his toned buns imprinted on the towel used to arouse me, but now there is only a hollow feeling.

Suddenly, anger bum-rushes me, wraps its boa tail around my neck, and constricts my heart. With the sheet draped around my nakedness, feeling so livid I could burst, I leap out of the bed and stalk him. "Don't patronize me, Marquise. Do I say that about your dream? Your running around all day like a little boy in a black uniform playing cops and robbers?"

"Oh, that's what you think?" Marquise spins around and throws both hands up in the air the way he does whenever he's frustrated.

"You've changed."

"You're crazy. Look. At least I get a regular paycheck. You must be PMS-ing again. Send out number seven. Now handle that!"

Marquise often says I suffer from multiple personalities throughout the month, so after throwing this snide remark over his shoulder, one of L.A.'s finest stalks into our master bedroom's adjoining bathroom and slams the shower door.

I go to my nightstand, pick up the copy of Patricia Anne Phillips's book, *June in Winter,* a story of infidelity, that I was reading the night before, and fling it at the bathroom door. "Handle that!" I shout, then slap my hands up and down in a "Take that!" sign.

Being married to a police officer is no joke. And Marquise has had a full-blown case of ego since he joined the LAPD three years ago, which doesn't help matters any. But to top that, as if Marquise's work schedule isn't a marriage ball buster, I have a business, which, for all practical purposes, is going "belly up."

Although we've only been married two years, we'd dated for five years after we met at UCLA. And, once again in our seven-year relationship, I'd just faked another orgasm. Moments earlier, when I held Marquise in my arms, I felt as if I were clinging to a glacier—following the sinking of the *Titanic*. I know orgasms have been called "*petit morts*"—little deaths—but what about fake orgasms? I guess those are the equivalent of grand mal seizures—the big deaths where we die inside a little at a time.

I sit back down on the bed and scratch my head. Thinking about number seven, I consider filing chapter seven, but I believe that's only for personal debts. Come to think of it, I have some other options here. I can file chapter eleven or chapter thirteen, or I can close my business. But no, I'm too stubborn. I still have one straw of hope. I have the possibility of landing that government contract, which I bid on last month. So far, I've let one employee go—my only white male employee.

Two weeks ago on Friday, I'd pink-slipped Ernest Schroder because he wasn't earning his keep. At the same time, I decided to keep my two reliable, mother-earth employees, Nadine Greer and Micaela Hernandez, who earned and created enough sales to make payroll for them from week to week, and even then, their future tenure with "Capri's Writer's Software" was uncertain.

In fact, I'd only hired Ernest Shroder to be in keeping

with the Fair Employment Act so that I would have a multicultural team.

After Marquise showers and leaves for work, I stomp into the bathroom and peer into the gold-veined double mirrors he's left fogged up. How many times have I told him to wipe the steam off the mirror? Anyhow, I have bags under my eyes that resemble kangaroo pouches, and they look even worse against my rust-colored complexion. Who is that old woman? I sure look older than twenty-nine today. I haven't been sleeping well at night—it's this recurring nightmare I have about drowning.

The weather is so humid outside for mid-September, I'm feeling clammy, and I guess we'll have an Indian summer this year. I study my reflection as I turn from side to side and examine my thighs and hips for new signs of cellulite. I admit I've gone from a 12 to a 16 in two years of marriage. Maybe this is what's turning Marquise off.

When I take my shower, I'm so bent out of shape, my stomach grinds as jaggedly as a garbage disposal. Just the idea that my husband made love to me, then blew me off as if I were some hooker has not exactly made my day. I feel worse than a whore. After all, I'm supposed to be the wife! I want a baby, but how am I ever going to get pregnant with our marriage going like this? Quiet as it's kept, I've never really experienced the ultimate of sex—an orgasm—but I figure in time I'll loosen up and it will happen.

I suds my body down with my usual blackberry soap and instead of feeling soothed, I feel violated. Yes, I'm still horny, but I'm so mad I can scream. As the scalding water pelts down on me, I squeeze my eyes tight and silently cry, my tears mixing in with the hot water. I've seldom let Marquise see me break—he always says that I'm a strong black woman.

I guess I'm remembering how we used to get quickies in

the shower before going to work and how we still left each other with our dignity. We also used to take a moment to spoon in each other's arms, even when we made love before we went to work. Although I've never had a real orgasm, I liked the cuddling part anyhow. But not lately . . . What is the matter? I decide I'll deal with Marquise and whether he is cheating on me later—much later.

It hits me again. *I am drowning.*

2

Marquise
7:00 a.m. roll call
Los Angeles Police Department, 77th Division

During roll call, my cell phone goes off with this funny-sounding version of a rap song, and Sarge gives me a look that could melt steel.

"Kill the cell, Officer Jordan." Sergeant Bellamy is a no-nonsense brother.

"Yes, sir."

A grin spreads over my face as I reach down to my waistband. Although I cut off the phone, I see the number in the screen before I turn my ringer off and jump back to attention.

I just hate that Capri is so psychic. Although I didn't tell her what I wanted to talk about on our so-called anniversary trip, it was as if she was a mind reader.

That day started like any other day on the beat. After roll call, I remember feeling a chill go through me, but I ignored it. When we got the call that there was an attempted rape situation at an elementary school on Central, I attributed it to the gut feeling I had that something bad was about to happen.

"Let's roll."

"Dog, you all right?" my partner Shank asks as we jump into the patrol car.

"I'm fine."

"How's Caprianna?"

"Fine."

"You guys get away for the weekend?"

I grunt, so Shank shuts his mouth. For a white boy, he's a little too nosy for my tastes, but sometimes when you share a space with another police officer, the boundaries such as race, gender, and creed fade. As partners, we often go to his house and so he thinks we're friends. Besides that, Shank thinks he's black since he's married to Coco, a sister.

A thud twitches in the pit of my stomach, but I ignore it.

"Let's hit it." Shank is riding shotgun and I'm the driver, so I push the throttle to the floor.

3

Capri
Downtown Los Angeles

An hour later I merge into the traffic on the Santa Monica Freeway at Sepulveda, which is near our Westwood home, and I'm bombarded with L.A.'s laid-back, but deceptively frenetic energy. At 8:45 a.m., the traffic is still bumper-to-bumper, but it's not the creeping and crawling gridlock it is at eight in the morning. As I cruise down the freeway to my office in downtown L.A., once again I'm glad I own my business and can go into work around nineish and miss the morning feeding-frenzy of workers fighting to get to the 2.9 jobs so many people in L.A. tend to hold.

Overall, since I moved from Oakland to L.A., I like the vibe. Los Angeles—the land of Botox, rappers, actors/actresses, Hollywood, blondes, Crips, Bloods, drive-bys, the "homeboy network and the hookup," panhandlers, ethnic markets, La Brea Tar Pits, and Disney. You can almost feel a throb in the air from the cacophony of contradictions. L.A.'s not for everybody, but with the ocean and the mountains right at my disposal, I'm content here.

That's another reason I have to fight to keep my business. I don't know if I'd like to work for someone again. With the economy in the state it is in and with the war, I don't want to look for a job again. And crazy as this place is, L.A. is now my home.

A smoggy day, and I'm almost downtown before I see the modest high-rise buildings in L.A. enshrouded by haze. A mixture of Mexican, Chinese, and Korean foods waft in the air. When I come up the freeway ramp and stop at a red light, a natty-haired derelict of unknown race or gender—the person is so dirty—rushes up and sprays my car windows, then wipes them clean with a crumpled newspaper.

"Only a dollar, miss. I need something to eat."

I roll down my window about two inches, just in case it's a carjacking. "Get away from me. You just want some drugs or alcohol. I got too many problems to listen to your mess today."

The dirty face creases in a vulnerability that you see in children, and immediately I'm ashamed of myself. I don't know what's come over me, but I'm so stressed out, I can't think straight. I try to make amends. "Here. Take this dollar and you better not buy any drugs with it." I thrust a dollar bill out the cracked window.

Now I recognize the dirt-caked face as that of a man's as the sad grimace leaves his face and he lights up. "Thank you, ma'am. God bless you."

"Yeah, right." I'm not feeling particularly Christian today. When was the last time I went to church anyway? I can't even remember.

When I arrive at my office building, a graystone in the garment district in downtown L.A., which was the cheapest rent I could find downtown, I climb the stairs to the second-floor loft, a spacious office. I step inside my domain, but today I don't revel in my décor of old seventies lime green and tangerine orange. Even the tinkle of the artificial waterfall in the corner doesn't soothe me, nor does the aroma of the brewing latte uplift me. I try to practice a form of feng shui and make sure my door is facing my prosperity by keeping the desks facing the door.

In fact, I'm feeling so down that when Nadine surprises me with a spray from her garden, my eyes flood with tears. She has what looks like herbs wrapped in a golden ribbon. Which reminds me that sometimes I bring in peach roses from my garden, but lately, I haven't been doing these little touches.

"What are these?" I inhale deeply.

"African lavender, basil, and tarragon."

"Mmmm. Smells good."

"Cheer up, Capri." Nadine envelops me in the wide girth of her bear hug, making me feel better. "Things are going to work out. You just wait and see. You've got to have faith in God, girl. Watch, you'll probably get that government contract."

Nadine's kind words and the pungent fragrances momentarily lift my mood.

"I'm okay." I manage a wan smile. "Thank you so much!" Impulsively, I hug her back and savor her maternal warmth. It's times like this that I miss my mother, who has been dead for seventeen years this fall. Out of the corner of my eyes, I watch Mica, as we call Micaela, give me a sidelong look sliced with disapproval. Then my eyes fell on what the culprit was. Now I know why she has a hair up her behind.

Next to Mica is the most scrumptious-looking German chocolate cake sitting on the dark cherry-wood desk. All of a sudden, I remember I was supposed to have bought the cake for Mica's birthday. Oooh, how could I be so thoughtless? It seems like the very earth is slipping out from under me and I am losing my grip. Obviously, Nadine has remembered and bought it for me. Thank God for Nadine.

I thump the flat of my palm to my forehead. "Mica, I'm so sorry about your cake. My bad. Marquise and I went away for the weekend and—"

Mica shrugs her shoulders. "S'all right, Mija." She tosses back her sable-colored mane, flicks her wrist in dismissal, and for the moment, my lapse is forgiven. I place my bouquet in Mica's vase as somewhat of a peace offering.

Yi-yi-yi. Nadine and Mica are worth every month I've struggled to keep them on payroll, not only because each month both women have increased their sales, but because they've been so supportive of my vision. So that's why I hate to tell my two favorite employees that I still might have to let them go at the end of the month—if I have to close my business. A vision of all the bills on the console at home flashes like a deck of flipping cards. I haven't even paid this month's rent on the loft, and I already have a three-day notice or quit. I'm hiding my car to keep it from getting repossessed.

Next, I trudge into my office, shut the door, and put my head down in my arms. I'm losing my business, my marriage sucks, but who can I turn to? Once again, I wish my parents were still alive. When I was twelve, both parents died in a freak bus accident coming from Reno. It's times like this that I wish I had a mother or even a father to turn to.

Not only have I lost touch with my sorority sisters in college, but also I no longer keep up with my former coworkers from my first job at L.A.'s City Bank. In fact, I haven't seen or talked to any of my friends or sorority sisters since my wedding two years ago. Even then, they were virtual strangers. I have met Marquise's partner Shank's wife, Coco, on outings to their house, but she and I didn't hit it off. I guess I'm suspicious of a sister married to a white man, although you wouldn't know Shank is white to hear him talk, but that's another story.

At any rate, people just don't realize how demanding a new business can be. I'll have time for my marriage and for making friends once I get my business out of trouble. Sad to say, this is the first time in my adult life, since I've been in control, that things have not gone well. I knew as a child, when my parents were killed, that you had no control when you were a minor. But as an adult, I've always tried to be in control.

Thinking back, I've been running scared since my parents died and maybe now it's catching up with me. First, I was scared that I wouldn't make it growing up without parents, scared I wouldn't finish high school, then college, scared I wouldn't find a job or make it in the business world, and now I'm scared that my business is going to flop.

For some reason, I gaze up and my eyes fall on the silver-framed picture on my desk. It is the picture of my deceased mother's stepsister. Aunt Mutt, who raised me after my parents' death. I guess she lived just long enough to see me get through grad school. From the hood I grew up in Oakland, this was no easy feat—the fact that I graduated with my MBA at twenty-two.

Poor Aunt Mutt raised me in a neighborhood of pimps, drug dealers, prostitutes, and players, yet somehow, I beat the odds. I didn't get pregnant as a teenager. I didn't get on drugs. I didn't drop out of high school. For a moment I wonder, why did God bring me through all this, to desert me now?

In fact, I have done everything on schedule or perhaps ahead of schedule. Unlike many of my generation-X contemporaries, I graduated from college on time. After I finished college, I moved to Los Angeles and started my own software business at twenty-four. Careerwise, I was on the fast track. After a five-year courtship, I had gotten married to my college sweetheart, Marquise Jordan, two years ago, so I had what I considered the American dream life. Three years after opening my doors for business, I even had three employees. As far as I was concerned, just two years ago, I thought the sky was the limit.

However, who could foresee the dotcom bombings, 9/11, then the war? Now with the economy down, writer's software is a luxury to most people.

* * *

Around ten-thirty this morning, Mica, who, in keeping with most small businesses' unwritten protocol, has an amorphous job description, and acts as a salesperson/receptionist/accountant, rings my office and speaks in a hushed whisper. "He's still calling, making threats and hanging up."

I suck my teeth, bending my elbows over my head. "There's nothing I can do," I say. "Don't worry about it. He's just talking out the side of his neck. He's harmless. Just a bunch of talk."

A knock resounds at my office door and I glance up to see that Nadine and Mica have eased themselves into my cubicle.

"Mrs. Jordan, do you think you should've told your husband?" Mica's thirty-something bronze face looks uneasy. I can see the Mayan blood warring with the restrained Indian blood in her face.

Without any of us calling his name, I know she is talking about Ernest.

"Yes, perhaps you should get a restraining order." Miss Nadine wrings her chubby hands.

We all shake our heads at the same time and suck in our breaths. Ernest has called and cursed me out twice in the past two weeks, but each time, I hung up in his face.

"Mica, Miss Nadine, I'm not worried about him."

"Are you sure?"

"No, I can handle it."

"Perhaps you should tell your husband."

"For what? Ernest is not going to do anything."

"Stop being so strong."

I laugh inwardly. If they only knew. After they close my office door, I grab my first cup of mocha latte and settle into work. We will sing "Happy Birthday" to Mica at lunchtime. I put that at the top of my to-do list, which has twenty other things on it, most of which I will never get to. The main priority—how to pay my rent on the office this month and keep my employees on payroll—is penned in invisible ink.

I decide to start with collections—something that might bring in some money and keep my doors open. "Ms. Josephson, are you sure that you can't make your payment today? Your invoices said ninety days. It has been 160 days. Does that make sense?"

"I'm sorry. I've been laid off. I don't have it."

"Ms. Josephson, I'm sorry that you've been laid off, but when I extended that credit, I gave it to you in good faith. Do you have a credit card I can put it on today?"

"I don't have any credit left on any of my cards. I've been paying my bills on credit and they are all maxed out."

"Can you make a partial payment?"

Finally, Ms. Josephson agrees to postdate a check. I place the receiver in the phone's cradle and shake my head. Now I understand how my bill collectors, who I'm ducking and dodging, feel. Lord, what a hypocrite I am.

Why didn't I incorporate and get some corporate credit to tide me through this cash flow crunch? But I started this business by the seat of my pants. For the past few months, I have been making payrolls out of my investments and stock from my first job, which I landed straight out of grad school when I worked for two years as an investment adviser at the bank. Let's just say, the till is empty.

My marriage crosses my mind and I vaguely remember a Web site where a guy says he can stop divorces. Maybe I should look him up on Google, then contact Mr. Stop Divorce or whatever he's called, but something makes me shrug it off. Marquise and I are just going through a phase. Our marriage is solvent. We're going to be okay. I just need to spend more time with Marquise. Then, maybe I can get pregnant.

Around eleven-thirty in the morning, the sun dances across my desk and I look up, feeling my mood rise with the late morning sun. Suddenly my cell phone rings.

"Hey, Capri." Talk about synchronicity. This time, Marquise's voice sounds a little humble. A funny feeling quakes through me as opposed to the thrills he used to incite.

I grunt in reply.

"Yo. Still mad?"

"I can't talk now."

"Can you pick my uniforms up from the cleaner's?"

"Sure."

My business phone line rings. As the queen of multi-tasking, I often juggle two calls at once, but today, for some reason, I'm eager to terminate the conversation with Marquise. "Gotta run. We'll pick this back up when I get home. I've got something I need to talk you about." I will talk about us getting pregnant when I get home, I think.

"Peace. Out."

I hang up and a thought occurs to me. Basically, my two employees and Marquise are my only contacts with the outside world. The rest are with suppliers, customers, and vendors. My business has consumed my whole life. I live and breathe my business. Sometimes, I even dream about my business.

As a rainbow team, Miss Nadine and Mica are part of the double whammy—minority females—African-American and Hispanic. I'd hired Ernest about a year ago because he had a background in computer programming and came highly recommended.

Five years ago, when I created a patented software for writers during the Silicone Valley heyday and before the dot-com failure days, the online and off-line sales had been modest, but at least the business was viable. With the down economy, I laid Ernest off. He always seemed like he was daydreaming and shooting off his mouth about what he used to do for his last software company in Silicone Valley. Not to mention, it did irk me that I sensed he resented taking orders from a black woman.

* * *

They often say that the craziest days of your life start out in the most normal way. I remember having my cup of latte with a dollop of French vanilla whipped cream as I usually do. By memory and rote, I go online and answer my e-mails. I make cold calls on other companies.

As soon as I settle back down with my second cup of latte, my business phone rings. A sultry voice hisses into my ear, "He doesn't love you."

"Pardon me?"

"Give him his freedom. He doesn't want you. He's planning to leave you."

"Wait a minute. Who is this?" I screech, voice cracking like a broken guitar string.

"This is woman-to-woman."

I put my left hand on my hip and raise my voice. "Take your tired, Betty-White-line-stealing, skank—"

I am in the midst of my tirade when I hear, but don't hear, the buzzer ring in the front office. In the backdrop of my rage, Mica must have buzzed someone into the building.

This anonymous woman's call has disturbed me for another reason, too. Somehow, her voice sounds strangely familiar. Now where did I hear that voice before?

I am so disgruntled, though, I don't pay any attention to the loud boom coming from the front office. I think it is a sonic boom or perhaps one of the construction teams working near our office, so I glance out the storeroom window behind my office. I don't see any construction crew working on any buildings outside. Then I hear a staccato sound and the walls reverberate and shake like they do during earthquakes here in Los Angeles. I wonder what the commotion is.

At the sound of a second loud blast, I leave my phone jangling, the alleged home wrecker on the other line to be dealt with later after I deal with whatever new emergency has jumped off. I figure it's an earthquake again. We've had an unseasonably warm September that tends to send us baking and shaking, as we call it in L.A.

"What is it—"

As I open my office door and sprint into the lobby, I cry, "What's going on?" but this is as far as I get. My jaw drops wide open.

If time is ever said to have stopped, it does for me at this moment. I freeze in my tracks. For a fleeting moment, I remember the dream I'd had of drowning last night, and oddly, I think of all the things going wrong in my life right now.

What I see next turns my blood to sludge. There in the entrance lobby are my two trusted employees—Miss Nadine and Mica—sprawled like red-stained limp rag dolls on the floor. One has been shot in the head and one in the chest. Their eyes are wide open as if they met death in sheer terror. Their crimson blood forms two spiderweb splats on the wall and the German chocolate cake resembles something a dynamite stick had been set off in the middle. Blood drips through the brown and caramel icing and splattered bits of chocolate and coconut paint the wall. My only thought is, *This can't be happening*.

Then, what I see is a bone-chilling glare I'll never forget as long as I live. It is Ernest, brandishing what looks like a shotgun. I've heard of employees going "postal," but good grief, I'm just a small business owner—I never thought this would happen to me.

For a moment, I digest the dirt ring around Ernest's collar, taste the sweat of his brush haircut, and inhale the day-old musk on his body. A wild deranged look glints in his eye. My rapid heart beats to the rhythm of too little, too late, too little, too late. Why didn't I recognize the signs? Too late, I realize Ernest is a loose cannon and now I know his threats have been real. Why hadn't I taken him more seriously?

Speechless, I swallow a wad of spit. Finally I speak up with a bravado I don't really feel. "Ain't this a trip? Ernest, put that gun down. Are you crazy?"

Ernest doesn't answer as he holds me in the dead silence of his stare. I'm hoping to unnerve him or even intimidate him, but I recognize the emptiness in his eyes and suddenly I know beyond a doubt, he is going to shoot me. With nothing to lose, I am engulfed by fear and rage. I am going to die, but oh Lord, not like this. I think of Marquise—how will he take it? Will he mourn my loss? Will he feel sorry for how rotten he's been acting lately?

I turn to flee but something knocks me to my feet. When the bullet first hits me below my waist, I don't feel anything. Then a piercing fire explodes and radiates through my hips. It takes a moment for the pain to register. The next thing that runs through me is, *How dare he? If I live, I'm going to wring his scrawny little neck.*

When I come out of shock, I crawl to the phone.

And with my last millimeter of strength, I dial 911. Beads of sweat pop out on my forehead. The smell of tarragon, basil, and African lavender fill the room. The acrid taste of salty blood fills my mouth. Out of the corner of my eye, I stare as Ernest turns and puts the barrel of the gun in his mouth. Streaks of blood cover the phone as I dial and the last thing I notice is that the German chocolate cake sticks to the wall and resembles a piñata. Just before I pass out, I called on a name I hadn't mentioned in a long time. "God, help me."

4

Elijah
Three months later
Pasadena, California
December 2003

Over his bowl of oatmeal, my son Cinque gazes up at me with his earnest mink eyes and says, “Daddy, do you think Mama is in heaven?”

I pause. “Yes, Cinque. I think that she is up there shining the stars and the moon that look at you at night.”

“Like the stars we saw at the planetarium on Saturday?”

Cinque is referring to our trip to the Science Museum this past weekend.

“Sure, Little Man.”

It is times like this he looks like his mother and I miss my late wife, Brooke, even more.

“Daddy? Can I show you my new magic trick?”

“Cinque, you can show me in the car. We’re running late.” I don’t add that I’d done my yoga exercises that morning, gone online, and gotten sidetracked.

“Aiiight.”

"What did I tell you about that word?"

"Yes, sir."

"That's more like it."

This morning after I drop Cinque at his bus stop where he is bused to a magnet school out in the San Fernando Valley, I drape my head in my arms on the steering wheel and pray. "Lord, help me be a better father to my son than my father was to me. I know I'm short with Cinque sometimes, but help me be more patient. And, Lord, let me find the right woman to be my wife and to be a mother to my son, if it is your will."

From there I head on to what has become an anchor in my life since Brooke's death—my job. I know some people say I have what other men would call a punk job, but I love it. For one, my job helps me forget. It helps me forget that I just evicted my tenants in the guesthouse behind my property because they were selling methamphetamines, better know as "ice," "Tina," or "crystal."

What makes me so mad is this back house cottage used to be Brooke's art studio, her sanctuary. Instead of a fence we used Texas privet, and within its low leafy border there were contrasting bronze and yellow kangaroo paws, sweeps of two-toned silverberry and mixed roses. I've tried to keep these flowers alive in Brooke's memory. I didn't know my tenants would use part of the plot of dirt to plant cannabis, better known as marijuana. I should've called the law on them.

But anyhow, I got through all this because of Cinque and because of my job at the rehabilitation center. This job also helps me forget how Brooke died of ovarian cancer two years ago. At the same time, it helps me to remember she would have wanted me to keep living.

Our eight-year-old son, Cinque, still cries for his mother, but he's beginning to settle down with school, and his new dog, Tupac, who is company for him.

I don't know how I would make it if it weren't for my sister Bianca and her husband, Larenz. Bianca babysits in the evenings, when I'm working overtime and on the weekends too. They also have two small children, Larenz Jr. and Tre.

As a physical rehabilitation and massage therapist, I have worked with cancer patients, the sick, and the dying. I believe as long as there is life, there is dignity, and for that reason, I took care of my wife the last six months of her life.

Before I went into this field, I was a trauma nurse in the emergency rooms of different L.A. hospitals. I swear there is something about the dying that you can feel. I've seen people walk into the emergency room, say, "I don't feel well," and the next thing, if no one takes action, they drop dead. It's never been scientifically documented, but I've seen it. In fact, I got so good at recognizing it, I lost the heart to be an emergency room nurse. Especially when I watched the one woman I loved slowly leave me and our son for good. Even when my mouth lied and I told Brooke, "You're going to make it, honey. You're a fighter," I knew in my heart, it was just a matter of time.

I cleaned Brooke's vomit, her stool, whatever it took to keep her clean and comfortable. Don't get me wrong. I didn't expect a badge or anything—this is what I felt to do. I loved her. I also found out the hard way how much work Brooke used to do once I began taking care of Cinque, washing his clothes, fixing his lunch, getting him off to school, saying his prayers. The list never ended.

But for some reason, I don't see that death aura, that dark halo around this new patient, whom I've been assigned to for the past couple of months, and I don't feel like she is going to die.

I call this one "the iceberg." I feel there is more to her than meets the eye. Although she is young, I notice no one visits her and she has been lying in this room for the past month. She never speaks. The report says she was a victim of employee violence on her job. Her eyes opened last week and I just know she can talk. There's something about the eyes that lets me know it. There is such a pain, like a wounded animal in her eyes. They say she had been in a coma for almost three months, and I overheard a nurse comment, "It's a damn shame how her husband doesn't come to visit her."

Besides the coma, they say she may be a vegetable for the rest of her life, but there's something about her . . . I don't know. I think she has a lot of life still left in her. There is something about her that I find intriguing. She's still bruised and swollen looking, but I think she's beautiful.

This morning before I left for work, I read the report on the Internet about cicadas coming in the spring, and I'm glad I don't live back East. I plan to start my garden early this year. Maybe those were cicadas that destroyed our elms when I was growing up in Columbus, Ohio. They come from underground every seventeen years, I understand. It makes me think of the life cycle. As long as there is life, there is hope.

Back to my new patient, I think her physical wounds have been healed but she is still weeping inside from her mental wounds. Something has told me to bring my wind chimes and put them by her bed.

5

Capri
Morning Glory Rehabilitation Center
Inglewood, California

The first thing I remember is waking up in this baby-poop-green room, the scent of old urine, fresh feces, and antiseptic cleaner assaulting my nostrils. The plopping of an ice machine resonates in the background. I hear a light tinkle in my ears. And I hear the sounds of raindrops. Where am I?

I try to think back and remember what happened. Then it all comes rushing back to me, reminding me of a horror movie on rewind.

I remember looking down the barrel of the shotgun that Ernest held. An image of my employees blown to bits as if they had stepped on a land mine hits me. Instinctively, I know Nadine and Mica are dead. My heart drops and guilt overwhelms me. Why am I alive?

Ernest, the wildness in his eye, the hysteria, the gun, the murders, then the suicide. Oh my God, why me? I wish I had a different life. This is unspeakable.

My first thought is, *This can't be happening.* I try to move my legs, but they feel like timber. I'm not getting up. Am I paralyzed? Where is Marquise? Maybe he had to work late.

What am I going to do?

I want to try to find words, but none come. This is the space where you try to say humans are this or that, but then you find out they lie, they steal, they even kill, but there are no words to express how abominable some human beings' behavior can be.

I study the man standing before me. A short, slender man wearing a short dreadlock ponytail. I listen to the splash as he pours ice water in a pitcher on my nightstand. He appears to be about five feet and a half and weigh about a buck twenty, so his baritone voice belies his diminutive stature. In the corner of my consciousness, I do remember hearing the timbre of his voice through the fog I've been in. This was the voice that went on and on and talked to me when I wouldn't—no, couldn't—talk. I wonder if he's a doctor.

"Hey, Sleeping Beauty awakes. You are awake, aren't you?" His voice is upbeat and chipper.

I haven't talked since I woke up a few days ago. I guess I've been fading in and out of sleep. I don't know how many days have passed. I notice a bedpan and a walker on the right side of my bed. There is an old lady who sleeps all the time in the bed in the corner.

I look under my hospital gown. I have what appears to be a colostomy bag on my side. I finally speak.

"Where am I? Is this a hospital?"

"No, this is Morning Glory Rehabilitation Center."

"How long have I been here?"

"A couple of months—give or take."

"Who brought me here?"

"An ambulance brought you from the hospital."

"Who are you?" I say.

"I'm Elijah Woods. Your physical rehabilitation and massage therapist. And you?"

I study the man closely. Despite his happy-go-lucky voice, I notice sadness in his teardrop eyes.

"Caprianna Jordan. People call me Capri."

"That's a beautiful name."

"Is it raining outside?"

"Yes."

"How long have I been out?"

"Almost two, three months. Do you know what day this is?"

"September something or other, 2003?"

"Can you see these two fingers?"

"Why are you talking to me like a child? Yes, I see your fingers. So what month is this?"

"December twenty-eight, 2003."

"You mean Christmas has passed?" I try to remember. What happened to October and November?

"This is your Christmas present. You came to consciousness at Christmas."

"Consciousness as in coma?"

The man nods. I'm flabbergasted. I've been in a time travel machine and don't even remember it. A wave of irritation ripples through me. "Hey, cut the chitchat. I'm outta here. Where are my clothes?"

"You don't have any clothes other than hospital-issued."

I spot a paper bag in the corner next to my bed.

Suddenly I notice the elderly lady in the bed next to me, who seems to be in a daze. Her eyes pop open, but they look vacant. I don't want to stay in the room with this zombie.

Okay, so I have a hospital bag and no clothes. Boy, this scenario is getting worse.

"Has anyone visited?" I probe.

"You see me every day."

"No, I mean a visitor."

"Not according to your charts. I think you need to take your time getting up and walking anyhow."

I'm so furious I don't answer. I can't believe Marquise has

not come to see me. How dare he? What about our seven-year relationship, our two-year marriage?

Mmmm. I let that one sink in. I change the subject. "What's that noise?"

"Wind chimes. I put them up. Feng shui. They bring life into a room."

I study the crystals hanging from the ceiling by my bed. When I calm down, I look around for a phone by my bed, but there doesn't seem to be one. I ask, "Do you have a cell phone I can use?" I almost add, "To call my husband," but I catch myself.

Elijah flips out a cell phone from his green hospital jacket pocket, then leaves the room so I can have some privacy.

Even as I dial the numbers, I have a feeling in the pit of my stomach that something is wrong. I call the 77th Police Division and I'm put on hold. What's going on? I think.

After a long wait, a female voice comes back to the line and says, "Marquise Jordan no longer works here."

"Well, this is his wife." I rattle out Marquise's Social Security number.

"Mrs. Jordan, I can't give you any more information."

"Can I speak to the desk sergeant?"

"Ma'am. He's with a client. He can't come to the phone."

"What do you mean he can't come to the phone? I will hold or I'll call up to the captain if I have to."

After about a five-minute wait, the desk sergeant picks up. "Sergeant Holmes. May I help you?"

I explain who I am—or who I used to be anyway.

Sergeant Holmes is quiet for a while. Finally, he clears his throat and speaks up. "Marquise Jordan no longer works here at the LAPD."

I'm humiliated that I didn't know this as the wife.

I hang up without saying good-bye. I decide to call the bank's automatic service. My business account has been overdrawn for two months and they are threatening to close it. Our personal joint account is closed.

Next, I call Marquise's stepmother, Grace.

Her voice sounds weird too. "I haven't heard from Marquise. He left us a letter saying he was leaving L.A. and would contact me and his father when he got situated."

"You sure you don't have a forwarding address?"

"Capri, I wish I did. How are you feeling? I'm so sorry about what happened to you."

"Thanks." I hang up again without saying good-bye. Is this the twilight zone or what?

I think about calling his partner's wife, Coco, but I'm too embarrassed. I'm also so pissed, I could scream.

I try to get up to leave this god-awful place, but I collapse back on my pillow. I'm just too weak to move.

I guess I have to accept the ugly truth like most people do in life. It is what it is. People are not always there for you.

6

Capri
Three weeks later

Last night, the lady in the bed next to me died and I'm kind of shaken up about that. They just took her out this morning. I think about it. I never even knew her name before now. It was Isabelle Lee. An old-fashioned name. They say she was seventy years old. She had no family or friends . . . just like me.

I really don't even want to stay in this room, but I find out there are no other vacancies. I have no insurance, no money.

Suddenly, that guy who's always making me exercise in my bed surprises me. "Hey, how about getting up and using your sea legs? I used to be in the navy and that's what they called them when you walk on a ship. That's how it's going to feel now."

"I don't feel like it." I shake my head adamantly.

"Look, I've been massaging these legs for some weeks now, you've had your physical therapy in the bed, so it's time to get up and put this show on the road. No more wheelchair."

"Leave me alone. I just want to rest today."

"I'm not leaving this room until you try."

I hesitate. Why is he torturing me? He stands by my bed as if he will never leave. Does he get his kicks out of making me miserable? When I see that he's not budging, I finally relent. "Okay, but I want that walker just in case."

"Do you think you can stand up?"

I struggle to stand up, then lean on Elijah and, for the first time, realize how weak I am. I feel limp as a jump rope. My legs buckle under me.

"Take one step at a time." Elijah steadies me on his shoulder. I finally adjust to the walker. It really is cumbersome. How do old people manage with this thing?

Although Elijah is a half a head shorter than me, he is strong and his arms are sturdy.

His voice is gentle as we slowly make our way outside the room. I get a glimpse of my reflection in the mirrored wall when we shamble past the ward and I almost faint. My hair looks sandy gray, it is so matted, tangled, and dirty.

A vampire doesn't have anything on me, I look so pale. No color. But it is my face that frightens me. My face is so thin and gaunt, I look like a scarecrow.

Lord, what is wrong with me? Who is that monster? Why didn't you just let me die? I can't stand the sight of my own face.

We shuffle past what looks like a recreation room. I see people in wheelchairs and on walkers slowly moving around. When I look at the silver heads, I look as old as any of the denizens there. I see a man with what looks like a steel halo around his head. How can these people go on living?

"What's wrong with him?" I whisper.

Elijah speaks in a low voice. "Neck and head injury. Quadriplegic."

Several people speak to Elijah as we plod our way down the corridor. I have to rest on the walker every few steps.

Elijah seems to know everyone. "Hi, Mr. Covington. How are you?"

"I'm tolerably well."

"Great. Hi, Mr. King. Are you keeping up your exercises?"

"Yes, Mr. Woods. I sure am."

Everyone speaks to Elijah with smiles in their voices.

"Where are you taking me?" I ask as Elijah turns down another long corridor.

"We're going to the garden on the grounds."

At last we burst out into a sunny day; the sun's glare hurts my eyes, it's so bright for January. I guess I haven't been outside in a while and it's a frightening experience.

"I want to go back in," I protest.

"Just wait a minute. I want you to see something."

Elijah guides me to the garden outside the nursing home's grounds. Bougainvilleas hang from the white fretwork, still vibrant with their bleeding vermillion colors. Late-blooming azaleas border the sidewalk.

"We're going to have a cicada spring," Elijah comments.

I look at him as if he's suddenly grown an extra head. "What's that?"

"Did you know that every seventeen years cicadas, which are sometimes called locusts, come from underground and invade the land? Some say they're harmless, others say they're not."

"What has that got to do with anything?"

"Life is full of rebirths."

I can't think of anything to say. I remain quiet. I feel as if I have stepped into a land mine of emotion. "What's left of my life?"

Elijah looked off at the late winter roses blooming in the garden. "It's a beautiful day," he comments. "We have today."

"Fuhgeddaboutit. Please take me back to my room."

Elijah doesn't budge. He just looks off into space. "This is a yellow happenstance rose." He points at a buttery rose.

I remain silent. Darkness engulfs me, and my mind relives the shooting. Moments like these, I even question if there is a God. Why hadn't I listened to my gut that morning? Like the time I was in New Orleans and had this eerie feeling so I didn't go out into the streets at night alone. I stayed in the hotel until I caught my plane back to Los Angeles. Later, I found out the hotel had been built on a slave auction block and was said to be haunted. If only I'd listened to my dream and followed my gut like I did before that time in New Orleans . . .

But slowly, with the wind caressing the back of my neck, the sun melting on my face, I feel something. Just a little inkling, but I experience a different feeling than I've felt since I woke up to this nightmare of a life.

At last, accompanied by Elijah, I hobble back to the room. With Herculean effort, I fall on the bed.

Elijah helps me settle into the bed and plumps up the pillow. "You want your bed put up?"

"Yes," I say, huffing and puffing. How can he be so patient? That makes me hate him for having such a pleasant disposition while I feel like such a bitch.

Elijah rolls up my bed to an upright angle. After I get my pillows puffed, an image of my hair standing up over my head like a werewolf's crosses my mind. "Got a mirror?" I ask.

"Sure."

I'm not quite as dismayed as the first time I got a peep at myself. I look at the thunder cloud of hair puffing up on both sides of my head. I take a deep breath. "Can you help me with my hair? Just maybe help push it down. I'm too weak to even brush it."

Elijah takes the hospital-issued brush and slowly untangles each section of my hair, braiding it piece by piece. I am amazed at the neatness of the braids. I wonder if Elijah is gay, but then I think of all the masculine things I've seen him do and I say to myself, *Nah*.

I'm curious. "How did you learn to braid?"

"My mother had a stroke while we were growing up and I had to learn to do my younger sister Bianca's hair for school. I also had an older sister, Janet, but by then, she was working."

"You've got good hands."

"Thanks."

Suddenly, I'm not feeling as irritable.

The next day I am looking forward to Elijah's shift. When he arrives, Elijah comes in with a Pinocchio puppet and a magic trick, which makes me crack up. For the first time in months, I laugh until tears roll down my face and I start to feel better.

7

Capri

"You were lucky, young lady. We call you the miracle lady." Dr. McGee pulls his stethoscope away from his ears.

I sit up, ears at attention, interest piqued. What is going on with me? I'm just beginning to feel tingles coming back in my legs. Elijah has been exercising and massaging them for the past month.

They say Dr. McGee was the treating physician at County General. The surgeon, Dr. Lyon, is credited with saving my life. Dr. McGee is following up from my last medical visit at the clinic where they removed my colostomy bag.

"Why?"

"You were hit full-blast with a shotgun, yet your main spinal nerve was not hit. I don't know how none of your main organs were hit. Even a fraction of an inch would have severed your main artery, and you would have bled to death. Even so, it was touch and go. We had to take a piece of your colon and reroute it. That's why you were wearing the colostomy, but as you see, you're able to make it without the bag now."

"Dr. McGee, will I walk normally again?"

"With therapy, I don't see why not. You have a lot of inflammation around your spinal cord. Spinal cord compression, they call it. You're a living miracle," he concludes with a smile.

"What do you mean I'm a living miracle?"

"Well, for one, the MRI you had the other day shows no sign of brain damage. That's a good sign after being in a coma."

"Why do they call me a living miracle?"

"Just read these hospital papers." Dr. McGee hands me a vanilla-colored envelope.

After Dr. McGee leaves, I read through the medical reports he leaves in my possession.

More and more, from the hospital papers I am learning the following.

I was pronounced dead at 1:15 a.m. on Tuesday, September 9, 2003. Somehow, just when they were about to zip me up in a body bag, an orderly saw two of my fingers move.

I have to sit and absorb this one for about an hour before I can read on. Did I have any out-of-body experiences after this near-death experience? I can't remember. It was like being in a deep well and hearing the voices around me, but I couldn't come out.

I am too astonished to even think. I sit there quietly for the longest time. Talk about second chances.

How can this be happening?

As if the hospital papers don't trip me out enough, I guess it is seeing the ink on the legal document that pushes me over the edge the next day. Without shedding a tear, I'd survived the shooting, the near-death experience, the coma, the struggle to learn how to walk again, but it is something about seeing Marquise's fancy handwriting that brings it all rushing back to me. He still has the same flourishes, the same curlicues in his writing, but now it seems menacing where it is signed on the dotted line of the divorce decree.

He is divorcing me. Bottom line. He does not love me anymore.

"Irreconcilable differences" are cited as the reason. All of a sudden it hits me. I have no husband, no home, no friends. All my hopes of a brown-eyed baby girl or baby boy are gone. Suddenly, I feel as bereft as if I'd just miscarried my unborn, unconceived child. I'm all alone. At least if I had a baby, I'd have someone to love.

As if my life wasn't bad enough before the shooting, now I'm faced with a divorce. Before all this happened, I was losing my business, which, in and of itself, was dreadful enough. Then next, I almost lost my life, and now I find out I've lost my husband and my home too.

I'm so blown out of the water, I sit still for a moment. I wonder if I can commit suicide. Do I have the courage? Sometimes it is too hard to keep living.

Like a fountain, my emotions burble up and find the path to my lips. I speak out loud to myself. "How could he? That no-good bastard. I hate him. I could kill him." Tears begin sluicing down my face.

Now I no longer have my health. I am too weak to fight back. I can see that the house is going to be sold during the divorce settlement, but how long is that going to take? I have no money and no place to call home.

So what were these past seven years? Was it all a pretend marriage, which was part of my pretend life? I take my fist and sock my pillow, wishing it was Marquise. More tears blind me before they rivulet down my face. *God, how could you let this happen to me?*

I think about it. I don't want to live. How can I go on with this mess of a life?

Suddenly, I am throwing the few toiletries on the table next to my bed and having a fit.

"Great job you're doing up there, God!" I ball up my fist. "I could tell you a thing or two if I ever came face-to-face with you. I'd spit in—"

"Hush, you don't mean that. Don't say something you'll live to regret." I look up and there's Elijah standing in my room. "What's the matter, Capri?"

I fling the divorce papers at Elijah as if he's personally responsible for them.

I'm so distraught, I don't care what Elijah sees. In a flurry of motion, he comes over and pins my flailing arms and swaddles me in his arms. "Calm down," he says in this low, soothing voice.

"I could just die," I admit between sobs. "I don't want to live. This is no life to have."

"Don't you die on me." Elijah's voice is suddenly brutal. He pulls away from me and looks me in the eye. His ambergris eyes turn a steely color like murky water. "I won't let you die on me like—no, you're going to live. Even if I have to will you to live myself."

Finally, after I've boohooed and boohooed until I'm tired, I sniffle and ask almost coquettishly, "Why do you care whether I live or die?" I peek out from under his embrace.

With a solemn look, Elijah releases me. He finally speaks. "Let me ask you something. What if this is the only life you're going to have?"

"So what is that supposed to mean?"

"You either accept your life as it is or do something to change it."

I'm too upset to respond. Finally, Elijah orders a mild sedative for me and I doze off into a fitful sleep. I don't know how long I am asleep, though.

During my induced slumber, I have the recurring dream of drowning, but then I hear my mother's voice say, "You can swim, Caprianna. You won't drown."

The next thing I know, my mother stands over my bed and says, "Get up out that bed, Caprianna. You can walk."

When I wake up the next morning, Elijah is sitting in the chair across from my bed, a look of consternation causing his eyebrows to knit together.

He is quiet for a while; then he says, "You okay?"

"I'm fine."

"I was worried about you."

"Why?"

"I just wanted to make sure you were okay. You were in pretty bad shape last night when I left."

"Don't worry. I'm not going to hurt myself."

Then I think about it. I'm not wired like that. No, other people can go out and kill themselves and escape their misery, but no, not me. I am made to just take it and take it, but Lord knows, I can't take any more.

At last, I find my voice. "Where am I going to stay?"

"I've got that solved. You can move into my back house at my place."

"But I don't have any money—any friends."

"You do now. I've looked on the Internet. As a victim of crime in California you are entitled to remuneration. But don't worry about moving expenses now."

"Let me think about it. I'll let you know later."

Elijah falls silent.

I think about it and I almost have to laugh at myself. Where did I get my pride, my hubris? Here I am, in this wheelchair 50 percent of the time, on a walker the other half of the time, just learning how to walk again, no visible signs of income, and, as poet Maya Angelou says about us black women, I act as though I've got "oil wells pumping in my backyard."

Suddenly I feel an anger, no, a rage coursing through my veins. How dare Ernest do this to me? How could he take away my means of livelihood? How could my husband, Marquise, abandon me at a time like this? How could my life careen so out of control? Why me, God?

I choose my words slowly as I try to frame some of what I'm feeling. "You know, I always prided myself on my instincts and intuition. But—" I pause. "How did I let this get past me? Why didn't I see this coming?" I don't know if I'm talking about my divorce or my shooting. Maybe all of this could've been prevented.

Elijah is silent for a long time. "We never know from day to day what can happen to us, Capri. You had no way of knowing."

Looking back, that day in September when I went to work, it started a whole chain reaction. Being in a nursing home is not exactly the life I'd envisioned for myself. At least before, I was healthy and felt like I could have turned my business around.

Elijah interrupts my thoughts. "How about let's make a bet?"

"What?" I wrinkle my forehead. I'm perplexed.

"Yes. I bet you will walk again."

"How much?"

"One hundred dollars."

"I don't have any money. I don't know."

"Well, if you don't walk, you owe me a hundred. If you walk, I pay you the hundred."

I weigh it. I have something to gain if I walk, so why not try? "You've got a bet."

Elijah changes the subject. "You know that cicada spring is on its way."

I give Elijah a look as if he's lost his mind. "Tell me more about it. You mentioned this before."

"It's the brood X, which will be attacking gardens."

"How do you know all this?"

"I'm a horticulturist by hobby, so I keep up with things like that," he adds as a footnote.

"Oh. So what's that noise? Is that the cicadas?"

"No, that's the wind chimes."

8

Capri

I heard somewhere once that in the barnyard, if there's a pig with an open sore, the other pigs will eat from it. Well, this must be open season on Capri.

Although one day melts seamlessly into another here and feels pretty much the same, this day stands out for me. This afternoon, I am already tripped out because I've taken my first shower that isn't a bed bath. Looking over my shoulder, I get a glimpse of my back wound and I almost pass out, my scar looks so bad. Although it has healed, there is a wide splotch of burnt-looking flesh that looks like the map of Africa. Also, I've lost so much weight, I almost don't recognize myself. I'm barely a size 10 now and at five eight, this makes me a rail. Strangely, I've still got the sister booty.

Then, I'm given another surprise. Internal Affairs comes to visit me.

One officer, Detective Briar, is white. The other, Lieutenant Wheat, is a brother. Detective Briar stands over six feet tall and Lieutenant Wheat barely stands five feet, but carries himself with a presence that commands respect.

"Mrs. Jordan, when was the last time you saw your husband?" Lieutenant Wheat absently brushes his thick black mustache with his right index finger.

"Why? Where is he?" I feel some of my old protective feelings for Marquise rising, in spite of my anger. Maybe he is going to show up and explain everything away. How he freaked out at first, but now he has come to his senses. Maybe he's going to ask for my forgiveness and call the divorce off.

"We're the one asking the questions, ma'am."

"Excuse me."

"So when did you last see your husband?"

"I saw Marquise that morning when I went to work."

"Do you know where your husband is now?"

"No."

"Were you having marital problems?"

"Not that I was aware of—that is until I got these divorce papers in the mail."

"Well, we're sending the FBI after your husband for questioning."

"Why?"

Both officers pause. Detective Briar speaks first. "Did Marquise have anything to do with your shooting?"

I draw in a deep breath of shock. I finally find my voice. "No, Ernest Shroder, my ex-employee, shot me."

I see the two men's eyes beeline into each other's and a look of shock crosses both of their faces. Detective Briar speaks up first. "Mrs. Jordan, are you sure?"

"I would know who shot me."

For the first time in six months, I retell the story as to what transpired that fateful day at the office. I had never told anyone. Just talking about it makes me relive the horror of that scene again. I begin to cry, and when I settle down, Lieutenant Wheat speaks up. "Well, we never knew who shot you before now."

"Why?"

"We found you unconscious at the scene," Lieutenant Wheat says. "Of course, there were the two other women victims."

Tears rush to my eyes. "Those were my employees—Nadine and Mica."

Lieutenant Wheat looks away uncomfortably. He clears his throat, then speaks again. "We just want to make sure there was no foul play. I'm sorry to ask this again, Mrs. Jordan, though we don't know any tactful way to ask, but are you sure that your husband didn't shoot you?"

"Yes, I'm sure!" I am adamant about that. How could they think Marquise, a man of the law, would shoot his wife and her employees?

The next question floors me. "Do you think your husband paid someone to shoot you?" Detective Briar stares at me with piercing sky-blue eyes.

I ponder my next words before I speak. "No, I don't think so. Wait a minute. Didn't Ernest kill himself?"

"Now who did you say is Ernest? We only found two bodies at the scene. You were found unconscious by the telephone."

I explain who Ernest Shroder is. My heart clutches and stalls out in my chest. I begin to sputter. "That means Ernest is still at large. Oh no! Am I safe?"

"We'll put out an APB for him," Lieutenant Wheat assures me.

"Let me rephrase this. Is there a chance this fool can come back and finish off the job?"

Lieutenant Wheat twists his mouth in a side grimace. "Perhaps you should move."

"But where? I have no money, no friends. Oh, this is friggin' great!"

If I've ever wished I had a friend, it is now. If I had a girlfriend, I could call her and she would be here for me. If I had a husband, he would be here for me. If I had my parents or

Aunt Mutt, they would be here. But I don't have anyone. After the police leave, I sit there and stew.

This night I realize I have given my all to this business, but what has this business done for me? It has cost me my husband, my friends, my credit report, and almost my life.

What am I going to do?

9

Elijah

The days are flowing into weeks and time seems to be flying by. There is something about this patient that makes me want to see her smile. The first time I brought in Cinque's Pinocchio puppet and some of his magic tricks, Capri laughed so I saw her face light up despite her pain. She'd seemed so despondent before that, I feared for her safety at first, but each day, I watched her grow stronger and stronger. As if she was determined to fight back and get her health back. I also bought her the Bible to read, but I notice it is still sitting where I left it on the corner of her nightstand. Oddly, I've begun looking forward to seeing Capri at work.

"You have a beautiful smile," I say one day.

"Thank you."

I keep reminding myself that Capri is a patient and I am her massage therapist. I really have to meditate when I massage her joints, her legs, her back. I do not want to cross that line. I lift my mind up high and close my eyes so I see and do not see her voluptuous hips. Although she looks like she's lost weight, her hips are still melon round. I numb my members, as the Bible says, and think of this as flesh I have to heal, nothing more, nothing less. I'm glad I know how to meditate and do yoga. I center my mind and the word I use in my head is this, *Freeze*. For that reason, I usually don't have to wear a jockstrap whenever I massage my women patients. Capri is the first one I've ever felt a strange attraction to. I try to carry on conversations as I do her massage to keep my mind occupied.

"Do you believe in God?" I rub eucalyptus oil and aloe vera gel on Capri's lower back, knee, and hip joints. I ignore her wound, which appeares to be healing nicely.

"I don't know." Capri sounds skittish today. Her limbs tremble and she feels nervous and jittery to my touch.

"What do you mean you don't know?"

"Well, I used to, but after my parents died in this freak accident when I was twelve, I'm not sure. I've learned you have to have strong self-determination and believe in yourself. And since this thing happened with my husband, I think it's all a big joke. I hate him."

"Him who?" I am afraid she means God and maybe she does. I don't want to push her into any more blasphemy than she's already done.

She pauses. "My husband, I mean my ex."

"How long were you married?"

"Two years."

"So you were married two years, and you're going to hate him the rest of your life?"

Capri doesn't answer that one. I don't say anything else either.

When I finally find the words to say, I confide in Capri something I've never told anyone. "I understand how you feel. I know my faith was shaken when my wife died two years ago." Then I tell her about Brooke and her two-year battle with cancer before she passed.

"I'm sorry to hear about that. How long has it been since she—"

"Two years. We have a beautiful son, though. Cinque."

"How old is he?"

"Eight. I'll show you a picture of him when I'm through working on you."

For a while, I can't think of anything to say. How can you tell a hungry person, "Go, be fed," when you haven't offered her anything to eat?

I speak up. "Sometimes you need more. Don't you believe in miracles?"

"I don't know."

"I believe anything is possible if you believe it. I still believe you can walk again."

Capri is silent for the longest time. She seems to be pondering over the steps she has been taking without the walker and without my help. She has now graduated to walking with a cane. But something seems to be pressing on her.

Capri looks away and gives a sigh of resignation. Finally she tells me what is on her mind. "Elijah, I have no place to go and now I'm afraid for my life."

Capri recants her visit from Internal Affairs. I try to hide my shock. This woman has gone through an absolute nightmare. Not only did her former employee shoot her and leave her for dead, her husband divorced her at her lowest point. Now she has found out the perpetrator is still at large. Heavy.

I ponder what I should do. How can I help Capri? I know she is a proud black woman, and the question I need to ask her has to be worded delicately. She turned me down once before when I offered her a place to stay.

I clear my throat and cough against my fist. "That offer still stands. Why don't you come stay in my guesthouse—just until you get back up on your feet?"

I am happy when I hear her answer.

"Yes. It doesn't look like I have much choice. It's either that or going to a women's shelter."

10

Marquise
February 2004

I know everyone says I'm a jerk. I can't help it. I hated to see Capri like that with tubes up the yin-yang and everything in the hospital, but I haven't loved her in a long time. I understand she's gone to a convalescent home now, and there's nothing I can do.

First, they told me she was dead, and then they said they had found a pulse—after they almost put her in a body bag. Now, with me being a cop and all, I tell you I've seen some crazy things on the street, but that's some scary shit there. I'm telling you, that is just a little too spooky for me. I can't live with her anymore. That's all there is to it.

Looking back, had I had the right feeling for Capri in the first place, I wouldn't have done what I did. If I'd really loved Capri, had really been into her in the first place, I'd have moved heavens and mountains to be by her side. Instead, I got in my car—I had already planned on leaving to move to Tempe, Arizona, where Sidra had just transferred her real estate job, and I just left. I left my job, my home, everything.

Sidra and I were both planning to leave our mates this year anyhow and we just wanted a fresh start.

I'm not even worried about the house. I left Century 21 in charge to have a real estate agent sell it. Capri can get her half of the profit from the sale of the house. We should each clear at least one hundred grand and this will tide me over while I'm trying to get on the police department in one of the smaller municipalities in Arizona.

I know you should stick by people when they're down, but I just couldn't do it. I hope this won't bring me bad karma.

I've never stopped loving Sidra, my first love. Since last summer, we had planned on leaving our prospective mates. In January we kept our New Year's resolutions. She has filed for divorce from her husband, and I have filed for divorce from Capri.

It's funny, but after all these years, when we ran across each other three years ago, we still had the same feelings. And, since I've made this move, I've never felt more alive. Life is nothing without the one you love.

I can't help it, but Sidra is my first and only love. I love Capri, but I'm not in love with Capri. There is a difference. Men know it. They will settle for a good woman because she may be there for them, but it's not the same as when you really love someone. Sidra was, and is, my soul mate.

I don't think I ever really loved Capri like I loved Sidra. I married my wife on the rebound. She has always been more like a sister and I have never had that feeling you should have for someone you're married to. She's a hardworking, industrious sister, but I've never felt that sparkle I feel with Sidra.

Sidra married another man when she went away to Stanford University for grad school, but now eight years later she has left her husband. They have a little boy, Kendall, but I don't care. I'll love him like he's mine because I love Sidra. You don't always get a second chance at love, and I think I'm going to go for it. It's as if time has stood still, waiting for this moment.

I realize I haven't been happy with Capri for a long time.

Our relationship had just grown stale. Once I hooked back up with Sidra, I felt like I was on a roller coaster. The hiding, the sneaking, the passionate sex. We'd been seeing each other on the down low for a year now. What I found is I never really had that feeling with Capri.

All Capri was worried about was that old silly business of hers, and from the looks of things, it was not doing well, even before the shooting.

When Capri gets on her feet, she'll just have to go get a job like the rest of us working stiffs. I've had it up to my eyeballs with paying all the bills. I had a little stash saved and I had already planned to get out of L.A. I'm sorry about what happened to Capri, but I'm not going to keep taking care of her and her selfish wants. Having a business, as far as I'm concerned, is not a need, it's a want.

I had planned to tell Capri that I was leaving while we went away for our second anniversary, but I didn't have the heart to tell her.

The day Capri was shot I was thinking about Sidra. Why should I let her go? Although I didn't want to mess up my home, I was torn inside. In spite of everything, I just couldn't let Sidra go. Not this time.

But the next thing I know, Internal Affairs is probing into my business, all up in my grill, up my ass with a microscope and saying that I'm a suspect. Once it was proven I was with Shank, I said to myself, I'm out of here. I don't know who shot my wife, but I'm sure not going to take the fall for it.

After I heard Capri was out of the hospital, I did what I had to do—I filed for a divorce. I also resigned from the department and moved to Arizona to be with Sidra.

The guys at work and the people in my family talked about me so bad, I just wanted to start over. Sidra and I moved here two months ago in December.

I just couldn't help it. Maybe I felt sorry for Capri because she was an orphan. I didn't know, but this I did know.

I couldn't continue this farce of a marriage any longer.

11

Capri
Spring Equinox

Pasadena is such a serene town, it's hard to believe it's so near the hustle and bustle of L.A., yet so far removed. I always think of it as the town of the Rose Bowl and Tournament of Roses Parade. Through the haze, you can see the San Gabriel Mountains looming in the distance. Lovely jacarandas light up the streets like lavender lanterns, and poplar, elm, and palm trees line the streets on both sides, forming a tunnel. The smell of chicory fills the air. Squirrels scamper between the trees and even come up to the houses.

"Okay, we're here. Welcome to the Taj Mahal," Elijah says as he pulls his Jeep up in front of a beautiful azure Cape Cod with a gabled roof. The landscaping around the house is breathtaking. Cactuses, black-eyed Susans, primroses, lilacs wrap around the outside of the front of the house. A large oak tree shades the front yard. Such a rustic, peaceful-looking place.

"Elijah, your home is beautiful."

"Thank you." Elijah flicks his hand in a modest dismissal.

When I step inside his living room, I see that he has books on horticulture, yoga, massage therapy, and reflexology piled on his coffee table. Cinque's backpack is strewn on the dining room table, which sits at one end of the oblong living room. Cozy and lived-in is the expression for this place.

His son comes running up when we step inside. "Capri. This is Cinque. Pick up your backpack, son." Without a word of protest, Cinque retrieves his backpack and hangs it on the coatrack in the corner. "Where's your aunt Bianca?"

"Aunt Bianca is out back, picking some flowers."

"Say hello to Mrs. Jordan."

"Hello, Mrs. Jordan. Pleased to meet you." Cinque has round button eyes that look so serious, they seem like he has been here before.

My word. A well-mannered eight-year-old to boot. I like him already.

Elijah talks in his authoritative father voice. "Mrs. Jordan will be staying in the guesthouse for a while."

"Aaiight."

Suddenly a large red terrier scrambles out from a back room in a blur of wagging tail and almost knocks me down. I have to hold on to my cane to keep my balance.

"Tupac, get down." Elijah pushes the dog aside. "Cinque, take 'Pac outside."

"Yes, sir." Cinque grabs Tupac by his collar and takes him out the back door.

"Your dog's name is Tupac?" I give a light chuckle.

"We both loved 'Pac', so that's why we named our puppy after him."

"How old is Tupac?"

"The dog? He turned one this summer."

"Well, he's surely big for a pup. I don't particularly care for rap, but I liked Tupac, too. The boy was a genius."

Elijah nods.

I glance around the room for a moment and notice Elijah's collection of jazz albums. "Jazz aficionado?" I say.

Elijah nods again.

I digest his bookshelves, which line one wall of the living room. Sun Tzu's *The Art of War,* and a copy of *The Complete Kama Sutra, the First Unabridged Modern Translation of the Classic Indian Text, Translated by Alain Daniélou,* stand prominently out on the bookshelf.

The entertainment center has a large-screen TV, a DVD player, and a VCR. A machine with two microphones sits on the mahogany étagère.

"What is that?" I ask.

"A karaoke machine."

"Yes? What do you do with that?"

"You'll see this weekend."

My eyes fall on an oil painting over the stone-faced fireplace of Elijah, a baby I assume was Cinque, and a beautiful beige-toast-skinned sister with faun-colored eyes.

"Was that your wife?"

"Yes." Elijah flinches. He is silent.

"She was beautiful."

Elijah nods.

Cinque returns to the living room. "Mrs. Jordan, you want to see some magic?"

"Not now, Cinque," Elijah interrupts.

"Please, let him show me," I protest.

Elijah nods at Cinque, who then proceeds to show me an elaborate card trick, and I must say he is pretty good since I never could pick the right card. After he finishes the trick, Cinque asks, "Ma'am, d'you want to play Scrabble?"

"Sure, let me get settled in and I'll be ready for you. Can you spell already?"

"Sure can. I won the spelling bee in my class last year."

It seems like these two things—watching Cinque's magic

tricks and later playing Scrabble with him—have won me a new little friend for life.

When we step outside, I meet Elijah's sister, Bianca, who is creating a bouquet from the flower garden. The fragrance is so overwhelming, the garden smells like a perfume store.

After the introductions, I ask, "What's that?" I point at a cluster of spiked purple flowers and Elijah says, "Verbena."

"How about those?"

Bianca answers, "Rusty red kangaroo paws."

Elijah speaks up. "We planted many of these flowers and plants when we got married."

I think about it. Elijah and Brooke even gardened together? When had Marquise and I ever done something as intimate as that?

Leaning on my cane, I ask, "How long were you married?"

"Ten years."

I do the math. That means they were married four years before they had Cinque. At this point in time, they would've been married twelve years had Brooke lived. I have a strange thought. Do people ever find true love again once they lose it?

Bianca says her good-byes and excuses herself. "I've got to get back to my boys. My husband, Larenz, is watching them while I drop off Cinque."

Something about her open face and dreadlocks seems so natural and down-to-earth, I immediately like her. "Bye. Nice meeting you."

When I step inside the cottage, I suck in my breath, it is so exquisite. The soft peach walls scream, "Quality of life." A small fireplace centers the front room. I can see how his dying wife would have loved this place as a studio. You can still see the artistic touches of Brooke's hands, by the fishnet hanging on the ceiling, the seashells on the bookshelves, and the few abstract paintings hanging on the wall. A crystal wind chime graces the front door. The inside of the cottage consists of one large family room, a small kitchen, and a bathroom with a shower stall.

"I'm impressed," I say.

Elijah has told me that the last tenants had demolished the place, but he'd spent the last four months renovating the back house. You'd never know it had been jacked up, it looks so neat and clean now.

"Why, thanks. I hope you'll be comfortable here. If you need anything, just whistle. Do you want a phone put in here?"

"No. I think I need time to myself to regroup."

"Okay, just let me know."

I don't know why I'm here, but I know I must catch my breath before I can get my life back. I have to find out what happened to Marquise and the sale of my house. I also have to find out what happened to Ernest. The last I heard he was still at large. I guess this will be a good place to lie low for a moment.

That night when I climb under the duvet of the let-out futon, I sigh. Maybe I have been wrong. Sometimes people are there for you. People you never expect to be.

This weekend, on Saturday evening, I get a chance to socialize more with Bianca accompanied by her other half, Larenz Payton. Larenz is a large brother, with a smooth dome head, and looks a lot like the actor Ving Rhames. He is a college football coach, so his schedule is lighter during the spring. Although they have their sons, seven- and four-year-old, Larenz Jr. and Tre, in tow, I notice that they are a couple whose marriage is centered in each other too. Cinque takes the smaller boys to his room to play Game Boy.

Right off the bat, Bianca and Larenz ask me to go to

church with them on Sunday, and I think they are going to be sticks-in-the-mud.

"I'll go too," Elijah volunteers, so I agree.

It is funny though. After playing a game of bid whist with them, I find they are down-to-earth Christians. The women play against the men and Elijah and Larenz win, and even run two Bostons on us. They talk smack throughout the whole game, and I see a playful side of Elijah that I've never seen while he was at work.

Music from a radio has been playing in the background throughout the card game. A song comes on and Larenz jumps up, holds out his hand to Bianca, and says, "Come on, baby. That's our song. Let's cut a rug." It's Chaka Khan and Rufus's "Ain't Nobody Love Me Better."

Without a word, Bianca falls into her husband's arm and they do a combination silky-smooth slow dance, part-calypso, part-tango complete with dips, which looks as choreographed as a modern dance. The chemistry between the couple is almost palpable in the room and I can almost smell the sensuality between them. Without a doubt, I know they will make love that night when they get home. It occurs to me that Marquise and I didn't have anything called "our song." In fact, we never did anything spontaneous like get up and dance at home or in front of any other couple.

I catch Elijah looking at me and I look away, embarrassed. It's as though I'm a voyeur looking in on the couple's intimate moment.

After Bianca and Larenz sit back down, Elijah changes the mood. "How about some karaoke?" he suggests and we fold up the card game.

This is when I learn how the machine works. We go into the den next to the kitchen. Sitting before the large TV set, where we read the words to the songs on the screen and use the channel changer to find the songs by a computerized code, we lip-sync to the songs in unison.

"Let's sing duets," Bianca clamors.

I am surprised at how well Bianca and Larenz sing together. They sing the Temptations and Diana Ross's version of "Ain't No Mountain High Enough" and I can tell by the glow in their eyes that they would take a bullet for each other.

"Let's sing a duet." Elijah hands me the microphone.

"I can't sing a note," I say.

"C'mon and try."

I finally relent and I'm glad I did. We have such a relaxing time. I remain seated on the love seat as I can't stand for long, but when we sing Marvin Gaye and Tammi Terrell's "Ain't Nothing Like the Real Thing," I hear Bianca chanting, "You go, girl. Sing it."

Next, Elijah chooses Rita Coolidge's "Your Love Has Lifted Me Higher."

As Elijah croons his words in his rich baritone, I get the strangest feeling in my gut, but I put it aside. This is business. He only feels sorry for me, I tell myself.

Bianca gets up and sings Tina Turner's "Nutbush," and I swear she sounds like Angela Basset in the movie, *What's Love Got to Do with It?* when she says, "Ike, I'm doing the best I can." We all have a good laugh since domestic violence seems like the least of concerns for Larenz and Bianca.

Watching this couple together makes me realize how lonely I am. I love how Bianca and her husband interact. They are good-natured and comfortable with each other. When it's time to go, Larenz helps Bianca dress a sleepy Larenz and Tre and carries them to the car.

I think of my relationship with Marquise. Although Marquise never hit me, we were never comfortable with each other like Larenz and Bianca. I have a feeling that Elijah and Brooke were the same way with each other.

I think about it. Who says domestic violence is the only way a person can strike you? Take Marquise. He didn't physically hit me, but when he hit me, he hit me with walking-out and divorce papers. Whoever said that sticks and stones may break your bones but words will never hurt you told a lie. Words can kill you. Even words on divorce papers. “Irreconcilable differences.” The words haunt me.

Several times throughout the evening, I catch a glimpse of Elijah studying me silently and a fleeting look crosses his face, but he glances away when I look back at him.

12

Elijah

"Ready to go?" I ask when Capri answers her front door.

"Yes. Let me get my purse." She steps outside smelling of soap and water, and dressed in a demure, white suit with a black camisole. Her low shoes are white-tipped with black patent leather points. Her twists gleam in the morning sun. She really looks great. Although she still walks with a cane, she seems to walk straighter and straighter now.

"I'm a little nervous," Capri admits. "I can't remember when I last went to church."

"Don't worry. I've been a stranger to the church's doorstep in the last few years too, but I think it's time for me to get reacquainted with God, too."

"Well, you make me feel better, to know I'm not the only backslider."

"Well, I'm sure God understands our circumstances."

"You look nice, Cinque," Capri praises Cinque.

Cinque hates wearing a suit, but he beams when he looks up at Capri.

We stop by Bianca and Larenz's and they follow us in

their SUV. They have both boys with them. On the drive to church, I smile inside. Talk about serendipity. I am so glad that Capri and Bianca have hit it off. It has made it so much easier to spend time with Capri and Bianca and her husband. Although we are not a couple, it sure feels like it when we are together. Finally, I have to face it. I am falling in love with Capri. What should I do? She is my patient. I can't do this.

Last night I couldn't sleep for thinking about Capri. What should I do? She is—no, she used to be—my patient. I couldn't do this, I thought, but then, again, I guess technically, she was no longer my patient since she was released from Morning Glory, but I am still in a quandary. Is this being disloyal to the memory of Brooke, my first wife, my child's mother? Wouldn't Brooke have wanted me to be happy though? My thoughts raced around and around.

Over the past few months, I've watched Capri blossom like a hothouse orchid. Something delicate, yet durable. I've seen her stay strong when most women would have crumbled. The tough veneer she had when I first met her has softened. Inside, she is this wonderful, caring woman.

When I think about her life story and how she's had to fend for herself since the age of twelve, I can see why Capri seemed so hard-core at first. I don't know what I would have done if my mother had not been there after my father walked out on us. My late mother worked two jobs for many years, yet she was the rock for her three children. I was raised in a houseful of women, and it just seems like it has only made me love black women all the more.

13

Capri

I am amazed at the edifice when we arrive at the church. The Macedonia Baptist Church possesses all the pomp and decorum of a large Catholic cathedral. High ceilings, tall stained-glass windows, organ music piping throughout the sanctuary, multiple steeples.

As we walk up the sidewalk this morning, I notice that many of the members have a downcast demeanor. As we enter the atrium, I hear someone tell Bianca, “Did you hear about Sister Winters? She and both of her children were killed in a car accident last night. A drunk driver ran into them.”

Bianca looks shocked. “I’m sorry to hear that.” She turns to me. “Sister Allison Winters was a faithful member of the church. She was only about thirty years old. She had a five-year-old and an infant. Oh Lord. Her husband must be distraught. Mmm, mmm, mmm.” She shakes her head, tears glistening in her eyes.

I don’t know what to say. Just last night while we were laughing and singing, someone’s life was being destroyed—just like mine was. Is there any rhyme or reason to life?

We trail inside the church and all of us, Elijah, Cinque, Larenz, Bianca, Larenz Jr., and Tre, sit on a front pew. A somber pall seems to fall over the congregation. Everyone looks down.

When Reverend Allen, who dresses in the regalia of the pope, takes the pulpit, he clears his throat and speaks with conviction.

"Today, congregation, friends, saints, and holy ones, I come before you with a different sermon than the one I had planned. I know you've all heard about Sister Winters." He repeats the information for those who might not have heard the bad news.

Reverend Allen continues. "My heart goes out to her family and especially to her husband, Brother Winters. Let's all pray for his strength in this tragic time.

"Today, I'm going to talk about the capriciousness of life. The Bible says, 'Unforeseen circumstances befall us all.' We must always remember this. We are all children of a moment's notice. We never know the day or the hour. At any moment, we can be taken away.

"In I Timothy 6:7, it says, 'For we brought nothing into the world, and it is certain we carry nothing out.' That's why we've got to get our hearts right. We never know the day or the hour.

"But the one thing we must learn to do is to forgive. We must even forgive the drunken driver who foolishly took a drink and has now caused three innocent lives to leave this earth prematurely. Why must we forgive? For God forgives us and God is love. To err is human, to forgive is divine."

I think about it. I'd already died and returned. Technically, I had had one hour of death, then a resurrection. It feels strange. Why has God given me a second chance at life? Why me and not Nadine or Mica or even Sister Winters and her young children? What am I still here for? Do I need to forgive Ernest?

After church, Elijah, Cinque, and I go to Gladstone's Restaurant on the Pacific Coast Highway overlooking the ocean. You can see the horizon from the windows of the restaurant, which is set on a pier. The cerulean sky boasts a cloudless day. The seagulls cry out to one another in mournful tones. In the distance, I see the families out on the beach, frolicking, picnicking, and enjoying the weather, the bicyclers pedaling up the bike path, the joggers running, and the planes flying overhead and I feel a sense of serenity.

When the waiter comes, we order a seafood smorgasbord, which includes lobster, oysters, and shrimp.

While we are eating, Cinque puts his fork down and gives me this quizzical look.

"What's the matter, Cinque?" I ask.

"Do you think it hurts to die?" Suddenly the sun illuminates something in Cinque's almond-colored eyes and I feel the presence of something otherwordly.

I pick my words carefully. "No, I think it's a wondrous moment—one of peace."

"How about Sister Winters and her children? Do you think they hurt?"

"No, they're in heaven now, Cinque. They're at peace."

"My mom died," Cinque says matter-of-factly.

Astounded, Elijah and I look at each other and don't say anything. That Cinque is so precocious.

Somehow, I find the words to respond. "She's at home, baby. My mom died when I was a little older than you are. But I carry her around in my heart." I point to my heart. "She's still here in my heart. Your mother will always be there, too, looking out for you."

Later, we stop by the beach at the Santa Monica Pier. We have a stranger take a picture of us on Elijah's digital camera. I can see the reflection of the picture in the lenses and I hate to say it, but we look like a family.

After we take Cinque to the different vendors and booths,

buy him ice cream and a hot dog, we stroll the beach. While Cinque runs ahead and roughhouses with other children, Elijah speaks in a solemn tone.

"I thank you for answering Cinque's questions. Sometimes I don't know what to tell him."

"Anytime. He's like an old soul. He reminds me of myself after I lost my parents. Anyhow, thanks for taking me to church. I needed to hear what the minister was preaching about today."

14

Capri

Since I've moved into Elijah's back house, he's kept our relationship very professional and platonic. I guess that's what you can call it. I never have considered him as any more than a friend. He's just been so kind to me, I am grateful. Maybe he feels a sisterly affection for me, so I dismiss my feelings that now and then surface when we're together. They make me feel uncomfortable. Technically, I'm still a married woman, but I guess the divorce will be final soon.

In any case, I begin to realize how much I look forward to him coming home from work at night. He always checks in on me before he goes to bed. At first, I didn't want a phone so I could keep my solitude. I've been able to make a lot of progress without the interruptions. Before I left Morning Glory, an unmarked box arrived, which I can only assume Marquise forwarded, with some of my home office equipment and some of my clothes.

The box also contained my laptop, so after a month, I've added a phone line in the guesthouse in order to add AOL to it. Since then, I've been able to apply for loans online, contact other victims of crimes online, and go into chat rooms.

I want to move on with my life, but, injuries aside, until I get some of this poison out, I can't.

The hospital referred me to a post-traumatic therapist, Dr. Medallion, who works in Beverly Hills. I feel like this is the first step to healing. I need therapy to talk out my feelings about being a victim of crime. I'm eligible for government-subsidized medical transportation. I arrange for a medical transportation service to come pick me up for a weekly therapy session.

In the meantime, I fill out my application for Victim of Crimes assistance, and while I'm waiting, I've done some small copywriting jobs for brochures and newsletters through my old client list.

My discharge social worker from the convalescent home has referred me to physical therapy at UCLA.

As soon as I get my first check from the Victims' Assistance program or disability, I'm going to find a private eye who will take a payment plan and find out what happened to Marquise. I also want to find out if Ernest's whereabouts can be located. If so, I will feel much safer.

I'm not in love with Marquise anymore, but I need to know. What happened to the life I had before I was shot and before I went into the coma? Was it all an illusion?

I also plan to pay Elijah back every penny I owe him when the house sells.

"I hate him! He took my life from me. Why did Ernest do this to me?"

My voice bounces off the high ceiling. I had started off in a normal voice and by the time I have talked a few minutes, I am shouting.

"Mrs. Jordan, are you still taking your Prozac?" Dr. Medallion's eyes narrow in stern caverns.

"Look, Prozac is not helping with how I feel. I need some money, Doctor. Look me in the eye." I take both index and middle fingers and point at my eyeballs. "I need some money."

"Well, it takes a while to get your disability."

The solemn eyes of Dr. Medallion continue to study me dispassionately from his high-back leather chair.

This psychiatrist's office is in Beverly Hills. I guess the Victims' Assistance program is going to pay for this. The whole room says, "old money." A vase with calyx and calla lilies are centered on a round table in the waiting room. The good doctor's office is no less inviting. Thick oriental rugs, high-gloss mahogany hardwood floors, high ceilings, ornate carvings on the wainscoting, floor-to-ceiling smoked windows.

"You have a lot of grieving to go through. You lost your employees who were also friends, you've lost your marriage, you lost your business, and you almost lost your life. It's normal to feel some of the rage you're feeling."

"Well, Doctor, when will the pain end?"

"Listen to you. You have become a victim twice."

"What do you mean?"

"You were a victim when your perpetrator shot you, and now, because you can't release the hatred, you're still a victim."

I fall silent. There is nothing to say.

Wringing my hands, I feel tears welling in my eyes. "Doctor, I feel so bad. Nadine and Mica were good people. Why did I live and they die?"

"You're suffering from something called survivor guilt. In a plane crash, whenever a few people survive, they generally have the same questions you're asking."

"What can I do about it, though?"

"Have you ever contacted their families and asked where Mica and Nadine are buried? Maybe you need to go and say your good-byes for closure."

"That's a good idea. I will, when I'm strong enough."

I decide when I feel it in my spirit, I will visit my slain employees' graves, yet only when the time is right. But not right now. I'm not strong enough.

Dr. Medallion gives me some thoughtful parting words. "When life is real painful, you have to learn to rise above it."

"What do you mean?"

"You have to remove yourself from the situation and look at it objectively. How about writing about it in a journal?"

I throw away the prescription of Prozac after I leave his office.

15

Capri
Summer solstice

I have been here at Elijah's house for three months. The past quarter of my life has been more relaxed than any period of my previous life, yet I'm slowly easing back into work and I'm beginning to feel like my old self.

It's something about seeing the therapist, which is making me less angry. I also keep my journal like Dr. Medallion suggested, and it is helping me release some of this craziness. Somehow, while I've been journaling, a character named Solange just leaped off the page and came to life.

I haven't told anyone, but I'm writing a screenplay about a woman suffering from amnesia whose whole life and identity have been stolen from her. That's how I feel. Like my life has been stolen. My script is called "Cicada Spring."

Strangely, I see the relationship of the resurrection of the cicadas after seventeen years to the renewal within my life. I wonder if it's connected to my parents being dead seventeen years too. Anyhow, I've never written a screenplay before, but from the software I created, I think I'm able to do it.

About a month ago, I also found a private investigator for a reasonable fee to look into Marquise's whereabouts and to see if he can find Ernest. So far, there's no sign of Ernest. He must have skipped town. Anyhow, the PI is willing to take a payment arrangement for now.

On my downtime, I play Scrabbble with Cinque after he's done his homework. I help him with some of his assignments. Every other day he shows me a new magic trick. I'm constantly amazed at his questions. He's like a little Buddha.

The other day, Cinque asked me, "Mrs. Jordan, where do we go when we die?"

I didn't know what to tell him. "I guess we go home to heaven."

That answer seemed to satisfy Cinque for the moment.

Tupac has become my constant companion and guard when I take my walks around the block. I'm thinking that maybe I'll get a dog when I move.

Meantime, I'm making friends with Bianca, and I'm realizing how much I've missed my women friendships since I'd started my business. I even enjoy babysitting her boys and Cinque when she has to go take care of business. She is a stay-at-home mom, and she's made me realize how important a job that is.

I can't believe this, but Bianca and I even talk on a daily basis when she drops off Cinque, which is something I have to get used to again—chitchat. In business, I only talked when it was about the business of making money. I'm learning the art of interacting with people again.

Each day I get up and go through my exercises for my back and my legs. I still need my cane to walk with, but I believe one day I will be able to walk without it. I have a medic transportation service, which transports me to UCLA for physical therapy and massages. Although I miss Elijah's massages, he seems to have drawn this invisible line now that I live in his back house.

* * *

Earlier this evening, when someone knocks on my door while a downpour of rain is battering my windows, I jump with a start.

I have no idea who it can be. I have been on a writing marathon since early morning, and I am just coming up for a break.

I'm surprised when I peek out the front door window and see Elijah holding a gingham cloth over something. He lifts the napkin, which reveals a ceramic tureen and a ladle. "You want some clam chowder?"

I open the door. A curly line of smoke rises from the bowl when he lifts the tureen's lid. I peek at the creamy white soup with lumps of potatoes and tiny chunks of clam meat inside and murmur, "Mmmm. Sure. Smells good. Thanks. Come in."

"Thanks."

"Did you make this?"

"No, Bianca cooked it and brought an extra pot over for Cinque and me. Is your heater working?"

"It's fine." I have a little room heater that keeps this two-room house with its half bath as cozy as a solarium. The houseplants are growing like weeds, too, and I talk to them every day. "Where's Cinque?"

"He's gone to the movies with Bianca and the boys, but she'll be bringing him home tonight. Anyhow, you mind if I make a fire and we can cut down the heater?"

I have noticed the fireplace before, but I have never used it. I've often wondered why it had glass at the bottom of it.

Elijah turns a long gizmo on the side of the mantel and the shattered glass in the bottom of the fireplace erupts into blue and orange flames. This was obviously some version of new fangled fire logs.

"Wow! Amazing." The fire casts a rosy glow over the room and mesmerizes me.

I sit before the fire, rubbing my hands together, savoring the warmth, enjoying the crackling sounds, and glad I'm inside instead of outside in the rain. Elijah lights a stick of lavender incense, then ladles up a bowl of soup for me.

"Have some with me," I offer.

"I've eaten already," Elijah says.

At last, I began to gulp down the chowder. Out of the corner of my eyes, I watch Elijah as he studies me while I eat. He has the look of a mother watching over her child.

I finally say it. "Why?"

"What do you mean, why?"

"Why this?"

"Why what?"

I fan my hand around the room, which is small, but so homey. The flames dance on the wall, reflecting our silhouettes on the wall.

"Why have you been so nice to me?"

"How about if I just say I'm a nice guy?"

"You are."

Elijah is silent for a while. He speaks up again. "I notice you've been working a lot lately. I see your light on late into the wee hours."

I smile, thinking of my secret. I decide to assure him that I'm not back into my workaholic mode. "This time, I'm working on my business and not in it. You know there is a difference."

"Oh?"

"Yes, before, I worked so hard, I had no time for people. I'm trying to be more balanced."

"Yes, I see. I notice you and Bianca are going places together."

"Sure are. We're going to catch a Tyler Perry play tomorrow night."

"That's good."

"Bianca is good people. She's been wonderful to get to know."

"She likes you too."

I smile. "Guess what? I read up on the cicadas on the Internet."

"Oh?" Elijah raises an eyebrow and gives me an amused smile.

"No worry about them coming to California."

I don't tell him about my screenplay. That is my little secret.

Elijah and I play two games of Scrabble and listen to some jazz. I don't know if it is the thumpety-thump beat of the rain, or the riffs of Charlie Parker, but for the first time in months, I feel something . . . I feel alive.

Elijah looks around the room and comments, "You know, this place hasn't felt this alive since—" He breaks off what he was going to say.

"That's all right. I know you miss Brooke."

"I miss her, but . . ."

Without warning, Elijah takes my bottle of gardenia oil off the dresser and begins to massage me in the slowest circular motions, causing me to close my eyes, to squeeze them tight and visualize all the colors in the rainbow. He starts with my back, then works his way down my spine, down my legs, down to my feet.

Perhaps all the pain from the gunshot wound has healed, because now all of a sudden, his hands take on a different feel. They are no longer just healing hands. They become magic hands. His touch is as gentle as a feather. *Oh Lord, this man is so sensual,* my mind screams. He massages as if he's conducting a symphony; there is much finesse in his movements.

Next, Elijah takes my boar hairbrush and begins to brush my hair until I can hear sparks fly. My hair has grown from the short ear-length bob to shoulder length since I started wearing twists. I'm glad I had washed it earlier this evening and I had not twisted it yet, so it feels bushy and healthy again.

The lavender incense burns in a seductive haze in the background and somehow the ambiance finds its way deep inside my thighs. A tingling starts in my loins, my nipples harden like diamonds, and I feel like I'm on the cusp of something. I have never felt this way with Marquise. I feel such a sense of intimacy, a connection. Marquise was never big on foreplay, and near the end, he didn't seem to care if I got anything or not out of our lovemaking. Here Elijah and I aren't making love, but it is like a slow adagio, so slow and leisurely that I feel like I'm being made love to. Although we're not talking, I'm feeling him.

I feel as if Elijah's fingers were Bird's fingers playing me like a saxophone. Fingers moving so swiftly that there is no science to it, only the rhythm of life.

In a way that seems as smooth as a calm sea, Elijah kisses me with the most soul-stirring kiss I've ever had. A roaring ocean pounds in my ears and I listen to the gallop of my heart. I feel the squish of my blood coursing through my veins. I begin to squirm, arch, and swivel to that ancient rhythm as he rubs me all over.

His hand finds my breast and runs it around and around it, causing my nipples to harden even more. I want him to kiss me on my breast, but I'm waiting for him to make the first move. I am getting so aroused I feel delirious.

The sounds of Charlie Parker's notes move in rhythm with his fingers.

I feel myself rising higher and higher, when suddenly, Elijah stops.

I moan, "Please, don't stop." I cling to Elijah and keep my arms clinched around his neck.

He slowly eases out of my grip. "We can't."

"Why not?"

"Bianca will be dropping Cinque off any minute. I want to take my time."

* * *

The next morning when I see Elijah as I'm taking my morning walk and he's putting Cinque in the Jeep to drive him to his bus stop, he looks sheepishly at me. He pulls me to the side.

"I'm sorry about last night. I'll never cross that line again."

"You didn't do anything I didn't want." How long has it been? Nine months. "Don't worry."

Once again I wonder, am I frigid? Once Marquise accused me of being that when I asked him to take his time with me. Thinking about it, I've never really reached a climax with Marquise, but last night I felt like I might reach one with Elijah.

The next weekend Elijah comes to visit and I am ready. I have showered, perfumed, and picked up a seductive teddy from Victoria's Secret. Bianca has told me that Cinque will be spending the weekend with her. I have lit vanilla candles all over the cottage and lit the fireplace.

When I answer the door for Elijah, we don't say a word, and as soon as he steps inside, I'm in his arms, lips locked to his. I notice that my being a little taller doesn't stop anything when it comes to kissing. We fit perfectly. For the first time, I learn what the songwriters talk about. Our clothes are spread like bread crumbs from the front door to the front of the fireplace.

We lie on a furry center rug I bought downtown in the alley and continue to kiss and slowly undress to the rhythm of the glass-burning fire.

Before Elijah enters me, he massages my entire body. While he oils my body, I feel his erection on my back and I'm so ready, I want to scream, "Hurry up."

"Let's go nice and slow," Elijah whispers.

So I try to slow it down. Following his lead I massage Elijah's body. I feel slippery as I sit on his back with the almond oil on both of my palms.

Before Elijah penetrates me, I feel like I'm going to explode like an oil rig, but he stops me. Over and over, he brings me to the brink, and stops me.

He slowly kisses my whole body, and I find erogenous spots I never knew I had.

Finally, when Elijah tries to enter me, I'm so tight, it feels as if I were a virgin and I tense up. No wonder. It has been over nine months since the last time.

Elijah begins to talk to me in this hypnotic voice. "Take it slow. Relax. Just breathe in and out. Lovemaking has the same rhythm. In and out. Don't rush." I catch the rhythms of the inhale and exhale of our bodies and we match our breathing.

Slowly, I begin to lubricate and Elijah slips on a condom before he penetrates. For a short man, Elijah surprises me. I guess that old saying, "Big things come in little packages," applies to him. I feel like I'm going to explode with each stroke as I experience the most pleasure I've ever known while making love.

As we work into a steady rhythm, I feel an ebb and flow start to build in my crotch and radiate through my hips, my spine, my breast, my mouth. I feel as if I were going over the edge of a waterfall and then waves of pleasure undulate through me. This night I learn the secret of not only having a vaginal orgasm, but having multiple orgasms. After the longest love session I've ever had, we both sing an aria to each other's name; you would have thought you were at an opera. At last, we collapse in each other's arms.

Elijah tells me something I haven't heard in a long time.

"I love you, Capri."

"I love you, too, Elijah," I answer with tears streaming down my face, tears that Elijah kisses, one by one, making me feel whole, making me feel better.

"How did you learn all this?" Elijah had done some things I've never even read about, let alone had done to me. If I was to compare, and I do, Marquise can't touch Elijah's lovemaking skills.

"*Kama Sutra*."

"What's that?"

"It's an old Indian lovemaking manual. Maybe one day I'll loan you my book."

I remember seeing it on his bookshelf and I say, "You're so bad."

"I didn't hear you say that a minute ago."

I chuckle and playfully push his shoulder.

Spent, we lie in each other's arms, spooning just the way I like to, and we talk about our whole lives until dawn. We talk about our hopes, our dreams, and our wishes. I am surprised when I even tell him about the shooting. Elijah just wraps me closer in his arms and I notice his face is wet when he kisses me again.

In Elijah's arms, I remember again that I've never had an orgasm before now. Now I've had several in one night. A word keeps running through my head. "Home."

16

Elijah
Two weeks later

Timing is everything in life, I decide. That's what I am thinking when I walk up the flagstone walk to the guesthouse.

I'd brought Capri a dozen red roses and had secured tickets to go to Sea World in San Diego for the next weekend since Capri had once indicated she wanted to go there on her birthday with Cinque. I wanted to surprise her and Cinque with the tickets.

But the biggest surprise was going to come first. I purchased a ring and was going to ask her to marry me after taking her to a romantic dinner at Spago's this weekend. I figure her divorce will be final soon, so it's not like jumping the gun.

I'm thirty-five years old, and although I'm considered to be a good-looking brother, even if I'm not that tall, I've never tried to be a player. I guess because my mother and older sister raised my younger sister and me by themselves, I have a love for black women and it just comes out in my dealings with them. It would be a mild understatement to say that I revere black women. I never ran around on Brooke, even when she was sick those last two years. I guess I'm a one-woman man.

I know by Bible standards what Capri and I did was wrong, but it felt so right. I try to be a Christian, although I know I haven't been going to church much since Brooke's death, but since I've started back I want to try to do right. I want Capri and me to be legally married the next time we make love. Since that first time we made love—and it was incredible—I have been real careful not to be alone with Capri. I've had to pray every night for self-control.

Over the last three months, Cinque has grown crazy about Capri. Even Tupac wags his tail when he sees her walk down the street on the cane. Recently, Capri has begun walking Tupac while she walks, and this is a good thing so that he's not sitting in the house going stir-crazy while I'm at work and Cinque is at school.

This evening when I get off work, I can't wait to talk to Capri. I want to invite her out for the surprise proposal dinner on Saturday.

When I knock on her door, a long silence ensues. I don't think I saw her leave or the med-i-cab come pick her up for her appointments that morning.

When Capri finally opens the door, with the way she holds her chin tilted upward, I know that something has changed. That is the most resolute look I've ever seen on a woman's face. Like her mind is made up.

"Hey," I say in a tentative voice. "May I come in?"

"Suit yourself." Her voice sounds petulant, yet cold.

She slowly eases open the door.

The first thing I see is her boxes packed and a small travel bag.

Trying not to seem too overbearing, too needy, though I need this woman like oxygen, I keep my voice calm. "What's going on?"

"I'm moving," Capri says simply.

"What? When did you decide that?"

"Last week."

"So you decide for the both of us?"

"No, I'm deciding for me."

I don't want to beg, but I can't just let it go. I can't believe what I am hearing. "Capri, didn't that night mean something to you? It did to me."

"This isn't about you, Elijah. This is about me. I've got to stand on my own two feet. I don't want to continue being a burden on you."

"You're not a burden. I love you."

"I've got to sort out some things first. Are you sure you are over Brooke?"

"You know I will always have a love for Brooke in my heart, but she would've been happy for me to go on with my life. If it were her, I would feel the same way."

Capri pauses. She seems to be picking her words. "We need some time. I've got to know you're not feeling sorry for me."

I am silent for the longest time. I think about the saying, if you love someone, set her free like a bird, and if she is for you, she will return.

Finally, I hear someone—not me, but my replacement—speaking for me. "Where are you moving?"

"I've found a place in Santa Monica."

"May I have the address?"

"No, not right now."

"Are you ever going to call me?"

"Yes. I will when I get settled."

"Capri, what happened?"

"Nothing. It's just time for me to put my life back together. Unless I do that for myself, whatever we might have will always be bogus."

"That's not true. I want to help."

"You have helped." Tears roll down Capri's cheeks. She

speaks in halting words. "You're the best man I've ever known in my life—since my father. But I've got to do this my way."

I heave a deep sigh of resignation, the thorns on the roses prickling my fingers. "Just tell me this. What are you running away from? Are you afraid to love again?"

"No, Elijah. That's not it. I can't talk about it right now. I've got to stand on my own feet again if we are ever going to be able to make it."

"Well, take these flowers." I hand over the bouquet.

"Thank you. They're beautiful."

I finally acquiesce. "Okay, I'll respect your wishes." I walk down the stone path, then turn back. Capri is still standing in the door. "By the way, I owe you a hundred."

"For what?"

"The bet that you could walk."

"No, that's okay."

"A bet's a bet now."

Capri finally smiles that grin I love.

"I'm still on a cane. Wait until I can walk without it."

"Okay. But I'll be here with open arms—when you're ready."

Capri nods. "Tell Cinque I'll call him when I get settled. I can't say good-bye to him right now." She closes the door behind her softly. As she disappears, I can hear the wind chimes tinkling a sour requiem in the background. I swallow deeply to keep the tears back that I feel threatening to come to the surface.

17

Capri
Three days earlier

I don't know anything anymore. I sit there, staring at the black-and-white photos, which the private investigator Charles Bryant has just dropped off. They are spread out on the small butcher block table in the kitchen. I'm too stunned to move. I can't believe what I'm seeing.

The woman in the picture with Marquise's arms wrapped around her waist is Coco—his partner Shank's wife. This has blown me away. Will wonders never cease? My ex-husband has taken a sister back from a white man. What is the world coming to?

I knew Marquis had had a girlfriend from college, but from what the report says, Sidra, which is Coco's real name, and Marquise had been college sweethearts.

So this is who he left me for? His partner's wife? Oh well, I don't really care, but I've needed to know the whole story so that I can move on. I've become numb when it comes to Marquise.

I love Elijah, but I can't stay here. Some of my money is

beginning to trickle in and today I placed a check in the mailbox to Elijah at Pasadena's main post office. I found a bachelor apartment in Santa Monica that I can swing. It is also near the address where my personal things are in storage. I plan to move this evening.

I guess if I lie low, I'll be safe from Ernest. The PI never found any evidence of Ernest still living anywhere in the L.A. metropolis.

I'm afraid, but I've got to take my chances. I'm on a mission and some things I must achieve on my own before I can become an "us."

I call Shank to be sure I haven't gotten this information wrong. When I get the answering machine, I leave a message on Shank's voice mail. He still has Coco's voice on the machine, as if he's waiting for her to come to her senses and return to him, and I cringe just hearing the sound of her singsongy voice.

That evening Shank returns my call. "Hi, Capri." His voice sounds depressed and subdued.

I cut to the chase. "Shank, is it true that Marquise left with Coco?"

He pauses. "Yes. I'm on sick leave now, this thing has blown me so away. I mean you know, Marquise was my boy, as well as he was my partner."

I have one more question. "What's your real name, Shank?"

"Kendall. They even took my son, Kendall Jr. I'm fighting to get custody back now."

"What is Coco's real name?"

"Sidra." So, the private investigator was right.

I can't think of anything to say. "I'm sorry."

"I'm sorry for you, too, Capri. How is your health coming along?"

"Don't be sorry for me. I'm going to be fine."

"Perhaps we can get together and talk some time."

"I don't think so."

After I hang up, I try to think back over our mutual get-togethers as two couples. Why didn't I see the chemistry between Coco and Marquise? Was I so busy I didn't want to see the signs? And then a chilling thought hits me. The voice. Coco's voice. That was it. That was the voice I heard just before Ernest shot me at my office. Coco's.

Why didn't I ever know that Coco was Marquise's first love? I wonder if that's why he picked Shank to be his partner, so that he could get close to Coco. I wonder how long the affair had gone on before the divorce. I wonder . . . Oh, what's the use?

Suddenly, I begin to cry so hard the bottom of my stomach hurts. It's not that I love Marquise anymore, it's just all the betrayal and drama. Now I know there's no way I can love Marquise again.

I am feeling so blue, I sob and I sob. I'm crying as if someone had died. Someone has died. A part of me. For the first time in a long time, I cry out to God. "Lord, help me. I can't go on. Please give me the strength and I'll listen to you."

For the first time since I've had it, I pick up the Bible that Elijah gave me. As if guided by some invisible hand, the pages fall open to Psalm 141.

Verse 1. Lord, I cry unto thee: make haste unto me. Give ear to my voice when I cry unto thee.

Verse 2. Let my prayer be set forth before thee as incense; and the lifting up of my hands as the evening sacrifice.

With difficulty, I get down on my knees and begin to pray.

"Lord, I know I haven't visited you in a long time, but please, don't forget your child. Please help me get through this. Help me not to lose my mind. Help me get closure about Mica and Nadine, so I can move on with my life. Help me get back on my feet so I can be a full woman when I come to Elijah, not an invalid. He deserves better than that. Keep me safe from Ernest until the police catch him. Amen."

When I clamber off my knees, I feel a sense of peace I haven't felt in a long time.

I hate that I have to move, but it's time to move on. I need to sort through things. I have to know I can make it on my own. I don't want to be a pity case. What is meant to be will be.

18

Capri
Six weeks later

"Mrs. Jordan, have a seat."

I'm at the William Morris Agency in Beverly Hills, sitting in this opulent waiting room. It reminds me of Dr. Medallion's office.

This last month has been a bipolar experience since I moved away from Elijah's. I didn't realize how protected I'd felt there. Now I feel vulnerable, exposed, and afraid. I've cried myself to sleep every night thinking of Elijah and Cinque, but I'm not ready to call him yet. I'm haunted by the hurt look on Elijah's face when he found out I was leaving. I hope he can find it in his heart to forgive me, but right now I don't know if we'll ever talk again.

During the day, I've kept busy, though. About six weeks ago, I'd e-mailed my screenplay to an agent, Frederica Lawrence, and I almost fell down when she called me on my cell phone yesterday. I don't have a landline at my new apartment, but I do have a cell phone now.

She got straight to the point. "Mrs. Jordan, I'm interested

in representing you. Can you come in tomorrow and sign the agent contract?"

So here I am, feeling like life is full of possibilities. I decide not to attach myself to the outcome. Whatever happens happens. This is the start of my new life.

Three weeks after my visit to the William Morris Agency, I receive another telephone call from Frederica. "Caprianna, are you sitting down?" she says.

"Uh-huh."

"I've sold your script to Paramount. Can you get ready for that?"

I pull my elbow down in the "Yes!" symbol. "This is great!" I let out a scream of joy.

"Please meet me at Katie Martinelli's Restaurant in Beverly Hills on Wilshire so we can go over the details tomorrow."

"What time?"

"Noon."

"You bet."

Good things tend to happen in waves. I can't believe how the tide of my life has turned around in these past three months.

Today, I open the mail and can't believe it. I have a government contract for Capri's Software. All this good news I want to share with Elijah, but first I have to take care of some unfinished business.

The divorce is now final, but the house is still on the market. One offer for the house has fallen through in escrow, so back to square one. Still, that's future money I have to look forward to.

I've joined a self-defense class, which is part martial arts and part yoga, and of course, this skill is making me feel less vulnerable as a woman. I've found a support group online for crime survivors. I guess I have survived.

Not too long ago, one morning I woke up and it occurred to me. I haven't had the drowning dream since my mother came to me in that dream while I was at one of my lowest points, when I was in the convalescent home.

I realize now, before the shooting I had my priorities screwed. I hope I never get it twisted again. There are only three things I have to do now. These are the things that matter.

For the past month, I've wanted to call Elijah, but I'm afraid he will reject me. I haven't talked to him in nine weeks. I miss him so much, my heart aches. Now I think of all the small things that he did that meant so much. The puppet he brought in to Morning Glory when I was feeling down. The flowers he told me the names of. Even telling me about the cicada spring, which gave me the title of my screenplay. Every day I take out the photograph we took at Santa Monica Beach and study it. Each time I see something different. I swear there is the lightest aura around all of our heads that look like halos. I think about how easy the relationship with Elijah was compared to my relationship with Marquise. Never an argument. Never a lot of drama. And I blush when I remember that wild night of lovemaking.

I guess I had always liked the challenge of Marquise, who was somewhat of a bad boy. I never dreamed I could fall in love with such a different man as Elijah, but I have. He's nothing I used to want physically in a man, such as the fact that he's not tall, yet he's the biggest man I've ever known.

A week ago, I dropped Bianca a postcard in the mail with my phone number on it and she called me the other day.

"How's Elijah?" I asked tentatively.

"Missing you."

"I miss him, too."

"Call him."

"I will."

* * *

On Saturday afternoon, I catch the bus from my Santa Monica apartment to midtown Los Angeles, then to east Los Angeles. I am surprised that both families of Nadine and Mica are glad to see me.

Nadine's children and her husband are at home in their stucco bungalow off Olympic Boulevard. Her children, Dyquaria, age fifteen, and Walter Jr., fourteen, are at home. They both welcome me with warm hugs.

"Nadine always spoke highly of you," her husband, Walter Greer, says. "She said she'd never seen such an ambitious young woman. She admired you."

"I'm so sorry about what happened."

"Well, young lady, we never know how long we're going to live. But Nadine was a good wife and mother, and she still lives in our hearts."

He tells me that Miss Nadine is buried at Inglewood Cemetery.

When I arrive in East Los Angeles, it's like I've entered Little Mexico. Mica's mother, Mrs. Hernandez, tells me through her heavy Spanish accent, "Mija, Mica was crazy about you. She said how you had inspired her and she wanted to start her own business one day."

Tears well in Mrs. Hernandez's eyes and she crosses herself with her rosary. "May she rest in peace. Do you think they'll ever find Ernest?"

"Mica was a good person. I'm sure she's in heaven. I believe the police will find him—one day."

Mrs. Hernandez gives me the address of the cemetery. I don't know if it's a coincidence, but Miss Nadine and Mica were both buried at Inglewood Cemetery.

I could've caught a cab, but I want to be out in the city among people. This is the first month I've walked without a cane. At the bus stop in Los Angeles, I see several men and women begging for spare change and I give them each a dollar.

"God bless you," I say.

Life is good.

On the bus, I use my cell phone to call Elijah on his cell at work. Bianca had told me that he's working this Saturday in Inglewood at the Morning Glory.

"Hi," I say, reluctant to say too much for fear he will hang up on me.

"Hi." Elijah sounds happy to hear from me.

I let out a sigh of relief. "How are you?"

"Okay. How about yourself?" The deep timbre of his voice sounds like music to my ears.

"I'm fine. I have a lot of things to tell you. But I have one more favor to ask of you."

"What is it?"

"Could you meet me at the Inglewood Cemetery?"

"Why?"

"I've got to say my good-byes to Miss Nadine and to Mica."

"I'll be off at three. Is that okay?"

"You bet."

"I'll be there."

"Thanks."

I get off the bus at Florence and Crenshaw where I see a street vendor selling carnations, roses, and gardenias. I buy two bouquets of mixed flowers for both graves.

I enjoy the walk, although it is hot. I sit at bus stops and rest as the walk is longer than I thought it would be. It's a sunny day for late August, and I wish I had worn a sun hat.

Finally, I arrive at the Inglewood Cemetery, which almost looks like a park, the landscaping is so beautiful. It's graced by sloping hills and winding drives, speckled with spruce, pines, and palm trees. However, there's a somber atmosphere here—as though the dead are whispering on the wind.

I wait for Elijah by the entrance at the black wrought-iron gates. A long funeral procession passes by and goes to a freshly opened grave slot near the front gate.

When Elijah finally pulls up in his Jeep, we walk over to the main office and get the mausoleum number for Miss Nadine and the plot number for Mica.

Together, we place flowers at each site. Mica is buried near a pond and I notice ducks and geese waddling around the grounds.

I talk to Mica's headstone, which lies flat in the ground. "Mica, you would like your final resting place. You can always see the ducks and the water. Yes, I know you would like this."

Elijah is silent as I do my rituals. At Miss Nadine's mausoleum, I say, "I thank you for being like a mother to me. And you were right. I am getting that government contract. And you're right about another thing. We have to have faith during the hard times."

After I leave both grave sites, I bow my head, close my eyes, and say a silent prayer for each of my former employees. I say my good-byes silently. Elijah just pats my back. I open my eyes and I'm almost blinded by my tears. Elijah just hugs me.

When we finally walk back to where Elijah parked his Jeep, he turns to me. "You want a ride home?" he offers offhandedly.

I shrug. "Sure."

"So it's all right that I'll have your address?"

"I'm ready now. Elijah, do you believe in life after death?"

"Oh, definitely. I believe in death while we're in life. Sometimes, we have to die in order to live."

"What do you mean?"

"An old part of us has to die in order for the new person to get out."

"That's deep." I'm silent for a while.

Elijah speaks up. "Capri, you think we can start over? Do you believe in second chances?"

I nod. Do I ever now!

"Let's start over as if we weren't two scarred people who had all this pain. Let's start over as if we hadn't dealt with all this loss and grief."

"Okay."

Elijah takes both of my hands. "Cinque has missed you. He told me you talked to him last week while he was at Bianca's."

"Yes."

"Why didn't you call me?"

"I wanted to see you face-to-face. To tell you how grateful I am—" My voice cracks. "To tell you—" My voice breaks off. Fresh tears spring to my eyes.

"I know. You don't have to thank me. Anyhow, here's your hundred dollars."

"No. I owe you."

"A bet's a bet. I said I bet you could walk again and now you're walking without the cane."

"Okay." I take the one-hundred-dollar bill and laugh.

We fall into each other's arms, which fit so comfortably, and kiss and laugh between our embrace.

"I love you, Capri."

"I love you, too, Elijah."

"Honey, will you marry me? That's what I wanted to ask you that last time I saw you."

Mmmm. I like the sound of the word "honey" on his tongue. "Yes," I say between kisses. "Yes, I will."

I don't remember what happened when I was pronounced dead, but this I do know. Since my resurrection, I imagine I have become like Lazarus, who after his resurrection probably saw life from a higher plane. I often laugh about how trivial things are that people think are really important. I'm beginning to see Cinque's magic in everyday life.

It's something about dying and coming back that makes you realize what's important. It is now important for me to make time for friends like Bianca and Larenz. It is important to take time to nurture children like Cinque, Tre, and Larenz. It is important as mortal man to have love, and I now have love with this wonderful man, Elijah. Most of all, it is important to have a spiritual connection with God.

At last word from Detective Briar, Ernest is still at large. I don't worry about it though. I have faith now that everything will work out.

They say, Job said, "I was born naked," and that is how I have felt since the shooting day to this day forward—naked. It makes me think of the story of Sambo. How he went into the jungle with a full set of clothes and came back out naked. I guess I'm like Sambo. I came out naked, but I'm still okay.

DETOURED

Michelle McGriff

1

He had dark eyes and a bright smile—almost like a perpetual grin—planted on his face. He wasn't very tall, but even for seventeen, he seemed quite muscular with his knobby joints and defined chest. That little bit of facial hair that had come out over the summer had Sonnet staring before she was aware. What a schoolgirl crush this was.

A mild look of confusion was on his face, him wondering if he knew her—ample as she was—wondering if perhaps she attended his mother's church or something. Maybe he had just seen her around. Maybe she was "somebody interesting's sister," for surely she wasn't anyone who had caught his eye before. It didn't matter; he was too busy right now to try figuring that mystery out. Hannah Judkins had just accepted his invitation to the movies on Friday and he was still on cloud nine—maybe even cloud fourteen. He just knew he had to find his buddies so he could brag about how easy it had been to get her to say yes. He would brag for at least an hour. Oh, and how easy it was gonna be to get in her panties . . . Hannah was the finest girl around—this week anyway.

He passed Sonnet without a second glance. Her heart sank. She felt like a nut, standing there gawking and staring.

By now she had to know that no boy was ever going to stare back, at least not with the same affection, especially a boy like Wilson Yant.

When boys stared at her, it was more to say, *Hey, who told you that you could fit those jeans?* or *Wow, you gonna eat all of that?*

Sonnet was seventeen and most of her adolescent life she had been overweight. It wasn't until today, the first day of senior year, that it suddenly mattered.

She turned, only to bump into by her childhood friend Justin. He was about six feet tall, give or take a couple of inches. He was fair skinned and well over 250 pounds.

Why were they friends? she often wondered. Maybe it had been his sad eyes on the playground ten years ago that locked her now into this life with him.

A bully had been laughing at him and Sonnet defended him by punching that boy out. Justin looked up at her innocently with those big eyes of his.

"Will you be my friend forever?" he asked.

"Always," she said, still huffin' mad, fist clenched tight.

He smiled at her then—and now—that's just how it was.

That's just how it is, Sonnet thought painfully to herself, as they sat together in the McDonald's eating their usual feast, two Big Macs, supersized fries and milkshakes, before going home.

She knew that her mother would have a full dinner ready by six; she always had dinner ready by the time her father would come home—but Sonnet would eat anyway.

Justin never even seemed to notice that she was so obese. He just seemed to like anything and everything about her. Something was wrong with that picture. What was wrong with a person liking the worst things about you?

Watching him eat, she hated how she felt inside about him. She didn't like the worst about him. She would give anything for him to change. Maybe it was time for a change, she thought.

Both Sonnet's parents and her younger sister were thin people. They would pretend not to notice, when out together as a family, how people would stare. People would stare, as if Sonnet were just a large stranger who had found herself a family to waddle next to. They would stare, as if she were some freak, let loose from her normal profession—as a circus act. Only once had Sonnet's mother tried to put her on a diet without her noticing. She was about twelve then—she noticed.

Sonnet's father, Frank, would only comment on her weight when he had been drinking. And he drank a lot.

"What's on your mind?" Justin asked. His eyes were dancing, the way they always did after he'd filled his belly. Eating brought him so much pleasure, Sonnet reasoned.

"Nothing," she lied. There was no way she was going to spill the contents of her heart again to Justin. For too many years she had told him all her most intimate secrets, all the details of her innermost fantasies. Anything deeper was saved only for Margaret, her sister . . . but that wasn't much, as Justin knew just about everything about her.

"Just tell me," he prodded, knowing she was holding back. She'd being doing that a lot lately. It bothered him, but he had just chalked it up to being a "girl thing."

"Nothing, Justin, dawg," she snapped. Her tone caught him off guard and his head ducked low. She hated when he did that; it was almost as if he had a fear of her.

"You wanna go?" he asked, finally, noticing her pursed lips and tight jaw. She sighed and nodded.

Sliding from the booth always brought attention, as Justin could never manage it without squeaking the faux leather under his wide rear. It would bring a chuckle from someone—never failed.

About that time Sonnet noticed her sister and Leita coming in through the front door.

Leita and her family had moved in around the corner. She was a plain skinny white girl with long, fine blond hair that didn't do much but hang there. She had never been popular in her old school and figured on the same treatment here. She had been right about that. It must have been Margaret's emaciated appearance and Sonnet's obesity that made those odd-looking sisters initially approachable; Leita seemed to take to them immediately and the three of them became the best of friends, right off.

Leita was a loving, sincere girl. She seemed to understand Sonnet and Justin completely. Maybe better than they understood themselves, she would wager. She thought it was cute that they had found each other.

It was more than their race and weight that brought them together, Leita knew that. It was more like the fact that they were meant to be. Justin's silent approval of Sonnet and Sonnet's acceptance of him, for who he was—this had touched Leita's heart.

And Margaret, her fear of everything hid behind her self-control. That's what it was that kept her from eating like she did—self-control, to the extreme. Leita felt that Margaret thought that if she could control her body, no one else could, and therefore nothing bad could ever happen to her.

Leita was a bright, intuitive girl, whose mother had always taught her that some people were just meant for each other and some things were just meant to be the way they were, and Leita believed that. She also believed that people should never have to change to suit anyone else. She had her own parents as proof of that. Although she felt that her parents were two of the most beautiful people on earth, they weren't exactly what most people considered "pretty people." She had been seeing a lot of pretty people since they moved to California just five years ago, and her parents didn't resemble any of them. But her parents loved each other dearly and they loved her and to Leita that was all that mattered.

Leita noticed Sonnet's wrinkled brow and decided quickly it was not a time to make any jokes. She loved to tease Sonnet about her lovers' spats with Justin. It would make her so mad—but tickle Leita to no end.

"You going home?" Margaret asked Sonnet, who shrugged her shoulders.

It was Monday night and that meant that their father would be home early. After the weekend, there was never much to do at the auto body shop on Mondays. Not for a detailer anyway. It wasn't until the middle of the week, after most of the cars had been worked on, that the washing and vacuuming and other detail work done on a car would be needed. It was Monday that usually determined the pace for the week in their house.

"Daddy home?" she asked, her voice carrying with it a secret code.

Margaret, catching it, smiled. "No."

"Oh well, I better get on home then to help Mom with dinner." Sonnet smiled back, glancing over her shoulder at Justin. "I'm gonna go on home," she told him. He nodded.

Sonnet never let him walk her all the way home. They usually got as far as this McDonald's, which was on the corner of her street. Justin sensed it had something to do with Frank Patterson, Sonnet's father, but didn't ask. Sonnet's mother was always nice, though. When she would come to the school for one thing or another—usually school plays, concerts, or things like that—she was always very nice to him. Justin couldn't imagine Frank Patterson being anything other than a hardworking man, who was strict about his teenage daughters walking home with boys—and he could understand that.

Justin's mother was a widow. She never remarried and, unless she had a great big secret, she hadn't dated either.

To Teri Hamilton, Justin was her life. She wanted him to grow up to be a civil service man or a teacher, anything other than the musician he was turning into. Justin played saxophone in his room most of his time at home, after school. He dreamed of being a jazz star, like his father. At least that's what his father was until he overdosed on heroin when Justin was only five. When her husband died, no one could blame Teri Hamilton for wanting to make the boy smile.

She knew she was overfeeding Justin, but in her mind, if she kept him happy, he would always love her—and never leave her.

He seemed so happy when she would make his favorite treats, so what was the harm?

Translate it into love, she would say to herself.

He was a good-looking boy, *Looking just like his father*, Teri noticed, watching him shuffle his large frame down the hallway toward his room. Take about a hundred pounds off him and he would *be* his father.

Ali Hamilton, Justin's father, had been a good-looking man too. He had many women, besides Teri, to prove it. There was no way Teri wanted to lose Justin to women like that. She didn't want to lose Justin to anything.

And nobody was going to convince her that she was just a lonely woman who was afraid that one day her son would leave her just like her husband did—that just wasn't true. Besides, she couldn't handle a thought like that anyway, so it never even entered her mind.

Teri heard the sound of his saxophone and it sent a chill through her. Justin didn't show it right now, but Teri knew about genes. She understood that the fruit might not fall far from the tree.

"But he's not going anywhere," she said to herself out loud. "Not if I have anything to do with it."

Besides, Justin liked simple things, school, food, and that girl Sonnet. And as long as it went in that order . . . she had no worries. Teri thought now about the pictures of Sonnet she found in the drawer of Justin's bureau. She would tolerate that horn for now. It was just a hobby, anyway. He couldn't help but want to play it, she reasoned. What with all the concerts she had gone to while pregnant with him, it was all he knew.

Unfortunately for Teri, Justin was good on that horn. But there was no way she would ever tell him. After he would play his little heart out for her, he would ask, “Mama, was I good?” and she would say, “It sounds all right.” It didn’t bother her at all to see his big eyes, the color of caramel, well up with tears. She knew it was for the best not to fill his mind and heart with such foolish things—like fame and the glamour—that came with being a musician. Playin’ that horn and being a musician, what kind of life would that be, for a good boy like him?

What Teri Hamilton didn’t know was that he was also a good pianist, trumpet player, and even drummer. Justin was good on any instrument he touched. She was almost right; it was in his genes all right, but what she didn’t realize was that it was also in his blood. And when he heard those words, “It sounds all right,” something in his heart would just freeze toward her and he was pulling away emotionally—leaving her. So all her efforts were for naught.

His bedroom door opened right on cue. It was his mother with a tray. It seemed that every time he would start to practice, he knew she would come into his room with something to eat. Perhaps she thought with a full mouth he couldn’t play, and it often worked.

When Justin wasn’t at home, he was with Sonnet. When together, the two of them never liked to talk about their home life much, and that suited him just fine. She had her secrets about her father, and he had his about his mother . . . it was fair. Of course, he had a secret too and that was his talent.

He hadn’t played his horn for her since they were little. She had no idea he was as good as he was. He had convinced himself that he didn't want to take up the time spent with her doing that. The truth was, he didn't want her to say those words he hated so much. He didn't want to take a chance that maybe Sonnet too would find his music merely—all right.

Justin knew that Sonnet had outstandingly high grades, but she never talked to him about them. He would just see her name on the honor roll list and things like that. She never even went onstage to collect her awards. She wouldn't even come to the assemblies. She never made a fuss over them, so he figured she wanted it that way.

They just talked about everyday things and he never pushed the conversation in any direction. He just figured one day it would all come together. He didn't know any other way to be with her. He loved her, he always had. He knew his love was growing into a deeper, grown-up kind of love—though he didn't have a clue what to do about it. He knew that one day they would marry—they had to. He had even written a song for her that he would play at their wedding. It was just what he figured was the way it was meant to be. He didn't think they needed to talk about it. They had spent nearly their whole lives together—surely she was thinking the same way.

Besides, even their friends took it for granted they were a couple.

Leita Gardner sure knew it and she was Sonnet's and Margaret's best girlfriend.

2

Margaret would never eat. Often Sonnet thought she might die. Sometimes Margaret would hide her food and give it to her late at night in their bedroom. Sometimes Sonnet could hear her throwing up in the bathroom when she thought everyone was asleep.

Once Sonnet asked her about it, but Margaret denied it, her eyes darting and squinting the way they did when she lied.

However, despite the lie that stood between them and total honesty and sister bonding, on the nights when their father would drink and fight with their mother, Yolanda, it was nice to have someone to be with. It was nice to have something to do besides listening to the yelling and swearing going on in the next room.

While their father would scream and curse at their mother on the nights he was drunk, the girls would giggle and eat cookies under the blankets on the floor. Sonnet could get Margaret to eat cookies sometimes, especially when they would play the fighting game. The fighting game went something like this—Sonnet and Margaret would eat a cookie for every time her father would call her mother a whore or slut. Once, they ate a whole package of Oreos before it got quiet.

"So, did Wilson talk to you today?" Margaret asked, licking the creamy middle out of the dark, hard cookie. Sonnet's eyes rolled as she crunched down on her treat, without bothering to twist it open.

"I told you not to ask me that anymore," she said with a sneer.

"Ah, shined you on." Margaret giggled, licking her cookie clean. From the other room they could hear the cursing.

"Wonder what Mom's gonna cook for breakfast," Sonnet mused, thinking of the norm.

On the mornings after a loud night like that, their mother would always be up early. She would be in that big old robe with the very long sleeves. When the girls got older they began to realize she wore that robe to hide the bruises that she had received from all of the pushing and shoving that had gone on.

Yolanda would cook such a big breakfast for everyone after a night like that. Lots of bacon and eggs and even biscuits made from scratch. She would kiss Frank and whisper how sorry she had been for everything. Sonnet always heard her, and the older she got, the more it would make her sick to her stomach. However, after such a good breakfast she would hardly think about it the rest of the day.

"I'm so sorry, Frank, baby," Sonnet whispered now, puckering her lips. Margaret's eyes widened, as the flashlight shone off her mortified expression.

"Oh my God, Sonnet, don't say that," Margaret said. "Don't play on what Mama says . . . after," she added, before stopping her words abruptly.

"Oh, come on, Marg, doesn't it just make you wanna hurl? Tell me it doesn't!" Sonnet said, tossing another cookie in her mouth, while they sat under that blanket, sharing their peace.

Just then the wall behind their closet rumbled, as they

both knew their mother was being bounced off it. At that, Margaret pulled the blanket from off their heads and leaped into her bed, covering her head with her pillow. Sonnet watched her younger sister, lying still there under the pillow—wondering if she was even breathing.

"Margaret?" she called.

"What?" Margaret's muffled voice could be heard answering.

"Wilson didn't give me the time of day," Sonnet admitted.

Justin lay still in his bed, unable to sleep, his mind filled with many things, yet nothing really connecting. He hated being seventeen. It was like the beginning of the end and yet—not. It was a senseless age, good for nothing but dreaming.

Soon he would be eighteen and all the answers to life would fall into his hands. He believed that.

He glanced at the clock; it was nearly 10:00 p.m., surely too late to call Sonnet. He had called once after nine and her father just hung up the phone on him without even giving Sonnet the message that he had called.

It wasn't as if he had so much he wanted to say to her right now, but hearing her voice would surely help him sleep tonight. Rolling over, he chuckled, knowing he probably was the furthest thing from her mind right about now. He wasn't stupid, Sonnet was changing and looking—and he was surely not in her sight. He had no idea why things were changing. Life was simple until now, and now—well, he didn't want to think about it anymore.

Lying in her bed, listening to the eventual silence of their house, Sonnet had time to think. She hated her life and the way things where. She hated the thought that everyone just assumed she and Justin would be together forever. They were just friends. In fact, she was planning on going to the prom with someone else. She was going to see to it!

She had had enough of those comments they would get, while walking together, kids acting as though an earthquake were happening, right when they would sit down at their desks . . . it had gotten to be a very tiring joke.

Sonnet had grown frustrated with Justin never noticing how smart she was, or how pretty she was. He hadn't even noticed how outstandingly large he was.

But then, it wasn't as if she had ever noticed what a soft pretty shade of brown his eyes were. She hadn't even looked lately.

Things were changing between them and he needed to get with the program. That was her opinion.

She chuckled to herself now, as she thought about the last three hours of her day—listening to her mother in the other room, imagining the scene. She had never seen her father swing at her mother, nor had she even seen him as the filthy words were coming from his mouth—it was almost as if they were listening to the television up too loud. It was hard to make it all real sometimes—what she knew to be the truth.

Even in the morning, when she saw the robe with the big sleeves and painful-looking, deep purple monkey bites on her mother's long cinnamon-brown neck, it was hard to imagine the scene.

What was left for her to think about but her life at seventeen?

3

Yolanda lay quietly staring out the window. It would be a while before daylight would come. She often wondered why the darkness stayed so long. So much badness happened after dark.

Stiffly, she attempted to look over at Frank, praying he didn't wake up. Her bladder was full, but the thought of getting out of the bed and awakening him was just not worth the relief.

Surely she would get another infection. She always got one when she would wait so long to go. Since she was a kid, she'd had that trouble.

Her mother would get so upset with her when she would come into the bathroom and find her on the toilet, crying from the burn of an infected bladder attempting to empty.

"It's not like we have an outhouse, Yolanda!" she would snap, cooling her off with a spray of cool water from the mister she used with her ironing. Yolanda would say nothing—she felt too stupid to speak . . . like now.

Frank accused her of having an affair with one of his friends from the Elks Lodge. A man she didn't even know. He hit her, pushed her, slammed her to the bed, climbed on her, and sprayed his putrid alcohol-smelling breath all in her face. It turned her stomach. Finally, she admitted to the affair . . . that made him happy. Then he could sex her. He would take her like a cheap whore—showing her he was better than . . . what's his name.

Yolanda felt stupid . . . and said nothing.

Finally, as the pressure got to be too much, she eased back the covers as carefully as she could, but sure enough it wasn't carefully enough.

"Yolanda," she heard him say. Her heart pounded loudly, her chest tightened.

"Yes, Frank?" she said over her shoulder. She felt his rough hand run down her back.

"Hurry back," he said.

She nodded.

Slipping into her robe and slippers, Yolanda greeted the morning on her way to the kitchen. She smiled, only because the night was over.

Opening the front door, she picked up the paper from the porch. She noticed Mr. Drake across the street headed for his car. He was a handsome man in his midfifties. His wife had died last year. So far he hadn't remarried. Apparently she had stood there too long; he waved at her.

"Hello there, Yolanda," he called out, with a bright smile showing. Yolanda smiled, brushing the loose hair from her face. "I noticed your roses are coming on up this year . . . they look really nice. You must be talking real sweet to them," he continued, almost in a tone Yolanda could have misconstrued as flirting . . . Surely not Mr. Drake . . .

Just then Yolanda felt herself being shoved aside and noticed Mr. Drake's expression drop.

"Hey, yeah, Drake . . . I bought some of that new stuff for plants. Grows the hell outta your flowers. Anything for the wife here. She wanted roses and so . . ." Frank went on.

Yolanda left the doorway.

Margaret pulled on her jeans; they were a lot looser today

than last week. She was losing weight again. She had to admit, she wasn't even trying this time. She glanced over at Sonnet, struggling to button her blouse, tugging and pulling at the buttons, forcing them over her ample bustline. Sonnet looked up, only to catch her turning away quickly.

"Mom shrank this," Sonnet said. Margaret turned back to her and smiled.

"I know she did," was all she said.

"You meeting Justin this morning?" Sonnet asked.

"Why would I meet Justin?" Margaret asked.

"Because I'm not. I'm not going to meet him this morning. I've got to get to school early . . . I'm, um, working on something," Sonnet said, moving in front of her vanity mirror and pulling her hair over her shoulder, flattering her pretty face. She applied some gloss, then held the tube out to her sister.

"Want this?" she asked Margaret, who refused. "You know, you need to stop looking like a boy."

Margaret looked down at her oversized clothes.

"I don't look like a boy," she insisted.

"You don't even have any boobs." Sonnet laughed, pointing at her flat chest.

Margaret's temper now came up. She hated when Sonnet did that.

"Why don't you gimmie some of yours? You gots plenty," Margaret bit out, poking her finger into Sonnet's soft chest.

Sonnet stood stunned, blinking away the instant hurt she felt.

Just then Yolanda came into the room. Both girls noticed the robe and instantly gave each other a knowing look.

"Breakfast," Yolanda announced.

4

It was Friday night and Leita Gardner was sleeping over. Sonnet and Margaret had said a silent prayer that their father wouldn't drink tonight. They had asked his permission for Leita to stay over, and he had said yes, so maybe that meant he wouldn't. It wasn't like Leita stayed over very often.

After Leita and her family had moved in around the corner, in the Johnsons' old house, the girls became friends. Aside from Leita and a couple of other girls they had known from elementary school, the sisters really only hung out with each other. Their being close in age made it very convenient to be their own social circle. Adding Leita in was a plus. Even though she was white, she seemed to be able to relate to a lot of different things, and their racial differences just didn't matter much.

"Maybe one day you'll notice that you're just a skinny white girl from the inner city," Margaret explained to Leita, sounding very deep and philosophical. Margaret prided herself on being the logical levelheaded sister.

"And that will make me want to do what?" Leita asked, a heavy Arkansas accent pouring from her lips. "Run down the street screaming or burn down the neighborhood?" she added with a giggle.

"I'm just sayin' sometimes youth blinds us to the realities out there, the hatreds and separations that make up our society, and so we, being children, have to ready ourselves for the possibilities of ending up on opposite ends of the fence once we get older."

"Well, for now, I just wanna sleep over tonight," said Leita.

"Yeah, yeah, it's not a problem—for now," Margaret assured her, sounding totally tongue-in-cheek, slurping down the last of her Diet Coke.

Leita noticed Justin, sitting alone in what was normally referred to as his and Sonnet's regular booth.

"Where's Sonnet?" she asked.

Margaret, quietly wondering, shook her head and shrugged. She prayed secretly that Sonnet wasn't somewhere making a fool of herself over Wilson Yant.

Sonnet sat, watching the cheerleaders, as they bounced around the field. She had a lot on her mind. Sitting in the bleachers, she tried hard to ignore the rumbling in her stomach that told her it was Micky D time.

That will be my first change . . . well, the second, after dumping Justin, she thought to herself.

Yep, a good night's sleep and an afternoon of watching Wilson at football practice were going to be more than enough to set her mind right again. It had been two days since her mother and father had had their blowout—long forgotten in their house. It was time to move on.

Just then, Sonnet thought she noticed Wilson looking her way. Before she could catch herself, she waved. The curve of his brow now told Sonnet she had been mistaken. The way he ran over to Monika, the head cheerleader, giving her a flirty swat on the butt, just brought the fact on home.

Sonnet watched the two of them playing slap and tickle until she could stand it no longer. Gathering up her backpack, she started down the bleachers.

Reaching the bottom, she was met at the gate of the track by two girls from the squad. One of them looked her over and giggled, the other punched her hard in the ribs.

"Girl, Shanelle is trippin', being hecka rude. My cousin is big boned—don't even sweat all dat," the girl, Tanya, said, with a jerk of her neck and a flip of her hair weave. Shanelle seemed to blush under her fair skin.

"Yeah, girl, I'm sorry. I feel your pain. You sittin' out here watching us and feeling bad 'bout choself—" Shonelle began. Tanya nudged her again.

"Dawg, Nelle . . ."

"No, I understand what you're saying, and actually I have been thinking of going on a diet," Sonnet divulged. "You know, maybe losing a few pounds."

Just then the two girls looked at one another and burst into laughter. Sonnet realized, again, she had been the butt of a joke.

"No, wait," said Tanya, between chuckles, catching Sonnet before she walked away. "What I was gonna say, before my girl here got all rude," she said, smacking her frost-colored lips, a color Sonnet wouldn't have dared try if her skin was as dark as Tanya's, but girls like her could pull it off, they could do whatever they wanted. "What I was gonna say was . . . try diet pills," Tanya suggested.

"Tanya, you ain't no doctor. You can't just say that," Shanelle yelled, slapping her arm.

"Look here. I see your name, uh, on the honor roll list and look here . . . why not be smart and beautiful?" Tanya smiled, reaching in her pocket and pulling out a small red pill. "These'll help. Get yo' mom to get you some . . . I mean, if she's big boned like you, they'll give her some and she can give them to you," she went on.

Sonnet took the pill and examined it.

"Well, my mother is thin . . . but I'm sure I can get some anyway," she said, almost mesmerized by the small tablet in her hand . . . the tablet that potentially held all the answers to her miserable existence.

"Thanks," Sonnet said, looking up, noticing the girls had wandered off without even saying good-bye.

"Would you girls like a treat?" Yolanda asked, as she peeked her head in the girls' room. Sonnet smiled and nodded. After that incident at the track, she could use a snack. Leita and Margaret declined.

The three of them had just eaten pizza less than four hours ago. Of course Margaret had had only one piece, but that was a lot for her. Yolanda smiled at Sonnet and reappeared in what seemed to be seconds with a plate of brownies fresh out of the oven. Leita ate one anyway, despite the fact that she was still stuffed from the pizza—to be polite. Besides, Mrs. Patterson was a great baker. Leita had seen ribbons from Yolanda Patterson's strawberry festival victories. Her strawberry pies and cakes won prizes every year.

"So, Sonnet, I hear that you're after Wilson." Leita laughed, as she nibbled on the brownie. Sonnet cut her eyes at Margaret, who held up her hands in surrender.

"Well, he noticed me if that's what you mean," Sonnet exaggerated, referring to that afternoon on the bleachers—he had noticed her. She also couldn't help but think about the afternoon that she bumped into him coming out of the gym and knocked him down, it wasn't so much her size that threw him to the floor as it was that he was just caught unaware. With his slender frame bouncing off hers and falling the way he did, onlookers got quite a chuckle. Sonnet was mortified—but he *had* noticed her.

"Well, I guess it's a good test for Justin," Leita went on.

"Test?" Sonnet asked, confusion showing on her face.

"You know, love test. What-will-he-do-to-keep-you kinda test." Leita's innocence was bubbling over so that she didn't even notice Sonnet's expression changing to irritation.

"Keep me? He doesn't have me." Sonnet put her hand on her hip in an arrogant stance. Leita laughed out loud, ignoring Sonnet's angry glare. "You're serious, aren't you? Me and Justin are just friends," Sonnet defended. "Why would you think more? Why would you say that?" she asked now, her voice hitting a high pitch. Margaret could tell she was upset. She jumped in, joking—trying to keep Sonnet from going off the deep end.

"Duh, you're always together," Margaret interjected quickly, trying to keep it light.

"You don't think I could get Wilson, do you? You think I could only get someone like fat slob Justin!" Sonnet challenged, her volume louder now.

Margaret and Leita began to squirm uncomfortably on the bed. Sonnet was angry, hurt, and a little embarrassed. Justin was her friend, but surely she could do better—she could do lots better. She had a pretty face—as pretty as any of those cheerleaders', her mother had told her as much. All she needed was the right motivation and she could get a pretty body too. She only needed to lose maybe fifty or sixty—okay, maybe eighty pounds. That wouldn't be so tough. Besides, the pill was burning a hole in her pocket. She was dying to try it out. Maybe she would just not eat, like Margaret.

It was September now and the prom was not until May of the following year, excluding the holidays and a few times that she might have to cheat. She would just cut back. Surely Wilson would *really* notice her and not by accident.

"I'm going to the prom with Wilson. Hell, prom? I might even marry him! You'll both see!" Sonnet snapped, sounding off the wall.

"I think Sonnet is outta her league," Leita said, after the

bedroom door slammed behind Sonnet, who exited without another word. Margaret knew what Leita had said was very true. Both of them had heard rumors about Wilson, and they weren't good.

Wilson Yant—his mother was a black woman from Panama and his father was a Jewish man. Even he knew his racial mixture looked good on him. He was dark and handsome and very forward sexually. He had even made a weak pass at Margaret once, which she pretended not to notice. Sonnet would have died if she found out—Margaret *knew that*.

She hated the thought of watching her sister try to be what others wanted her to be—especially someone like Wilson. Losing weight for him would not be an easy road, a hard road with only disaster waiting in the end. But Margaret decided she would keep silent.

Later, after Sonnet calmed down and returned to the room (and the plate of brownies), Margaret and Leita sat on the bed watching as Sonnet dusted the crumbs of her third brownie from her chest. Both girls knew her plan was going to be a challenge, if not impossible.

The night went smoothly. Frank got in from work and watched a little television—sober. Margaret found herself so tense by the anticipation of the night going bad, she vomited several times. It was on the last time back to the room that Leita caught her in the hallway.

"You sick?" she asked.

Margaret jumped, startled.

"No, I mean . . . yes. I think the pizza got to me," she lied, as they entered the bedroom.

"Well, it didn't get to me none. And it sure didn't bother your sister," Leita said, without thinking.

"I heard that," Sonnet mumbled from under the covers.

5

"Mom, I've decided to go on a diet," Sonnet announced at the dinner table Sunday. The silence was deafening, as everyone just looked at one another dumbfounded. Yolanda had made one of her specialties. She had pulled out all the stops too. For a second Margaret noticed an expression of hurt feelings cover her mother's face at the thought of Sonnet maybe not enjoying the meal to the fullest.

"What brings this crazy talk on?" Yolanda chuckled, setting the large bowl of potatoes in front of her—her actions unconsciously encouraging Sonnet to dig in.

"A boy," Margaret snapped. Margaret was hoping her parents would support her stand as a nonconformist and not encourage this stupidity any further—Sonnet dieting for a boy.

"A boy?" Frank asked. There was nearly a cheer in his voice as he dug into the bowl of mashed potatoes. "My, my, a boy. Is it that time already?"

Yolanda chuckled.

Margaret's heart sank. She sighed. "What superficial madness this all is!" But no one heard.

The phone rang. Frank went to answer it. "It's that Justin *boy*," he called out. Usually Sonnet would have had a fit if he had said something like that, but not tonight—tonight she didn't budge.

"Tell him I'm busy," she said, sounding cocky and even a little stuck-up.

Margaret caught her mother's eye for a second before she went back into the kitchen to get more salad for the bowl—since that's all Sonnet was going to be having tonight. Yolanda had a little bit of apprehension showing, but not enough to fight what was going on here.

"You can do better than that guy, anyway," Frank said when he came back to the table.

Margaret was shocked by the statement. He had never said that before about Justin—how dare he? He didn't even know Justin, Margaret thought to herself.

All these years and now the truth came out. All he saw in Justin was a fat little boy and now a fat teenager. He didn't know anything about Justin the young man, the talented, bright, loving, and kind young man. Margaret was feeling a deep hurt, like a dagger's cut.

"You're gonna be able to get somebody better soon," Frank added.

Now Margaret was angry.

After Sonnet passed on dessert, Frank grinned like a clown.

"See, Yolanda, our girl will be back soon. At this rate, she'll be a cutie little somethin' in no time," he said.

Margaret was growing ill, but again she hid her true feelings. Once again, her mother disappeared into the kitchen.

During the night, Margaret could hear Sonnet in her bed. She was tossing and turning—starving. Margaret had only consumed about five hundred calories that day herself, but that was a way of life for her. It had been that way for her since she was thirteen. But for someone like Sonnet, it had to hurt, and it hurt Margaret now to be able to see her sister in this pain . . . and for what? *For the approval of a boy? For the grins of their father?*

It was the first night that Margaret realized how much Sonnet had disgusted their father. He was a prideful man from a large family. His mother was from Africa and he was very proud of that. Sure, he was proud of Sonnet's grades, but not of her. That was obvious. And now with the prospect that she would be thin, and pretty, he was happy. Margaret could see that.

Monday came finally, and Sonnet had her mind made up. After the weekend of revelation and successful dieting, she knew her life was about to change. There would be nothing holding her back.

She would have to break away from Justin in order to make a real life for herself—to make all her dreams come true. Without Justin hanging on, she would have a chance at a real life—a life with the beautiful people where she belonged.

She had gotten Margaret to style her hair differently Sunday night before she went to bed. She had wrapped it tight in one of her mother's head scarves. And now it hung full around her shoulders, instead of up in that tight bun she normally wore. She even wore makeup.

"You look great," Margaret admitted.

With confidence, Sonnet sauntered to her locker around the time she knew that Wilson would be coming from his class. Having her locker located right outside his math class was what had started this whole thing to begin with. She would never have seen him so up close and personal had she not had her locker here. She was close enough to smell his cologne when he walked by.

The bell rang and the door sprang open. Having gym this period, Sonnet was usually out way before he was—one excuse or another always kept her from dressing out for gym.

So again today, she waited. When he walked out, he was talking to Cathy Crowley, a blond girl from the flag squad. Cathy was cackling like a hen and flipping her hair and Wilson—he didn't even look Sonnet's way. Trying to hide her feelings, she threw her books into her locker, causing a cacophony of sound, and slammed the door.

Cathy wasn't even pretty, she thought to herself. All that stringy blond mess . . . and her skin . . .

Sonnet shoved her hand deep into the pocket of her jacket; it ran across the little red pill. Just then, when she looked up, she could see Justin smiling as he neared her. He was always smiling, she thought to herself . . . and for what?

Sonnet wanted to pretend she hadn't seen him, but that would be too obvious. She wanted to run, but that was impossible, not without everyone in that hallway getting a total freak show, so she waited. They walked to class together—again.

Again today, Justin ignored the jeers from their classmates . . . and again today, Sonnet knew this life with Justin would have to come to an end—soon!

Teri opened the mailbox. She saw the New York return address. Justin's grandparents had written him.

Why were they doing this to her? Didn't they know she was not going to send her son to them? What was their problem?

"Hey there, Teri," Julie, her neighbor, called out, as Teri closed the lid of the trash can. Startled, Teri unconsciously jumped.

"Oh, hey there, Julie." Teri smiled overly wide—guilty.

Justin cleaned his plate; it was easy to do that night, as Sonnet had stood him up at McDonald's after school—this was becoming a habit with her. Leita and Margaret had showed up as usual, but no Sonnet. And when he called her, her mother had said she was busy. He didn't know Yolanda Patterson well, but he could tell a lie in anyone's voice.

"Justin, is there something on your mind tonight?" Teri asked, guilt apparent in her voice too.

What was up with everybody's mothers tonight? Justin thought to himself.

"No," he lied.

"I mean, you seem kinda out of it," she continued. Justin could not stop his eyes from rolling. Teri caught it. "What the hell you looking at me like that for?" she snipped.

Justin sighed.

"Nothing, Mom . . . Gawd, stop pushing me," he answered.

"Take out the trash!" was all Teri had to say in retort to his foul attitude.

Justin jumped up from the table and grabbed the small trash receptacle and slammed out the back door. He was angry and didn't even know why.

Reaching the trash can on the sidewalk, he flipped on the flashlight and opened the can. Out of reflex, he glanced inside—possibly to make sure there was room for the trash he was getting ready to dump—and that's when he saw it, the New York postmark. Justin dropped the trash bag and reached in the can to retrieve the crumpled letter. His heart was pounding. His mother hadn't even bothered to open it . . . or tear it up! Looking toward the house, Justin could see his mother moving about the kitchen, unconcerned about what he had discovered—what she had hidden. He shoved the letter deep in his pants pocket.

He knew in this letter there would be some answers to his burning questions. The questions about his life—he just knew it.

* * *

Yolanda was shocked to find Justin at her front door the next morning. He never came all the way to the house to pick Sonnet and Margaret up. Frank usually made him feel so bad, Yolanda didn't blame him—but today, here he was, Justin Hamilton. Behind all that baby fat stood a handsome young man, with kind and gentle brown eyes filled with laughter. Just looking at him made her smile.

"Justin? Uh, Sonnet and Margaret both are already gone," she said.

Disappointed, but not deterred, he smiled, thanked her, and hurried off. He seemed to have no idea that Sonnet had no desire to see or talk to him. Of course Yolanda didn't agree with her daughter's decision, but it was Sonnet's to make. Besides, it kept Frank happy and that's all that mattered.

Yolanda thought about her daughter all afternoon—to the point of distraction. Sonnet was so much like her in so many ways. Or maybe it was just high school . . . with its pressures to blend in, to be like everybody else.

Back when she was in school, though, being like everybody else only meant a small circle of blacks—all who lived on your street—who attended your same church . . . still, you had to fit in. Yolanda remembered how different she was than most of the ones in that small world of colored girls. They only wanted to see how close to the edge they could get, how much they could get away with.

Even her best friend, Clara . . . she got herself in trouble. The boy wouldn't marry her, so she had to go live with her grandmother in Texas. How horrible that was. It had scared them all for a while, that is until the next dance.

Frank had asked her out the first week they moved into the neighborhood. So many girls had wanted to go out with Frank, *but he had asked her.* . . . However, it had only taken a couple of dates to know that Frank wasn't who she wanted to go out with—that he wasn't the right guy. But when she told him she wanted to break it off, he nearly broke her wrist. He apologized, of course, blaming it on being upset, but it scared her. She never told her parents.

She just continued to date him. That is until Joseph came along. . . .

6

Sonnet saw Justin coming, full speed. She slammed her locker and started for class, as if she hadn't seen him. He called out loudly for her. She froze—mortified now. She noticed Tanya and a couple of the other popular girls look over in her direction and shake their heads—whispering now. Sonnet wanted to scream.

"Sonnet, I need to talk to you about something," he said, sounding out of breath from the hurried pace.

Sonnet was livid. Embarrassed at the outburst and the attention it drew and angry that he felt he had a right to call her that way.

"I'm busy, Justin. I have a test first period and—"

"I know, but listen," he went on, disregarding her.

Sonnet was shocked. She was wondering what had come over him when he pulled the smelly letter out of his pocket and fanned it in her face.

"My mother threw this away," he began. The late bell rang. Sonnet moved toward her class. Justin out of reflex grabbed her arm.

Sonnet didn't pull away. At first she thought about making a scene, jerking her arm from his grasp, but why? Justin was her friend; despite her desire to move on, he was, after all, her friend.

"And rightfully she should have. It stinks," she said, carefully taking the letter from him to read it. It was from his grandparents. They were asking him to come to New York. In the letter they mentioned how long they had been asking his mother, but now, with his eighteenth birthday less than a year away, they decided to ask him.

"And so . . ." Sonnet questioned the importance of the letter.

"Don't you see, Sonnet?" he exploded, wide-eyed. He had forgotten that there was no way Sonnet could see. He had not told her about the music in him. He had not shared that part of his life with her. She didn't know about his father. She just knew that he was dead. She had no way of knowing he had been a musician and that his grandfather was also a musician.

"No, Justin, I don't see. Tell you what . . . call me tonight. We'll talk about it," she said, gracefully blowing him off.

He stood watching her walk away.

Yes, something indeed had changed between them.

7

As Sonnet became more and more obsessed with her weight loss over the next few weeks, Margaret noticed Justin. He seemed so lonely. She and Leita began to join him at McDonald's after school, as Sonnet was always headed to the gym now as soon as the bell rang. Frank had even given up a whopping thirty bucks a month to get her into Lady Fitness. She loved his attention. Every day she went. Her overworked endorphin glands had kicked in, apparently, quickly giving her an addicting rush, and she was loving that too.

"Where is Sonnet?" Justin asked, as Leita and Margaret slid into the booth across from him. They looked at each, other trying not to show amazement at the amount of food that sat in front of him. Margaret had hoped he had ordered for Sonnet, hoping she would join him. There could be no way he had ordered all that stuff for himself.

He is really hurtin', Margaret thought to herself.

"The gym," she answered.

Justin looked down at his food and then at the two scrawny girls sitting across from him in that small booth.

"Want some?" he offered. Margaret shook her head. Leita took some fries to be polite. "I don't see her anymore. What's up with that?" Justin asked, as he began to inhale the burgers.

Margaret's stomach began to feel queasy.

"Oh, I dunno," she lied quickly.

"She's tryin' to lose weight," Leita blurted. Margaret's eyes rolled, giving her the signal that she had said too much. Leita just shrugged and sighed, shifting her eyes toward Justin, gritting her teeth. Justin's face read "instant confusion" after hearing Leita's words. It was almost as if a foreign concept had just been introduced.

"Losing weight? The gym? Why is she doing that?" he asked.

"What's wrong with it? Why shouldn't she want to do that?" Leita asked. "Do you feel threatened?" she prodded, with hopefulness filling her tone.

"No, of course not. I just wondered why she wants to do that." He licked the dripping ketchup from his fingertips.

"Maybe her health?" Margaret said, with sarcasm in her tone, handing him a napkin.

Justin shook his head and smiled. "Or maybe Wilson Yant," he said, looking at both of them directly.

Leita's mouth dropped open in surprise.

"You know?" she gasped.

"Of course I know—who doesn't know? She makes a fool of herself every time the guy comes near her."

"So you think it's a mistake too?" Margaret sat forward now, thinking finally she had someone to help her with her cause—saving her sister.

"No, no, I don't. Sonnet is a beautiful girl. I've always thought so, anyway. And if she feels that she wants somebody like Yant and melting away to nothing is the way to get him, then that's her business," Justin said, with finality in his voice.

Leita looked closely at him to see if he was faking sincerity. She was hoping that perhaps inside he was really all broken up over this new change from the way things were. But Leita could see nothing except the brown of his eyes. It was then she noticed the freckles against his light skin. Leita had met his mother once and didn't remember her having any freckles. Perhaps he looked like his father—so many things about Justin none of them knew.

"Well, I think it's disgusting." Margaret pouted, folding her arms tight across her chest.

Just then, Wilson and his entourage entered the McDonald's. One of the boys with him noticed Justin immediately. There was no way he could resist a little harassment, noticing all the wrappers on Justin's tray.

"Hey, is there any food left in here?" He laughed out loud. Wilson looked over in the direction of Justin, Margaret, and Leita. He noticed Margaret. Wilson had always found her very pretty. Maybe a little thin, but her face was smooth and brown and her fingers were long and thin, as if she played the piano . . . just like his mother did. Her neck was long and so were her legs. She always wore that ankle thing tied around one—he found that very sexy.

She didn't look anything like her sister, Sonnet, even though, now that Wilson thought about it, there was something kinda different about her lately too. Of course, no matter what was different on Sonnet, she wasn't Margaret. Margaret was so cool, mysterious, and hard to get . . . he liked hard to get.

The winter festival dance was coming up and he was going to ask Margaret to go with him. That is, as soon as he dumped Marcia.

"You have to stop her, Justin," Margaret was pleading now.

Justin shook his head. "Nope, she needs to get it all out of her system."

"But what about you?" Leita asked sincerely.

Suddenly, Justin looked embarrassed. He began choking on his soda.

"Me?" He smiled, showing the blush under his skin. "I'm just her friend and I always will be. I mean, she knows I'm there for her—if she ever needs me," he continued the strong front.

Leita still watched him closely as he spoke—waiting for the flinch.

Perhaps all this time she'd had been wrong and Sonnet and Justin were just meant to be friends—collaborators in their bingeing dysfunction. And Justin, now that Sonnet was on to something else, would just binge alone or find someone else to share his problems with. Leita thought all of that, but in her heart was not thoroughly convinced of any of it, and Justin's lackadaisical attitude—acting as if he didn't care—wasn't going to convince her of anything.

"When are you gonna play that thing for us? You've been bringing it every day for weeks now," Leita said, pointing at his saxophone case.

Justin had been working on some special projects with Mr. Park, the music teacher. Mr. Park was sure Justin could land a scholarship to the School of Fine Arts, if he just applied himself a bit more.

"Never," Justin answered, draining his drink, making a loud slurping sound that brought waves of laughter from Wilson's table.

"Doesn't any of that bother you, Justin?" Margaret finally asked, the question burning in her for a long time.

Justin shook his head. This time Leita caught a smidgen of pain in his eyes.

8

Yolanda looked at herself in the mirror a long time, studying the new lines coming around her eyes. She was looking older—feeling older. How had her life gotten so off track this way?

She looked over at Frank in bed. He was snoring loudly—as usual.

He wasn't so bad. He was handsome enough, with his high cheekbones and smooth face. Sure, he drank too much . . . but even that was getting better now that Sonnet was losing weight.

The connection? Yolanda could only imagine.

She looked at herself in the mirror again only to see the scowl in her brow and the smirk on her lips. She shook the obscene thought from her head.

What's the matter with me? Frank's not like that, Yolanda thought now, smoothing out the new facial lines she had just put there.

Sonnet was on diet pills. Yolanda shook her head. She couldn't believe that Frank had told her to get them for her.

"But, Frank, diet pills? Diet pills? She's just a kid. She'll grow out of that baby fat. It's just baby fat," Yolanda had argued.

Frank held up his hand to silence her.

"Get them," he said, grabbing up his lunch and leaving for work. "I'll be home late," he added.

It was December now and it almost seemed that the obsession with Sonnet's weight loss had brought peace to the household. Frank had only been on one small rampage since September and immediately Sonnet had reached for ice cream. When he saw her, to the amazement of everyone, he apologized for his loss of temper. He put his beer back in the fridge and went on his way. Everyone was stunned.

Sonnet had lost about thirty pounds and he was ecstatic. That was obvious to everyone in the house.

"Mom?" Sonnet asked her mother, while watching her fill the dryer with laundry.

Yolanda turned to her. "Yeah?" She asked without looked at her.

"You ever like a boy?" she asked.

Yolanda smiled.

"I mean, besides Daddy?" Sonnet asked, her voice unconsciously lowering, overhearing her father in the living room enjoying his sports program.

Yolanda glanced in the direction of the living room and then back at Sonnet.

"No, of course not. Your father was my first and only," she answered.

"You're kidding. I don't believe you," Sonnet said, showing true surprise.

"No, I'm not kidding. And what's there not to believe? I've only loved your father. You need to know what you're doing when you decide to *date* someone—when you decide to *like* someone," Yolanda lectured. "You make the wrong choice and . . . well, your life could turn out—not quite the way you planned," she said, sounding very reflective, and then going back to her chores, humming mindlessly.

Sonnet realized suddenly that their conversation was over. On her way back to her bedroom, she glanced in the living room at her father, sitting inches from the TV, beer in hand, cussing and swearing at the teams.

"I don't believe her," Sonnet said out loud, without drawing his attention to her.

9

It was the week before Christmas break and the girls were up late. The excitement of having two weeks off coming up could be felt everywhere. The air at school was nearly electric. Sonnet couldn't wait until she would be included in the plans of the popular. The thought of spending two weeks shopping the mall with the girls like Tanya nearly made her head spin. Sure, she was vain, but that was a front—surely. Sonnet thought about the day at the track again. At first she thought they were making fun of her, but the more she thought about it—they had suggested the diet, hadn't they? Well, it didn't matter, they wanted her to lose weight, and they wanted her to fit in with them.

Besides, Margaret and Leita had begun to take her place in Justin's life. Sonnet had figured it out after seeing the three of them together on several occasions. Sonnet was glad that they were taking care of Justin. She still cared about him, but she had taken off a lot of weight already, and surely Wilson had taken note—or was about to, anyway. She wasn't going to let sentiment over Justin and their relationship get in her way.

There would be no stopping her now.

Unfortunately, Sonnet had reached a plateau and hadn't lost any weight in two weeks.

Sonnet asked her mother, Yolanda, to get her a refill of the prescription diet pills. She seemed more than willing. Sonnet could tell she was enjoying being a part of her weight loss. She had said it made her feel needed. Sonnet noticed her father being happier with her mother too. Truly she had brought the family together.

"Well, how much have you lost?" inquired Margaret, while nibbling on a cookie from the stash drawer they kept. Sonnet had long since abandoned it and now it seemed that Margaret was dependent on it.

"Not enough," Sonnet answered, swallowing the diet pill.

Margaret sat up in the bed. "What was that?"

"What?"

"What you just took."

"A diet pill. Mom got them for me, I've been taking them for a while now," Sonnet defended. She was shocked at Margaret's ignorance.

Margaret moved to the edge of the bed now. "Sonnet, this is getting crazy."

"Margaret, I've been taking them for weeks now, where have you been?" Sonnet asked.

"I thought you were just working out . . . I thought . . ." Margaret stuttered.

"What, you scared I'm going to be thinner than you?" Sonnet asked, her words sarcastic and stingingly cold.

"Sonnet, what are you talking about?" Margaret asked, her face flinching as if Sonnet's words had slapped her.

"Oh yeah, I forgot, that's impossible. If I did that I'd be dead." Sonnet snickered now, sounding like someone else.

Margaret felt instantly cut to the heart. Sonnet had never said anything so mean to her before.

"I tried to copy you with the throwing-up thing, but it hurt my throat," Sonnet went on, as she began braiding her hair.

Margaret's eyes burned, as she fought back the tears. They had never talked about Margaret's eating problem so casually before and never with so much thoughtlessness. Yes, there was a problem, Margaret would be the first to admit it . . . but it was her problem, not Sonnet's, and she had no right to joke about it this way.

"I haven't done that in a long time," Margaret defended weakly. Sonnet climbed into her bed, appearing bubbly and carefree. She reminded Margaret of the cheerleaders at school—self-centered, thinking only of their own vain existence.

"Yeah, I know, now you just pig out with Justin," Sonnet finished up, turning her back on Margaret.

Sonnet couldn't stop the words from coming; she knew the words were killing Margaret and that now she was crying. Never before had she ever addressed Margaret's eating "thing" as if it was just a weird quirk. Sonnet wanted to apologize but she couldn't. She simply left Margaret hurt and confused.

Her mood swings had been erratic for weeks and now she was hurting Margaret. Maybe it was the pills, she thought to herself, but it would be over soon. She would have Wilson and things would be right.

She'd apologize then.

Sonnet flipped over and quickly turned off the light, putting them both in the dark, without looking over at her sister. She didn't want to see Margaret sniveling, rubbing her eyes with her fist. Instead, she lay there, staring upward in the dark listening to her sister's heavy sighs as she attempted to cry quietly into her pillow.

When Sonnet woke up, Margaret was already dressed and gone. Sonnet looked at the clock; it wasn't even seven. Her head was spinning and her ears were ringing. This must be what a hangover felt like, she thought to herself. The doctor had prescribed stronger pills this time. Suddenly, she noticed blood on her pillow. She wiped her nose and felt the dried blood.

Margaret waited outside Justin's house until his mother noticed her from the kitchen window. Teri opened the window and called to her, "Margaret, is that you?" Margaret nodded shyly. "Well, come on in," Teri invited.

Never before had Margaret eaten so much, though nothing on the plate had much taste. She just felt like eating.

Justin was surprised to see her eat this way. He often wondered how she stayed alive. She was so frail and thin.

A strong wind could just take her away—easy, he always thought.

Justin could see that Margaret was growing uncomfortable as his mother babbled away. He knew Margaret's thinness made a lot of people nervous, and his mother was no exception. He knew his mother was used to Sonnet and her healthy appetite and appearance.

Finally, they left for school. Justin stayed quiet for a long time, seemingly waiting until he was sure they had cleared his mother's watchful eye.

"What brings you to my house?" he finally asked.

Margaret just shrugged her shoulders. She didn't look like she felt well.

"Are you all right?" he asked her.

She shrugged her shoulders again and then darted behind a large tree, vomiting violently.

Justin didn't know what to do for that time, so he stood perfectly still until she finished. Finally, she emerged from behind the tree. Tears were streaming down her face.

"Ate too much?" he asked, softly draping his heavy arm

around her shoulder. She nodded as he pulled her in close while she wiped her face dry with her coat sleeve.

Justin was like a big teddy bear and Margaret instantly felt safe. She decided then that Sonnet didn't know what she had in this big ol' wonderful guy.

10

Sonnet took a deep breath before approaching Tanya. She waited until she was alone. She wasn't ignorant—image was everything and being seen with a *nobody* could definitely put a crimp in her social life.

Margaret had been hard to find today, but that was okay. If she had seen Sonnet talking to someone like Tanya, it would make life hard around their house.

Life was just so hard sometimes. . . .

"Tanya, I need to talk to you," Sonnet began.

Tanya turned to her and looked her over. Suddenly a smile crept to her lips.

"Hey, yeah, I remember you, the big-boned girl from the track. Girl, you dropping down some," Tanya said.

Sonnet's heart leaped. She couldn't have heard anything better. She almost forgot what she had wanted to ask.

"Yeah, I'm taking those pills," Sonnet began shyly.

Tanya smiled.

"Cool, cool, and they're working." Tanya giggled, tossing her long braids over her shoulder.

"Yeah, and I was just wondering . . ."

"Wondering what?"

"Well, I want to go to the winter formal and I wanted to know if I should ask this guy," Sonnet said.

Tanya looked her over again.

"You do whatever you want," Tanya encouraged with a wink. The bell rang. "Do whatever," she added, walking away.

Sonnet moved slowly between classes, hoping to run into Wilson. She was going to ask him to the dance on Friday, since it didn't seem like he was ever going to get around to asking her. Besides, Tanya had said go for it, and she should know.

It was lunchtime before she finally saw him. Wilson was standing alone for once, by the vending machine. He was banging on the soda machine and cursing at it for taking his money. Sonnet quickly took out a dollar and walked up to the machine.

"Oh, damn, is it broke? And I wanted a Diet Coke, too," she said, trying to find her most alluring voice.

Wilson looked her over. Her jeans were tight, but look at all they had to cover, he thought to himself. She had a pretty face. Her skin wasn't too bad. His mind wandered until suddenly he recognized her, she was Margaret's sister. What a lucky break, he thought, now was his chance to see if Margaret was going to the dance with anyone.

"You're Margaret's sister, huh?" Wilson asked. Sonnet batted her lashes. He noticed her big brown eyes.

"Yup," she flirted. "I'm Sonnet."

She outstretched her hand for a handshake. He looked at it, snickering as he shook it. *What a weirdo,* he thought.

"Isn't a sonnet a song or something?" he asked, patting a rhythm against his tight chest.

"Well, more like an elegy, a poem—like a love poem," she explained.

"Yeah, cute . . . uh, you going to the winter dance?" he asked, showing total disinterest in her brief English lesson.

"Not yet, but I can be ready by six," she said. She couldn't believe she had said it. It was a line she had practiced for months, and she actually had said it.

"No, I meant," Wilson began before he caught himself. "Cad that he was, he wasn't cruel. Even when he dumped a girl, she would all but say thank you for the chance to be dumped by you." He had class if nothing else and he wouldn't ruin that reputation— not over *this* girl. Pity actually could add some stars to his rep.

But how would he get to Margaret now?

"Yeah, maybe we could, uh, double-date or something," he suggested, hoping his first thought would be the solution to his Margaret dilemma.

"Double?" Sonnet asked, confused.

"Yeah, my best friend and your sister and me and you," Wilson said, leaning against the vending machine.

Sonnet noticed his muscles through his T-shirt. Her heart began to pound. *How could anybody be so fine?*

"Sure! I know she's not going with anybody. That'll be cool," she spouted.

Wilson smiled his winning smile and blew her a kiss as he strolled down the hall to class.

Sonnet couldn't believe it, her first real date and it was with Wilson Yant, the best-looking and most popular guy in the school. Life couldn't get much better than this.

11

Leita and Margaret sat with Justin on his favorite bench. It was an out-of-the-way spot but he liked it. He had agreed to play the saxophone for them today and Leita, for one, was very excited.

"I get to hear a star before he becomes a star. This is the coolest thang," she said, unable to keep the giggle from her words.

Justin rolled his eyes. He really liked Leita. She was so open and real. He often wondered if everyone from Arkansas was that way.

"Look, Leita, you can hang out with us, but you are gonna have to stop acting so square, hear me?" he said, imitating her accent.

She slapped his big arm playfully. He pretended injury and insisted he couldn't play now.

"I'll break your other arm. Now come on and play," she begged.

Justin proceeded to play his horn. He first played the school song and a couple of pop tunes from the radio, which very much impressed Leita, but Margaret knew there was more in him than just those few elevator tunes; he was saving up something special, for someone special. However, she wouldn't push . . . not today. Maybe one day he would really play that horn, maybe one day he would really play that horn—for her.

"You guys going to the dance?" Leita asked.

"You?" Margaret asked, surprised at her question.

Leita smiled and blushed. Justin and Margaret laughed heartily, as they had never seen Leita so flustered by a simple reply.

"I got asked this morning by Dorky David Summerland.

"Well, are you going?" Justin asked.

"You betcha! In a heartbeat." Leita giggled on, almost uncontrollably now.

Justin looked at Margaret and then at Leita.

"Me and Margaret are going," he announced.

Margaret was taken aback in surprise.

"Not on your life," she retorted.

He looked at her sterner now.

"Why?" he asked.

"I'm not going to a stupid dance with you," Margaret answered, still chuckling. Leita noticed Justin's serious face and punched her hard.

"I'm not your type, right? No, I'm too much of your type, right? Get it? Too much." Justin laughed sardonically.

Margaret frowned.

"No, Justin, you're too stupid. Don't you know I'd go anywhere with you? You're my friend," Margaret said, sounding very serious and grown-up.

Justin, caught off guard, swallowed hard.

"I just think school dances are for losers," Margaret added, looking deep into his eyes, hoping to share a moment.

"Well then, I guess we all better just go then," Leita suggested. "Losers that we are," she added.

They were all quiet for a second and then they bust into laughter.

Just then Sonnet appeared. Justin quickly put away his

saxophone before she noticed it. She had come to see Margaret.

"He asked me!" she exclaimed.

"Who asked you?" Margaret asked.

"Wilson! Wilson asked me to the dance." Sonnet continued to bubble over.

Justin suddenly felt a tinge of jealousy and then just as suddenly, he felt a strange—nothing.

Why should he feel anything? She had made her choice months ago and without so much as a warning or good-bye. He looked at her. She was almost too thin now, in his opinion. He wasn't even sure if he liked it. However, as she jumped up and down in those tight jeans, he felt a little bit of a sexual tingle. It embarrassed him slightly, though he knew no one had noticed.

"He wants you to go with his friend—like a double date. And I told him great. I said we'd be ready at six. I said the line—remember the line—and it worked."

As she spoke, Margaret's anger rose to her face. She stood.

"Look, girlfriend—ol' sista of mine," Margaret began, with her finger pointed in her sister's face. "You don't need to get my dates for me. Especially after how you've been acting lately, and besides, I already have a date," she said, with a harrumph.

"With who?" Sonnet asked, truly surprised.

"Justin," Margaret answered with confidence.

Sonnet didn't even turn to look at him.

"Be serious. This is Wilson and his best friend we're talking about here," she said, as if Justin were not sitting there.

"Forget it and forget you," Margaret said, slamming herself stubbornly on the bench with arms folded.

Justin began to feel uneasy, as Sonnet turned and glared at him. She hadn't looked in his direction in weeks, and now that she had, it was with so much animosity he couldn't stand it.

"Look, Margaret, it was a joke really. I can't go to a dance like that. You know that," Justin said, backing down. "I can't even dance." He giggled.

"No!" Margaret screamed.

A couple of people turned around to see what the commotion was all about.

"We are going to that dance together if I have to kill you!" Margaret yelled, turning back to Sonnet. "You just work it out with your *boyfriend*, sister girl," she said, and snapped her finger at her.

Sonnet was livid. How could Margaret have turned on her this way? And for what . . . Justin? This wasn't happening. She had been working so hard to lose this weight, and Wilson had noticed her after only thirty pounds.

Her heart was pounding so, she felt almost faint. Leita had said nothing. After a moment taken to gather herself, Sonnet stomped off.

She didn't need Margaret. She would think of something. She didn't need anyone. She had it all under control.

"She's outta control," Leita said finally.

Margaret sat in an angry huff. Justin gathered his things, as lunchtime was nearly over.

"You should have told her yes," he said.

"To hell with her. Do you know what she said to me last night?"

"No," Justin said softly.

Margaret thought about her hateful words, more hateful words from her sister . . . they had been coming fast these last few weeks.

"Well, it was really mean and I don't care about what she does anymore."

"Wilson asked her for a reason, and maybe it's a bad one," Justin added, noticing Wilson and a couple of his friends pointing at Margaret from across the quad. Margaret hadn't noticed them.

"Go with them. I don't need to go to the party," Justin assured her. "She might need you there to protect her."

Margaret looked at him, searching his eyes for a meaning to his words.

"From what?" she asked.

"Easy sex," Leita answered, matter-of-fact. They both looked at her. "Wilson probably thinks she's easy."

They all knew, in those sincere words from Leita, that Margaret would have to go.

"Just call me. My mom will let me use the car and I'll come get you if I have to," Justin added, while they walked back toward the classroom hallway. Margaret finally, though reluctantly, agreed.

Sonnet had dropped another seven pounds by Friday and was thrilled. She was able to squeeze into a size 16 now.

She was about five feet five. Margaret stood about the same height, though she appeared taller with her dress draped loosely on her shoulders.

"Get a size three," Sonnet insisted, as Margaret stepped out of the dressing room with the size 5 hanging badly on her.

Margaret glared at her.

"Get a size twenty," she remarked in a cold retort.

Both girls had been carrying on this way for days. The biting comments were getting worse. Sonnet wanted them to end, but she didn't know how to stop them. Margaret was only being reflective and Sonnet knew it. Sonnet knew she was the reason Margaret was so angry, she couldn't help it—it wasn't her fault.

Wilson hadn't said much to her at school since that Monday, but each day, Sonnet would confirm their date. He would just smile and sigh, verifying the time. He would also make sure that Margaret was coming—for his friend, of course.

The night of the dance came. Frank took the girls' pictures and Yolanda, instead of making cookies or a sweet snack, had made beautiful corsages for their dresses. As she fluffed Sonnet's hair and tucked in Margaret's safety pins, she had never felt so proud of her girls. Maybe she had been wrong. Maybe beauty was still an important component to happiness.

She remembered being in high school. Of course, there had been Frank, but lots of other boys "wanted" to date her, too. She was talented with her hands and smart. She was very pretty and so fair skinned that even a white boy had asked her out once. Of course, her parents said no, but Yolanda always knew that being both pretty and smart she could have any life she chose. But she chose Frank, and Frank had chosen her because she was pretty . . . only because of that. But no sense in thinking about all of that tonight. Yolanda sighed, thinking about her father's famous words, "You made your bed . . ."

Yolanda knew in her heart that as soon as she could, she would have to get out of this life, even if it was just vicariously through her daughters. Life with Frank had been hell with a smile.

Frank answered the door. It was Wilson. He was dressed in a dark shirt and slacks. His shoes were two-toned and he wore a large watch. Frank sized him up immediately.

"You look really pretty, Margaret," Wilson said right away, noticing Margaret over Frank's shoulder. Frank frowned. Yeah, he sized him up right away.

"Oh, and especially you, Sonnet," Wilson said now, covering his faux pas, noticing Frank's instant disapproval of his attraction to Margaret.

The girls were off on their first real date.

The banquet room was crowded and Sonnet was thrilled to be there. It showed on her face. She was so thrilled that it didn't even bother her that Wilson asked Margaret to dance first, leaving her at the table with his friend.

Wilson's friend was a white boy who dressed like a rap singer every day. His name was Clyde, but everyone called him Starbuck. Supposedly his father had apparently been a musician in the disco era and used that name, so Clyde, though he had no musical talents, adopted it, thinking it made him cool.

Margaret looked around for Leita only to see her also on the dance floor with Dorky David Summerland. She seemed to be having a great time. Tall, lanky David Summerland had no sense of rhythm, but neither did Leita, so they made a good match tonight. Margaret looked back at Wilson, who was staring at her—deep into her eyes, with a wicked smile on his lips. He made her uncomfortable. Margaret was only dancing with him because she thought Sonnet was too embarrassed to get on the dance floor in that tight dress. Margaret wanted this evening to be over—like now.

The slow music started and Sonnet took the floor with Wilson, hanging on tight. Little did she know that while she thought they were making a "groove thang," Wilson was making faces over her shoulder to Clyde at the table. Margaret was fuming but kept quiet.

Finally, the evening ended.

"The boys want to go riding," Sonnet said excitedly to Margaret while they stood at the entrance, waiting for the boys to retrieve Clyde's parents' car.

"Riding?" Margaret asked, shock showing. "Well, I don't," she snapped. Sonnet sighed heavily and then hid her disappointment behind a fake smile as Tanya and her date walked by, smiling. Margaret was shocked—since when did someone from the "in" crowd speak to Sonnet?

"Come on, Margaret, don't start this." Sonnet stomped her foot.

The boys pulled up and Sonnet climbed into the back with Wilson. Margaret hesitated and then got in the front with Clyde.

* * *

They drove for a few miles and then pulled into the turnout of the Holiday Inn. It was an area called the Point. It was on the cliffs overlooking the ocean. There were several other cars parked there already. Sonnet's heart raced. She had heard about this place but never dreamed she'd come here with Wilson Yant!

From under the seat, Starbuck pulled out a fifth of gin. Wilson rubbed his hands together eagerly. Margaret's eyes grew wide. She looked at Sonnet, who was looking only at Wilson. Suddenly Wilson kissed Sonnet quickly on the lips, catching her off guard. Margaret glared at Clyde, who was leaning toward her.

"Don't even think about it," she whispered sternly and folded her arms tight against her chest.

Clyde backed away and took a swig from the bottle. He ran his fingers through his hair in frustration and handed the bottle backward to Wilson in the backseat.

Wilson took the bottle and moved close to Sonnet, offering her some. She looked at Margaret, who was turned around in the seat staring at her now. Margaret shook her head, but Sonnet just rolled her eyes and took a drink. It burned her throat as it went down, and with the help of the diet pills in her system, the effects were almost immediate.

The giggling started now and the close quarters of that small car had everyone growing uncomfortably warm. Sonnet removed her jacket and Margaret did too. Wilson immediately noticed Sonnet's large breasts and grew excited. He had never been out with a girl *this* size before.

It wasn't so bad, he thought, and besides, she was going to be easy if nothing else.

Wilson felt his teenage hormones surge, starting between his legs. He looked at Margaret, her curled lip and bad attitude—"hard to get" was not his preference tonight. He would have to get back to Margaret at a later time, he thought now, burying his face in Sonnet's cleavage.

Sonnet couldn't believe what was happening. Before she could react, Margaret reached into the backseat and pulled Wilson's hair. Both he and Sonnet yelled out.

"Let's go home!" Margaret yelled.

Clyde grabbed Margaret's arm hard, hurting her. "Look, skinny Minnie, you need to stay out of it," he said, in a mean voice.

With her small fist, she hit him square in the eye, causing him to yelp. Sonnet knew then that this evening had come abruptly to an end. She reached forward and wrenched Clyde's hand free from her sister.

"Look, don't put you hands on her," Sonnet growled in a threatening tone. "I'll have to break you in half," she added with a clear threat. She knew her unfeminine threat would turn Wilson off, but her loyalty, after all, was to Margaret.

"And big mama will do it, too." Wilson giggled. He was drunk already.

He patted Sonnet's heavy arm. "Look at these muscles. Wrestle me, baby," he continued, snickering, slobbering. Clyde laughed out loud while holding his sore eye. Margaret jumped out of the car.

"I'm walking home! No, I'll just call Justin," Margaret exclaimed.

"Oh, I'm really scared now . . . that tub-of-lard bodyguard," Wilson slurred, groping out the window for Margaret. She stepped out of his reach.

"Hey, how 'bout a little threesome?" He smiled and winked.

Margaret wanted to hit him right in the mouth and break those perfect teeth.

Sonnet, still in the back seat, reluctantly put on her jacket.

"Where ya goin', tub 'a love?" Wilson asked her, rubbing on her arm moving his hand up to her shoulder.

Sonnet's heart sank. She would forgive him tomorrow, she knew that, but tonight, she was hurt.

* * *

The girls started walking back toward the hotel where the dance had taken place. Margaret said nothing. She was livid. She had left her jacket in the car, but she was so hot with anger, she hadn't noticed the cold.

When they reached the lobby, she went to the pay phone to call Justin.

"Please don't call," was all Sonnet could say.

Margaret glared at her without saying anything in response. "Hello, Justin, can you pick us up?"

Sonnet felt ashamed and embarrassed. Margaret had called Justin, and from the sounds of it, he had been expecting the call. It was if he knew ahead of time what Wilson was going to do.

They waited in silence for the dark green Camry to pull into the parking lot.

Justin had come in ten minutes. He was smiling. *Always smiling*, Sonnet thought to herself, releasing a sigh as she climbed into the backseat, despite the fact that Margaret had offered her the front.

"Hey, it's Friday. Let's go into the city," Margaret suggested suddenly. Sonnet was instantly surprised at Margaret's sudden change of mood.

Now she wanted to go out?

"No, I want to go home." Sonnet pouted.

Margaret turned around in the seat. "Well, I don't and neither does Justin, right?" she asked, playfully hitting him on the arm.

Justin noticed Sonnet's irritation in the rearview mirror. She looked very pretty tonight.

Sonnet noticed Justin's clothes. He was dressed up. Perhaps he assumed they weren't going right home.

They would be in the city in less than an hour.

"Fine," Sonnet said, giving in to Margaret's and Justin's good mood.

There was a club for the younger crowd downtown and though they had never gone there, they had heard many of the kids at school talk about it. Justin had money and paid their way in.

The music was loud and lively. Soon Sonnet found herself dancing to all the fast songs and never leaving the dance floor.

The three of them danced together, the two of them circling Justin on the floor. They stayed until closing at 2:00 a.m.

Justin had told his mother he was with Sonnet and Margaret, so he had no worry about the time. He could just enjoy the wonderful night he was having with his two favorite girls.

The only thing missing was Leita, but they were all certain she had made her own memorable winter night with Dorky David Summerland.

12

During the winter break, Justin went to New York. He had taken the check from the tossed envelope and, against his mother's wishes, cashed it and gotten his plane ticket. He knew she hated him for it and would never forgive him for going against her this way . . .

But enough was enough.

Things were changing in Justin's heart and though he was going through a lot of it alone, still he had to go through it. He had to figure out where he would end up. He had reluctantly given up on his hopes of marrying Sonnet, so he now figured, when he graduated, he would probably give in to his grandparents' urging and move to New York.

Even after the night in the club, he could tell there was nothing in Sonnet's heart for him. He would have to plan another life now. A life with his music, and that would mean, unfortunately, a life without his mother too.

At first he nearly gave in to depression. Loneliness was his only thought for his future, but as the plane lifted, Justin's thoughts became filled with excitement. He began to feel freer with each new state he crossed.

His grandfather had been in the philharmonic orchestra

many years ago. He was one of the first Negroes accepted. Of course, his skin was very light and he had passed as white. He had opted to not make history by exposing the fact that he was black, so no one ever knew, except his family.

"Just do what you do . . . and do it good. Don't matter who knows you're doing it," he would say. He was a quiet-natured man and Justin saw a lot of himself in him.

Ali Sr. was crazy about his grandson, Justin, and loved having him around. Justin's father, Ali Jr., had been an only child and now Justin was their only connection to their son who was gone. They wanted the best for Justin and they could afford to give him the best. They had even offered to move Teri and Justin out to New York with them right after their son died, but she wanted no part of that. She always took everything they did as a threat.

In their minds, Teri was killing Justin. She was breaking his spirit and his heart. Maybe she wasn't doing it on purpose, but Ali Hamilton Sr. was not going to tolerate it any longer. Justin didn't know it yet, but his life was going to change for good, he was going to see to that. Too many years of not having Justin around was going to end.

Now that Justin's grandmother, Zenobia, was retired from her teaching job, she was home all the time. Having Justin around was a good idea to her too. She had often spoken with him over the phone. He sounded just like his father and she wanted nothing more than to have Ali Jr. near her again. She longed to hear the music coming from that bedroom at the other end of the house again. She wasn't obsessed, nor did she think of her feeling as unreasonable. Teri had been the one acting unreasonably, in her opinion.

Maybe it was selfish of her to covet Teri's son this way, but that's just how it was for Zenobia; she wanted Justin in her life and she was going to have him.

Both Ali Sr. and Zenobia just knew Justin was in love with the idea of living with them in New York. They only wanted the best for him and he would understand and not take it as a put-down of his mother—after all, they weren't putting her down. She had been a good mother, as far as "good mothers" go.

When Justin stepped off the plane Zenobia burst immediately into tears. She hadn't seen Justin since he was five. He was so tall, so large, but that smile, that smile was Ali Jr. all over again. Behind Justin's empty eyes, Zenobia saw life. A life waiting to emerge, and she would help him.

Ali Sr. hugged his grandson tight and together the three of them walked out of the airport to the car.

Justin nervously tapped on the leather seat of the large car. He sat alone in the backseat, taking in the view as they drove from the city to the county. He noticed his grandfather looking at him in the rearview mirror. It was a strange feeling looking at the stranger in that mirror, yet feeling so familiar.

"Justin, let's get it out in the open now," his grandfather finally started.

Justin looked at the reflection.

"Do you want to stay?" Ali Sr. asked bluntly.

Justin stared into the rearview mirror, his heart pounding. His mind soared. He had only packed for a few days, but even then, he had packed everything important to him—clean underwear, his horn, and a picture of Sonnet. Justin nodded slowly into the mirror and watched his grandfather's eyes tighten with his broad smile.

Zenobia laid her hand softly on her husband's thigh as she looked out the window, pretending not to notice that her prayer had just been answered.

That night Justin sat in his father's old room playing his horn. There were no interruptions, no food, just his grandmother sitting there smiling, listening, and after Justin finished, for the first time he was applauded.

13

During the vacation, Margaret fell sick. Possibly the night in the cold, after the dance, was the cause of her landing in the hospital with pneumonia. It was then the doctors found out, during their examination, that she had stopped menstruating along with the other assorted health problems that her anorexia nervosa had brought on, the worst including the weakening of her heart.

Sonnet sat by her bedside one afternoon, reading a magazine to her as Margaret lay staring out the window. Her lunch tray had been set before her almost an hour before—in case she wanted to eat.

Margaret had refused to eat when she was first brought in, and after two days she was force-fed intravenously. Now at the end of the first week they brought in the tray at least once a day to see if she would cooperate and eat on her own. But again today, the tray sat untouched.

"It says here that cheesecake is one of life's favorite things." Sonnet chuckled. Margaret turned her head to her, and then attempted a weak chuckle. Sonnet was pleased to hear it.

"Hey, look, you've got cheesecake on this tray. It's disguised as some green beans but still," Sonnet went on.

"Trying to tempt me to eat? Well, it won't work," Margaret said softly, before closing her eyes.

Sonnet grew frightened. What if the doctors were right and Margaret was going to die if she didn't eat? Who would she have?

Sonnet didn't want to be alone; she didn't want to be without Margaret. She was feeling very confused.

The night of the dance had disillusioned her and now she was confused about everything. She had always been sure of three things, Leita, Justin, and Margaret. She was scared now for the first time that she would never have them together the same way again. Life had changed overnight and she hadn't even been notified.

School was back in session now and the pretty people, the popular people had replaced Justin, Margaret, and Leita, and now Sonnet wasn't sure she wanted to belong with that group. For some reason, the popular people were calling her now, inviting her places. One side of Sonnet wanted Margaret well so she could go, the other side just wanted Margaret well.

Leita stopped in one afternoon to check on Margaret. She was bubbling over with the exciting news about Dorky David.

"You're still seeing him?" Sonnet asked. "I didn't know that."

Leita just smirked and rolled her eyes. "I don't think me and David run in your sights," she said, not meaning to sound as cruel as it came out.

Sonnet felt very "put in her place" and stayed quiet.

That had been her second humiliation that day. Earlier she had opened a letter from Justin that she had assumed to be for her—she was wrong, it was for Margaret. It was a very personal letter to just Margaret; Sonnet got that from the first paragraph where he began to tell her about his grandparents and his issues with his mother—deep stuff. Sonnet felt the need to tape the letter back together.

When had it all happened? When had she stepped so far out of their close circle?

Later that night Yolanda stopped in to see Margaret. Margaret attempted to sit up in the bed.

"Where's Dad?" she asked.

Yolanda said nothing, but continued to straighten the covers around her and pulled the bed table to Margaret's lap. She opened her large purse and pulled out a thermos. Opening it, she poured some of the hot soup into the top.

"Margaret, you are going to have to eat. I need you and you're not going to do this to me any longer. I don't deserve it," Yolanda finally said, holding the spoon to Margaret's lips. Tears were forming in her eyes. "Maybe I do deserve this, I don't know, but I do know this, you can't do this anymore," she finished.

Margaret, noticing the bruising on her mother's wrist, began eating obediently from the spoon her mother fed her from.

"Where's Daddy?" Margaret asked again, between bites.

Yolanda paused and sighed heavily, rubbing her forehead. "He's home."

"Is he drinking again?" Margaret asked.

Just then, Yolanda took a large piece of pie from her purse. It had been Margaret's favorite kind once upon a time.

"Oh, man, you remembered." Margaret lit up at the special treatment. She knew in her heart that her mother was being punished for all of this coming-to-the-hospital stuff. All this time away from Frank was surely unacceptable to him, and now today—she had come at night.

Her mother was always at home, her father made sure of

that. Frank hadn't come to the hospital once in the three weeks Margaret had been there.

Suddenly, Margaret wondered how her mother had gotten to the hospital this evening—so late. They only had one car, but she never drove it. It was too late for her to have taken the bus. . . .

Margaret watched her mother's face as she fed her the pie. She smiled and talked about the talk show she had seen on television that afternoon, the article she had read in her periodical that came in the mail . . .

She felt sad and happy all at the same time at her mother's effort to be there for her. Margaret knew the risk she had taken to come and the price she would pay when she got home.

"I love you, Mama," Margaret said.

"I love you," Yolanda said, kissing her forehead before she left.

Margaret decided that night that she wouldn't stay much longer in that hospital, she wouldn't put her mother in that position again.

Starting the next day, she began to eat and soon her body responded to the medicines she was being given.

Before long, her father showed up, for the first time—to take her home.

14

Margaret was feeling better now. However, due to her inadequate immune system, she had to remain on home studies. Her doctor wanted as little exposure as possible to virus and germs. Although she looked healthier, having gained about twenty pounds in the hospital and even having menstruated once, she was fighting depression; she felt she was no longer in control of her life. Margaret felt she was now a part of the dysfunction around her.

Sonnet had lost fifty pounds. The stronger diet pills seemed to be working even faster now. She slipped easily into a size 14 without any trouble. The nosebleeds had all but stopped. She was thrilled. She was addicted to diet pills.

Frank had gone back to drinking and fighting with Yolanda; apparently with Sonnet's weight loss came new friends—not what Frank had in mind. He had no control over Sonnet's comings and goings like he thought he would have. So he took it out on Yolanda. Margaret's health was something he had no control over, so again he punished Yolanda for that.

No one cared that Margaret was bloated from the protein

drinks and now Sonnet was disappearing from starvation. No one had noticed that Justin hadn't come back from New York. No one noticed that Margaret wasn't handling life very well anymore.

15

Yolanda sighed heavily, looking at her reflection. Her lips were growing larger with each moment that passed. How would she hide this? What would she say?

On New Year's Day, it had been easy enough to claim drunkenness as the reason for the knot on her head.

"I fell," she explained to the mailman, who inquired. "A little too much celebration." She chuckled. He didn't buy it, she could tell.

But there was no way she was going to explain that Frank had used her head like a basketball, acting out his frustration over the hospital bill that had come in the mail. That bill had put quite a pinch in their savings, despite having insurance.

What was the reason this time? Yolanda didn't know. But for whatever reason, she deserved a slap.

Maybe it was the shorts that Sonnet had on when she got back from the gym.

It was the middle of winter and here she was parading around in spandex. This weight loss thing was causing problems for all of them. Yolanda sighed. When she glanced at the picture of her two daughters, sitting on her vanity, Yolanda felt instant remorse. How unfair of her to blame Sonnet or

Margaret for her troubles. Had she taken another direction in her life . . . had she chosen differently . . .

Frank groaned.

“Come to bed, Yolanda,” he said. “Come on now, girl,” he repeated, grinning at her now.

She saw his face in her mirror. She knew what that grin meant.

He threw back the covers, exposing his readiness. Yolanda’s stomach tightened, as she stood from her safe place—her mirror—and returned to the bed, to her wifely duty.

16

Sonnet's excitement over her acceptance into the world of popularity was short-lived to say the least. Maybe it was the way everyone started calling her to meet with them at the local coffee klatch, to join in their study groups right around the time of winter midterms. Sonnet was far from stupid; she had lost all this weight, only to be finally noticed for her brains—something she always had going for her. How back-ass-ward was that?

Wilson had been all but invisible.

One spring Saturday afternoon, Wilson had returned Margaret's jacket. He was hoping to get a look at Margaret, having heard rumors about her, but instead, he noticed Sonnet. He had been avoiding her at all costs for months, but suddenly today when she opened the door in that skimpy little sundress, he noticed. He'd been hearing how she headed the study group for Gamble's history class back when finals were happening—everyone in her group passed with flying colors. He remembered seeing her name on the honor roll, too.

Despite the hum around school, there was no way he was dating a fat girl just to get an A. He still was trying to live down the winter formal—what he remembered of it.

Looking her over now, though, Wilson noticed the ankle thing Sonnet had around her now very slender ankle. It was sexy. He was amazed at all the new things he was noticing about her today. Where had he been for the last three months?

In thinking back to the formal, all he remembered were her large breasts. Though they weren't as full now as that winter night, they were still ample. Her face was not made up and her hair was pulled back—she was pretty.

He needed something to say to her.

"Hi, I wanted to bring by your sister's jacket and, uh, congratulate you for making honor roll." He smiled.

Sonnet smirked.

"I always make honor roll," she said.

Where had he been? Oh, that's right, before when she made it, she was a fat girl on the honor roll. She saw his eyes widen when she opened the door. She saw them cover her from head to toe.

"Come on in," she offered.

Just then, Margaret appeared from the kitchen. Her chubby cheeks and plump body, bloated from the medication she was taking, shocked Wilson so that he gasped. Margaret rolled her eyes and disappeared into her bedroom.

There was an awkward silence between Sonnet and Wilson before she took the tiny jacket from him. Margaret couldn't fit it anymore anyway.

"Would you like to go out sometime, Sonnet?" Wilson said with a smile.

Sonnet thought about the winter festival.

Forget it! was her first thought.

"I don't know," she said instead. "Margaret won't be able to—"

"No, I mean, like, you and me," he said quickly. "Do you have a date for the prom?" he asked.

Sonnet thought about the promise she had made herself last year. She thought about Justin. He hadn't come back, nor even written her. He'd written Margaret only that once. Sonnet fought the fact that inside, she was hurt and angry with him for leaving her that way.

He hadn't even given her a chance to *be* sorry for treating him the way she had, let alone tell him how sorry she was.

"No, I don't," she finally answered.

She didn't have the heart to tell him at least eight guys had asked her to go with them, all thinking she was a new student in the school.

"Is it a date?" he asked in a nearly pleading tone.

Sonnet found herself giggling, listening to him as he flirted.

"Of course, silly," she said, finally accepting.

Only this time, things would be on her terms, she reasoned. She would be the one in control.

The senior prom was four weeks away. It was nearly April now and she was a svelte 130 pounds even without the gym, which she had abandoned months ago. The magic pills did everything she needed them to do all by themselves. Every time she hit a plateau, she simply had her mother get an "upped" dose. It was easy enough.

Sonnet stood in the mirror admiring herself. The stretch marks were very ugly, but in time they would fade, she assured herself. If not, maybe her father would swing for laser treatment. She had heard about it from one of the girls in her new crowd. It sounded not more painful than a tattoo, which she was contemplating.

Just then, she turned around to find her father looking at her. He grinned at her. She grew uncomfortable. He had never looked at her that way before.

"You look just like your mother," he said with the crooked smile still on his lips.

"I do, don't I?" She giggled, taking the strange comment as a compliment.

Sonnet had always felt her mother was beautiful. Too beautiful to have settled for her father the way she did. Though she loved him she had to admit her mother and father didn't seem to be very well matched. He was rough around the edges and uneducated. She was bright and her looks glamorous. Yolanda had been honor roll all four years in high school and had even received a scholarship through the United Negro Fund to the college of her choice, but she married Frank instead and settled into this life. She could easily have been an actress or a model—yes, they were not very well matched at all. Kinda like her and Justin would be now—mismatched.

The thought of Justin ran through her mind—she wondered where he was.

Well, it didn't matter, Sonnet was going to get Wilson and they were going to make a better life for themselves than the one her father had made for her mother and them.

17

Justin worked hard all winter while living with his grandparents. They lived out in the outskirts of the city and so it took nearly all day for him to get from there to school, then to his part-time job and then back home again at night. It was a tough regime but it was worth it to Justin to work at that recording studio. His grandfather had gotten him the job through his connections in the music industry. Justin was just a gopher for the owner, but he loved it. He'd met so many famous people in such a short time. Through running errands, he met many of his favorite musicians and even got to watch a recording session of one of his favorite jazz bands. He had never been happier.

The best part of it all was the fact that he often got to play his music at work and even more often when at home. His grandparents never seemed to tire of listening to him. There were no more interruptions, ever.

Winter ended, the snow left, and soon the sun broke through. It had been months since he'd made any contact with anyone from California, and he missed everyone a little, even his mother. She had written once around February to tell him that she had started seeing a postman. Justin was a little surprised but figured maybe in the end, they had been holding each other back . . . now they could both be happy.

It was a Friday afternoon and as was Justin's regular routine, he waited for the train to take him into Manhattan to the studio. He had become a true New Yorker, minding his own business and not talking to anyone around him.

Just then, he noticed a young black woman waiting for the train as well. She looked to be in her twenties. She smiled at him.

Why was she looking at him? he wondered.

He tugged at his large pants.

Maybe that was it, perhaps she thought he was homeless or a bum or something.

Nothing fit anymore, as he was nearly disappearing from the workout that came with his busy lifestyle. That was okay though, he didn't need food, he was happy.

Suddenly, the young woman approached him. He looked around to make sure it was actually him she wanted to speak to.

"You play that horn?" she asked, noticing his case.

Her voice was sultry and her eyes were dark. Justin realized then, his heart was pounding very hard. He nodded.

"I would like to hear you play. You see, I'm in a band and we are looking for some new talent. Oh, forgive me, my name is Donelle, Donelle Christian," she said, and smiled again, handing him her card. He took it from her, and inadvertently touched her hand in the process. Justin went into a temporary trance.

"I've been seeing you for a while now, catching this train, and I've wanted to talk to you. You look . . . I don't know, you look like a deep guy," she went on. Justin was barely listening though, for all he could hear was the melody of sound her voice made, and all he could see was her smile—she was beautiful.

He went with her that afternoon instead of to the studio.

* * *

When Justin arrived home that night and told his grandparents about the woman at the train and about her band, and how now he would get a chance to play his music for real, they almost couldn't believe it. Justin was going to play backup for the band. The saxophone, the piano . . . whatever was needed . . . and after graduation, he would travel with them. His dream was coming true, his dream and what was always his mother's nightmare. His grandparents were excited and happy for him, so he decided to put off telling her.

18

Sonnet moved across the room gracefully. Margaret was just now noticing how graceful she had become. She was beautiful. Margaret raised the covers to get a better look at her thin legs, black and blue from the bruises that came easily whenever she bumped into anything. She looked at Sonnet's legs, smooth and shapely.

When she sat on her bed, gathering up her homework pages, she slung her hair. It moved easily, and then came to lie on her shoulders. She had added some highlights to it, which accentuated her light eyes.

"Sonnet," Margaret called. Sonnet turned to her, a smile on her lips.

"I miss you," Margaret said to her.

"Miss me? I'm not gone anywhere." Sonnet chuckled, her forehead wrinkling.

"You're all . . ." Margaret hesitated. "You're all different now," she finished.

"I'm not different. I'm just who I'm supposed to be," Sonnet said.

"Am I? I mean, look at me." Margaret sighed.

Sonnet noticed the dark circles under her eyes and her

dry lips. Margaret was such a pretty girl. Sonnet always felt Margaret was prettier than her, with her high cheekbones and dark eyes. She looked just like their father—exotic actually. If only she wasn't so thin—and now so bloated and out of shape . . .

"Tell you what," Sonnet bubbled, closing her textbook. "I'm gonna give you a facial."

Margaret's eyes lit up.

Emptying her vanity of all her cosmetics, Sonnet began her magic on Margaret. Smoothing on the foundation, perfectly matching her tone. Adding the subtle colors, copper and corals . . .

"Do your lips like this," Sonnet said, showing her how to blot the tissue. Margaret imitated her.

"Perfect. Let's show Mom and Dad," Sonnet suggested. Margaret climbed out of bed and slipped into her robe.

They walked into the living room where their parents were watching television.

"Tada," Sonnet introduced. Margaret stepped from behind her, grinning proudly. She had hoped for oohs and ahs, but instead, before her mother could give the praise Frank was on his feet, cursing and spitting. He threw his beer toward the girls, nearly hitting Sonnet. She had to duck.

The girls ran back to their room, locking the door. Margaret was so scared, Sonnet had to help her back to bed, as she had begun hyperventilating.

"Frank! There's nothing wrong with it!" they heard their mother cry out.

"Sluts! Both of them!" Frank yelled, his voice coming closer to the door.

In her growing panic, Sonnet jumped into the bed with Margaret, who was crying now and rubbing the makeup from her face with her blanket.

"I never want to wear this stuff again," Margaret cried.

Frank's fist hit their door once, before it hit their mother.

"All of you are just a bunch of sluts," he was heard saying, along with more foul swearing. The front door slammed.

Slowly, Sonnet pulled the cover from her head. She listened closely for the sound of the house—was it peaceful or violent? She heard nothing.

She crept from the bed, out of the room, and down the hall to her parents' bedroom door. All she heard was her mother's sobs.

How much longer could she ignore this?

19

Wilson stayed close to Sonnet every day, almost like insurance, until the day of the prom, confirming their date constantly. Margaret was still in shock that Sonnet was actually going out with him again.

"I thought you were just playing him," Margaret said, while watching Sonnet dress and apply the finishing touches to her outfit.

How pretty she was tonight. She had made it down to nearly 125 pounds.

"Like Marilyn only with a butt," Sonnet had said laughingly when she stepped off the scale at the doctor's office. Though the doctor didn't seem too overly interested in her health care—the way he would basically give her any dosage of diet pill she wanted—he did think her comment was funny.

Margaret had to admit it—though reluctantly—the results now seemed worth the effort.

Sonnet had Wilson eating out of the palm of her hand and it was funny to watch. He had been calling every day. Sometimes Margaret would pretend to flirt with him, just to see what he would do. Wilson would stammer and stumble.

"But I thought you liked me," Margaret would say, before bursting into fake sobbing and then hanging up.

Sitting there on the toilet seat, watching Sonnet, Margaret suddenly remembered the letter she had gotten from Justin.

"Oh, gosh, I forgot to tell you! Justin wrote me, he's in a band!" Margaret bubbled excitedly, hurrying back to their bedroom and retrieving the letter.

Sonnet stepped from the bathroom into the doorway to see Margaret's face when she came out of the room.

"A band? What kind of band?"

"A jazz band," Margaret said. "Yeah, and he's real excited about it," she went on.

"He plays an instrument? How come I didn't know that?" Sonnet asked, thinking out loud. Margaret laughed a little. Sonnet looked at her, with confusion showing on her face.

"He plays a lot of instruments. Where have you been? You never noticed that black case he always had with him?" Margaret asked her, taking the bobby pin from between Sonnet's lips and pinning up her hair.

"So what else did he say?" Sonnet asked, sounding rather sheepish, pretending she was only remotely interested. Truth was, she was very interested. She missed Justin very much.

"Do you mean, did he ask about you?" Margaret asked, looking at her in the mirror.

"Maybe," Sonnet answered.

"He asked about everybody. Justin is a *good* friend."

"And you are implying I'm not?" Sonnet asked with a snip in her tone now. She turned to her sister.

Margaret backed away slightly. "No, I'm just saying that you are doing your own thing now, that's all."

"Like when Leita comes over and you two hide out in here and giggle—you guys are, like, inviting me into your world when you do that?" Sonnet snapped, her jealousy showing now. "I miss Justin too, ya know."

Margaret grinned. She never thought the day would come

when she would make her sister jealous, or admit her feelings about Justin. Margaret could tell by the tightening of Sonnet's jawline that her words carried no more intent than normal sibling bickering.

"Look, go out with your Wilson and have a good time. Get all this madness out of your system—then you can come back to earth. Leita is staying over tonight and we'll wait up."

"You don't need to wait up for me. You're not my damn mama," Sonnet whispered through gritted teeth, wrinkling up her nose.

Margaret giggled now. It had been a long time since Sonnet's words had carried the sting they once did when she had first start losing weight.

Suddenly their playfulness stopped. Sonnet looked serious.

"But Dad's drinking," she said.

Margaret had been unaware. She had seen him take one drink earlier that day, it was Saturday, his day off, but for some reason seeing him take the one drink hadn't made her think that he would continue. Besides, he had said Leita could stay over. Why would he continue to drink?

"Maybe I should call Wilson and cancel," Sonnet said, before suddenly Frank came down the hall toward the bathroom with Yolanda close behind him, looking nervous and wringing her hands. He stopped and stared at Sonnet a long time before finally he grinned. It was a nasty lecherous grin that made Sonnet's stomach tighten.

"You look just like your mother used to in that damned blue dress," he said, touching the fabric. "She thought she was too good for me that night, too. But that Joseph Brown taught her a thing or two and she came running back." He laughed loudly. "When that little nigga Jew gets through with you, you'll come running back too," Frank slurred. "You'll come back to your daddy," he added.

Sonnet had never heard her father speak to her this way

before. It scared her. She looked to her mother for answers, but there were none coming, only the movement of her mouth. Margaret was silent. Suddenly Frank looked at her and scowled.

"You're sick and ugly, go to bed," he snapped.

Margaret looked at her mother, who was shaking her head and mouthing the words *I'm sorry* behind his back.

Margaret felt truly sick now and ran into the room, slamming the door.

"Why would you say that?" Sonnet asked, thinking she could reason with him, talk to him.

"Are you a whore now?" Frank asked Sonnet, closing in on her. Yolanda grabbed his arm, and Frank pulled away.

Sonnet's eyes widened now, in a new fear, the fear that perhaps he would hit her—like he hit her mother.

"Frank!" Yolanda screamed. "Leave her alone, you're drunk," she said, tugging at his arm again. Suddenly, Frank seemed to calm down as Sonnet stood stone faced and silent.

"You're precious, Sonnet," he then said, with words dripping with sarcasm.

The doorbell rang. Sonnet ran to answer it. It was Wilson. He was gorgeous in his dark tuxedo, but she didn't have time to stand and admire him now. "Let's go," she blurted, hurrying him from the house.

As they drove away, she didn't see Leita on her way to the house. No one had been able to warn her.

20

Sonnet thought about the situation at home nearly all the way to the hotel. However, as soon as the doors opened, she was instantly mesmerized by the lights, the colors, balloons, music—and pretty people.

Sonnet danced that night away. She knew her life would never be the same after tonight. Everyone was looking at her as Wilson spun her on the floor, showing her off like a prize. Tonight, no one was looking at her like a freak . . . tonight everyone was looking at her as if to ask, "Who told you that you could look so good?"

Tonight Sonnet knew she had even outshone Cathy Crowley, the homecoming queen.

Her mother had worked hard on her dress and it was the most perfect shade of midnight-blue satin.

"I wore blue satin to my prom," Yolanda had said, sounding reflective.

"And what did Daddy wear?" Sonnet asked.

Sonnet suddenly remembered her mother had never answered.

Wilson was very attentive to her—making sure she had punch and that no one else got near her. And when the photographer took their picture, he held her tight around her waist, pulling her close. *What a memory*, she thought to herself.

This was the most perfect night of her life . . .

Unlike the scene going on at the house . . .

Frank was going berserk, breaking things and screaming. His voice carried all over the entire house.

Margaret had never seen him this way. She locked the door, hiding Leita and herself in the bedroom.

When Leita had arrived, Frank hadn't started his tirade. Yolanda had just opened the door and without thinking told Leita to go into Margaret's room. Yolanda wondered now why she hadn't told the child to go home.

"Maybe we should go through the window and I'll get my dad," Leita suggested.

"No offense, but my dad will kick your dad's natural ass," Margaret said while she pressed her ear against the door.

Leita thought about it for a moment. Her father wasn't nearly as big as Frank and now, in Frank's crazed drunken state, her father didn't stand a chance. But still, they needed to do something.

Frank was ranting and raving about Yolanda and the past, about how much of a tramp she was. He was going on and on about how she had never thought he was good enough.

That is, until she got in trouble and needed him to fix it.

He was screaming something about "fixing Joseph's dirty work."

Margaret couldn't get it all, but from the sudden commotion in the hallway, she just knew he was hitting her mother.

"Good Lord, Margaret, I never knew you lived this way! You've got to call 911 or something. I think he just hit your mother," Leita screamed, panicking.

Margaret tried to think. The telephone was surely off the hook, as her father would always take it off when he beat her mother. Suddenly Margaret felt a wave of emotions, from guilt to anger . . . and then shame.

"He'll stop in a minute," she said, lowering her eyes.

She wanted to crawl under the bed and disappear. She wanted to vomit. She wanted to scream, but instead, she began to wring her hands and pace the room. Never had she been without Sonnet on a bad night like this.

"Margaret, are you gonna do something?" Leita asked, her eyes wild with fear. She grabbed Margaret by the shoulders. Margaret was nearly limp.

"I don't know what to do," Margaret answered, her voice just above a whisper now, as both of them heard Yolanda cry out as she hit the wall.

"Well, I do! This is crazy!" Leita said, before opening the door and running from the room.

Frank had chased Yolanda into the kitchen. He had her by the front of her blouse and her lip was bloody. Just as he was about to strike her again, he saw Leita in the doorway.

No one had ever seen him hit Yolanda before. He usually beat her in the privacy of their bedroom.

No one since Joseph, that night at the prom seventeen, almost eighteen summers ago, had ever interfered with the way he *handled* Yolanda.

That night, Yolanda had gone with Joseph to the prom, instead of him. Joseph was new in town. His folks were from Texas. Yolanda had broken it off again—or so she thought—and had tried to move on, with Joseph. Joseph was loud and instantly popular, smart and good looking too. Yolanda had a crush on him immediately.

That night of the prom Frank caught them. He had followed them to the place where lovers went to be together. Joseph had that fancy car and all. Frank spotted them right away. He waited in the dark, watching them. Watching that car sway back and forth, as they made love in the backseat.

Frank remembered the looks on their faces when he approached and swung open that door, and dragged Yolanda out by her hair, and slamming his fist into her face, and tearing her dress. She was screaming and there was blood.

Joseph tried to fight him but he was stronger. Fed by his alcohol and anger, he hit Joseph so hard he was knocked unconscious with one hard blow. Frank then threw Yolanda into his car and drove away with her. Frank was wild with anger that night. He couldn't believe how Yolanda had held him off all this time, sexually, but without a second thought, she had given her virginity to Joseph Brown in the backseat of his car.

Frank threatened to rape Yolanda that night, but instead chose to humiliate her in the worst way.

He then took her home—walking and bloody. He then explained to her parents how they had gotten into a car accident.

"I pushed her out, because I thought we would be killed," Frank lied, smoothing down his ripped shirt, which he'd torn himself. He looked at Yolanda, daring her to challenge his story. She was silent, running to her room, unable to listen to the rest of the lie.

Yolanda conceived Sonnet that night. She knew it right away. Loving Joseph had been so sweet, so wonderful it couldn't have caused anything less.

Her fear of what Frank would do drove her to make the biggest mistake of her life . . .

She slept with Frank as soon as she missed her first period.

However, Frank wasn't as naive as she wanted him to be.

She had slipped him into her room while her parents were out one afternoon. She flirted and teased, thinking she was winning him over. Once in her bed, Frank was rough and uncaring as he sexed her. Yolanda had no idea sex could hurt like this. With Joseph it had been so wonderful . . . even in the backseat of a car.

Yolanda thought about Joseph the whole time Frank rode her, grunting and sweating, until finally he came. She pushed him off quickly and hurriedly gathered up her clothes to dress. She sat at her vanity, putting her hair back up, looking at Frank, lying in her bed—in no hurry to get up—with no plans to leave. He was cocky and confident.

"So, you're knocked up, eh?" Frank asked her, out of the blue. She looked at him in the reflection of the mirror without turning around. She watched him while he laughed at her.

She then told her parents she was pregnant by Frank and then, despite his efforts to see her, she told Joseph that she didn't care about him and that he needed to go away and leave her alone.

To this day, Yolanda could see still Joseph's face—how sad he was. How confused and hurt. He left for Texas to live with his grandparents.

Yolanda's plans to go to college were bypassed, her plans to live in that small town, near her parents and her friends, changed, her chance at true love diverted. In the wink of an eye, she was married and off to the big city. Her once simple life's dream had turned into a nightmare.

All she felt was shame and the sense of complete failure.

Frank's jealousy over Joseph was unrelenting, growing worse and worse with each day passing until one night, three months after the birth of Sonnet, Frank, drinking heavily, came home after working as a janitor at one of the downtown office buildings, beat, and raped her, begetting Margaret.

21

Leita was stunned when she saw Frank, whose hands were around Yolanda's throat. Margaret reached her, grabbing her by the arm. She looked at her father and mother, who stopped, as if frozen, where they stood. Margaret felt weak at the sight and fainted. Leita fearlessly ran to the phone.

When Margaret came to full cognition, the police were at the house and Frank was in handcuffs. She attempted to rise up from the couch, but Leita held her down.

Yolanda was giving a report to the female officer while she applied a cold pack to her face. She turned to Margaret and smiled just a little. Margaret, looking at the bruises on her mother's face, closed her eyes tight.

After the police left, the girls sat on the sofa as the radio played. They sat quietly for a long time before finally Leita smiled. "You know, we're gonna look back on all of this and smile one day," she said, softly touching Margaret's arm.

"Why do you say stupid things?" Margaret snapped.

Leita bit her lip and pulled her hand back into her lap.

"I didn't mean it," Margaret apologized and then hugged Leita tight. They hugged a long time, as Margaret suddenly felt that after tonight their time together was about to be shortened.

"Yolanda, what are you going to do?" Leita's mother asked her. Yolanda looked off, avoiding her face.

She and Roslyn Gardner had never shared too many deep conversations. They both knew it was because of Frank they had not become better friends.

"I don't know. I haven't known for a long time," Yolanda admitted.

Roslyn moved from her side of the table around to Yolanda, and wrapped her arms around her shoulders, comforting her.

Roslyn assisted Yolanda to her bed. With Frank securely behind bars for the night, Roslyn and Leita planned to stay the night.

22

This time Wilson didn't suggest a drive, he pointed upward.

The prom was being held in the ballroom of the Howard Johnson Hotel, but still, Sonnet was a little bewildered as to what he was pointing at, that is, until she noticed a few couples leaving, heading up in the elevators.

The lights had gotten dim and the music was very mood-setting, but Sonnet still wasn't sure about all he was implying.

"If you change your mind we can come down. Richard got a big suite up there and everybody is mostly going up there to drink a bit and then come back down," Wilson whispered in her ear—clearing things up.

"Mostly?" Sonnet asked, finally catching the innuendo.

She had to admit she was intrigued with the idea—curious even. He was so handsome tonight—how could she refuse? It would just be a couple of drinks and then they'd come back down, that's what he said. Unconsciously Sonnet looked around. She saw all the loving couples, moving to the music coming from the stereo—and their hearts.

Who knew what the rest of the summer would bring?

Sonnet was up for a scholarship to UC Santa Barbara, as well as Sacramento State and even one right there in San Jose—as if she wanted to stay home. She was ready to leave—to take one of the out-of-town scholarships. Sonnet was ready to get out of the life she had there. The memory of her father's face flashed before her eyes and then she looked back at Wilson, who was smiling at her.

She might never see Wilson again, after she went away to college.

When they walked in, Sonnet's eyes scanned the room for anyone she might recognize. But the room was crowded and felt unfamiliar. Couples were sitting around the suite drinking. Just then a couple came from the bedroom. The pretty, dark-haired girl was smoothing her hair and the boy was putting his jacket back on. Wilson held Sonnet's hand as he made his way through the crowd to the bar. He poured them both a drink.

"Here, baby, drink this, it'll calm your nerves," Wilson said, handing her a drink.

Sonnet didn't like the taste of the drink, but it seemed to make him happy for her to drink with him. He began to kiss her neck.

"Don't we have some unfinished business?" he whispered in her ear. She leaned back and looked deep into his eyes. Her belly fluttered. She set the drink down and held her hand on her stomach to calm it.

Biting her lip nervously, she looked around, almost hoping that Margaret would suddenly appear to break this up, as she had that night at the Point—at the winter dance.

Wilson smoothed back the comforter on the bed with one hand as he loosened his tie with the other. Sonnet didn't move. She stood by the door watching.

Maybe she would change her mind now. Maybe he wouldn't mind if she ran out.

She looked down at her hand on the doorknob. When she looked up, Wilson stood naked before her. She had never really seen a naked man before except in a movie. It wasn't the same at all.

Wilson was quite erect and ready for her.

"Aren't you going to undress?" he asked, pressing against her, raising her dress high around her waist.

"Okay, I change my mind now," she said under her breath. He chuckled. The heat of his breath was causing the hairs on her neck to rise. Suddenly he bit her bottom lip hard and hung on while he pulled her to the floor. He straddled her while rolling down her stockings and underwear. He didn't even take off her shoes before he parted her legs and forced himself into her. Sonnet felt suddenly light-headed as her legs numbed while she surrendered her virginity.

She had never before felt the pain she was feeling now while she gripped the shag carpeting of that luxury suite.

Sonnet didn't fight him—what would be the point? she thought. She had asked for this—hadn't she? All that work, all the plans, all for this—

Her mind soared as Wilson moaned and humped her. She thought mostly about Justin.

It just wouldn't have been this way with him. Not on the floor in a strange hotel room with her dress hiked high around her waist and her stockings around her ankles. Justin wouldn't have humped her like an animal, without even kissing her or looking at her the whole time.

Finally, Wilson grunted, releasing all he had to offer inside her. He pulled himself from her and rolled off. He was breathing hard and smiling. She closed her eyes tight and then opened them again. He was already standing and starting to dress.

"Hurry, we need to get back down there," he said, tossing

her a towel. She looked at it and then him standing there over her, looking down on her.

"It's clean, don't worry. They keep lots in here," he continued, as he now smoothed back his hair.

She wiped herself dry and pulled up her underwear and stockings. She smoothed down that beautiful midnight-blue satin dress that her mother had worked so hard to get perfect. She was humiliated beyond words.

But the evening wasn't perfect—not anymore. Reality had hit hard, and it was ugly.

Wilson didn't even know it had been her first time with sex. He hadn't even noticed the blood on the towel. And he didn't seem to care either.

He hadn't used a condom. He had just taken it for granted she was protected by birth control pills, like all the other pretty girls in that school. Sonnet had heard them talking in the gym about their pills and doctor appointments.

She knew about pills and doctor appointments, just not for birth control.

"You were pretty good," he said to her with an impish grin, when he handed her the little blue-sequined bag that matched her dress so perfectly. "Just think, last year I wouldn't have even been able to find it." He chuckled.

Sonnet's eyes began to burn, but still she couldn't respond to his words. She didn't make a sound.

They walked out of the room, and suddenly Sonnet felt sick to her stomach.

"I need to go home," was all she could finally manage to say.

"Wait, let's go downstairs a little while longer," Wilson said. His voice sounded soft now—almost warm, almost caring. He reached for her hand, only to have her pull away.

Sonnet rushed through the suite, avoiding the stares and empty laughter. She ran quickly to the elevator. Wilson called for her, but she didn't stop.

* * *

The fresh air hit her face when she exited the hotel lobby to the street. She stared walking. Soon her hair began to fall. She began pulling the bobby pins out, one by one, and throwing them, as far as she could. As they flew into the darkness she found herself chuckling at how stupid her actions must look. Again she thought of Justin.

There would be no calling him tonight, she thought to herself.

Her legs throbbed; she stopped to rub her thighs a little. It was then she realized that Wilson hadn't even come after her.

Oh well, so much for Mr. Perfect, she thought to herself, fighting back the tears, fighting off the degradation.

She looked in her purse to see if she had enough money to call a cab. Her mother had apparently slipped her twenty dollars in addition to the seven singles she already had.

Ignoring the cabdriver's attempts at conversation about her prom night, she sat in silence all the way home. She never wanted to think about her prom night again.

She stared out the window.

As the cab pulled up in front of her house, she could see the living room light was on. Margaret had waited up just as she had promised.

What would she say to her?

Before Sonnet walked in, Margaret knew immediately things had gone very wrong. Why else would Sonnet be arriving home in a cab?

She looked over at Leita, who was asleep on the sofa. Roslyn had gone to bed in the spare room.

Sonnet walked in. The two girls stood facing each other, looking each other over, sizing up the moment.

Margaret's eyes were puffy from crying, her size 7 jeans hugging her body so tight that she could barely manage to shove her hands into her pockets, Sonnet's hair a mess and her mascara running down her powdered cheeks.

"I saw Daddy beating Mama up," Margaret finally said, her words nearly stopping Sonnet's heart. "We had to call the cops on him," she added. "Mr. and Mrs. Gardner had to come and now everyone knows," she continued, holding back her tears. Sonnet took her in her arms, holding on tight.

"I'm here now and everything is going to be all right," she comforted.

Margaret shook her head. Sonnet pulled her face close to hers.

"Yes, it's going to be all right. I'm not going to take those pills anymore and we're going to call Grandma and ask her if we can come stay awhile with her. And everything is going to be all right."

"What about graduation?" Margaret began. "You graduate in a month—"

Sonnet put her finger to her sister's lips, shushing her.

"Don't even worry about all that right now," Sonnet said.

"That's right, you can stay with me until graduation," Leita said, sleepily rubbing her eyes.

What a good friend Leita was.

23

Sonnet had never remembered her grandfather being so old before. Perhaps it was seeing Yolanda so mentally scattered that had aged him. He had always been so optimistic for her, wanting so much. Seeing his daughter so devastated was nearly too much.

There was an empty feeling deep inside Sonnet as she watched her mother and sister ride off in that big Town Car headed for that little nowhere town in the San Joaquin Valley.

There were no pretty people there, just hardworking farmers and lots of agriculture.

"So where you gonna go to school?" Margaret had asked, while Sonnet hoisted the heavy bags to the living room. Packing had taken most of the night. They were both exhausted. Yolanda hadn't helped much as she seemed to be drowning in depression.

"Fresno State," Sonnet answered.

"Fresno? You didn't want to go to Fresno, did you?" Margaret asked, carrying a smaller box of trinkets.

Sonnet smirked and glared at her, noticing their mother sitting in earshot.

"It's okay. I'll do what I have to. We need to go to Grandma and Grandpa's," she said, sounding in control.

Margaret noticed Yolanda too—sitting there, silent.

"Do you think she regrets what she did to Daddy?" Margaret whispered. Sonnet shook her head.

"No. But I think it's gonna take some time before she can cope with everything. Mrs. Gardner said it's just gonna take some time," Sonnet said, lugging another large bag into the living room, to wait for their grandparents to come.

When Sonnet had called her grandparents the night before and told them the abbreviated version of what had happened they were ready to come get them in a flash. They had been in the dark for so many years; it was both shocking and refreshing to be finally brought into the light.

They were both saddened and excited at the prospects of having their daughter back home and proud of Sonnet for making the call.

"You'll come and finish school here, Margaret," they assured her. "And, Sonnet, don't you worry, you'll have full support with your schooling until you girls and your mother can get on your feet."

Sonnet watched the big Town Car pull up. Her grandparents had a small dog named Boots and Margaret seemed to draw comfort from him immediately as he jumped all around in the backseat. It only took minutes to load the trunk with the few suitcases and boxes they'd packed. They drove off, taking most of Sonnet's belongings with them. She couldn't wait to see them again.

As they rounded the corner and out of Sonnet's sight, she lifted a small bag with only a few necessities, and prepared to make herself comfortable in the Gardners' home for the next few weeks.

The weeks flew by and before they knew it, Sonnet and Leita were at the Greyhound bus depot preparing to say their good-byes. Sonnet now was headed out to that nothing town to go to school and become, "A teacher?" asked Leita, sounding quiet surprised. Sonnet nodded.

"No glamorous life, no fancy college," she said. She had come to accept it.

Graduation had been a blur. She saw Wilson in passing, and he just smiled and kept walking. He must have noticed she was gaining weight. She had stopped the pills and had put on about ten pounds very quickly.

Leita and Sonnet sat in the café at the depot thinking about their lives and what they had planned to do with them. Leita was not going to college at all when she graduated next year. She was going to work at her father's store and keep seeing ol' Dorky David Summerland.

He had become a pretty permanent fixture these days. He wasn't so bad; besides, Leita was crazy about him and visa versa.

Sonnet told Leita about the night at the prom—everything. She hadn't told Margaret or her mother, but she knew she would probably have to as she was late for her period. She was hoping it was a side effect from getting off the diet pills.

"We can only hope," Leita said with a weak smile. "Oh, Justin wrote me," she added, hoping a change in subject would make the awful possibilities of what Sonnet had suggested go away.

"I saw the letter on the table yesterday," Sonnet admitted.

"And you didn't open it?" Leita giggled. "You know you were dying too."

Sonnet rolled her eyes, feeling the heat coming to her cheeks. Her embarrassment surprised even her.

"Yup, he's going on tour with his band. They made a record and he is sending me a copy of it."

"I'm sure he is going to send Margaret one too," Sonnet said with an empty smile. There was nothing but a feeling of loss in her voice now.

Leita had written and told Justin of all of the events that had led up to Yolanda Patterson and her family having to move. He hadn't written back much in reply to that information except to say that he hoped all was well and to tell her about his music. Leita was surprised that Justin didn't seem as if he had a stake in his and Sonnet's relationship either.

Maybe Sonnet really had killed his love. Or maybe he was as empty as Sonnet looked and sounded right now—rattling on about becoming a teacher as if that was all she wanted in life.

Leita didn't know that the day before, Sonnet had gone to say good-bye to Justin's mother but she wasn't home. She was hardly ever home anymore.

Sonnet hadn't seen Frank since the night she left for the prom. He had come to the Gardners' home one night looking for his family, but Mr. Gardner lied and said he didn't know where anyone was. Sonnet hid in the back room. Frank never returned.

Sonnet noticed that the house had emptied and gone up for rent by the end of the month.

Margaret called and had told her that Frank had showed up there drunk and their grandfather pulled a shotgun on him.

The call for the bus came and Leita burst into tears and so did Sonnet.

24

The band sat in excited suspense as the doors of the record store opened. They were going to be signing CDs that day. They had released their first single last week and it was flying up the charts. Everyone seemed to love their sound and Donelle's voice was haunting.

It was hard at first for Justin to get used to all the attention and fan mail, especially from the women, both old and young alike.

Grant, the leader, knew his stuff when he suggested their pictures be on the cover. People noticed him everywhere he went now.

"We are some pretty-azz people." He laughed, admiring the picture that was to be on the front of the CD, and he was right. Justin had changed into one of the pretty people without even trying. He had made it to the "in" crowd without even endeavoring to do so.

Tonight they would celebrate his eighteenth birthday. His grandparents were very proud of him. He liked to think that his mother was too, though she hadn't answered any of his letters or even responded to the copy of the new CD he had sent her.

Justin had written Leita a couple of times, and though she tried to put him in the know about what was going on with the Pattersons, he could tell there had been some gaps. Fresno State had never been on Sonnet's list of schools to attend. Being a teacher was not one of her "glamorous" goals.

One day he would go back to California. One day he would fully understand. But for now, he had his new life in New York. He was fulfilled, or so he thought.

"I love you," a heavyset blond girl, who looked only about fifteen, said to him as he signed her CD. He felt his face grow hot.

"Love yourself first," he said to her. She stared at him for a second as his words sort of slapped her into reality and then she took the CD and walked away.

Donelle overheard him talking to the girl. She liked the way his lips moved when he spoke. She liked the way his dimple would come to his cheek when he was embarrassed. She had been watching him transform right before her eyes, from the chubby boy in the baggy clothes standing in that subway station, to this tall, lean, handsome man, signing his name to his music here in this Broadway music store. He was a good musician, and a kind person. He had grown to love himself, too, which had given him confidence. She liked a man with confidence. Donelle knew she had become infatuated with Justin, although she was at least ten years his senior. But she knew, deep inside, he loved someone else—it showed. But that had never stopped her before; besides, whatever he felt for that girl was just puppy love. . . .

Grant had told Donelle to watch herself for publicity's sake. After all, until today Justin had been a minor, a boy, but after tonight, well . . .

* * *

After the signing, they all went back to the hotel suite and the party began. Many people came, more than Justin had ever remembered at any of his birthday parties before. Famous people were there. Rich friends of his grandparents were there. Nearly every important person to know was there, but the most important people to Justin were painfully missing.

He slipped away amidst all the smiles and congratulations to call. The only number he had was Leita's, so he called.

"Ohmigod, Justin!" she exclaimed.

Justin found himself grinning at the sound of her voice.

"It's my birthday," he began.

"I know. And you called me. How special is that, Teddy Bear?"

Leita had given him that nickname a long time ago but had never told him until now. He laughed out loud at the sound of it coming from her.

"Are you going to call Margaret and Sonnet too? They would love to hear from you."

"I don't have their number."

"Well, get some paper," Leita requested, sounding motherly.

"Okay," he agreed, still holding on to the smile he had planted on his face. He could clearly see Leita's face in his mind . . . her goofy, crooked grin and stringy hair. She was a mess . . . but a good friend.

He turned to grab a tablet and suddenly was shocked to find Donelle standing in the doorway. She was so pretty.

"ET phone home?" she asked, her voice sultry and arousing. It would rumble inside him when she spoke, and when she sang to the music he made, it would almost make him cry. He had played the song for her that he had written for Sonnet, for their wedding day. It all seemed like a childhood dream now.

Donelle had put words to the piece. He had told her it was for someone special, someone from his past. Grant fell in love with it, and so, after a little beefing up, they released it on the CD, titling it “My Sonnet.”

Justin hoped that just maybe, maybe if Sonnet heard it, she would just know it was written for her—or maybe not. Maybe now her life had changed. Maybe now she was thin and beautiful and in love with Wilson Yant.

“Justin,” Leita called from the other end of the phone.

“Let me call you back, all right?”

He quickly hung up the receiver.

Donelle closed the door and locked it. Justin’s heart began to pound with each step she took toward him.

“My grandparents are out there,” he began, as she moved in on him. There was no mistaking her intent tonight. He always knew she was a flirt but often wanted to make himself believe that her attention was never really directed at him. There were no doubts tonight.

“Good, I would hate it if they were in here.” She giggled.

She had been drinking. He could tell by the taste of her mouth when she kissed him, her tongue hungrily searching for his. She tasted like sweet wine.

As she crept up on him, moving like a cat, he became engulfed in unfamiliar feelings—hot, but shaking from a chill all at once. When she began to unbutton his shirt, he felt that sexual tingle again, only this time, Donelle noticed. She unbuttoned his pants and began to fondle his sex. The sensation overwhelmed him. This was nothing like the few times he had masturbated, this was real . . . this was intense. He quickly moved away from her, holding up his hands to hold her off—just for a minute at least. He needed to think. He needed to pull himself together. He needed to . . .

“You’re legal now, baby, and legally mine,” she vamped, opening the sarong. She was naked underneath.

Justin felt weak.

“Oh my Gaad!” he cried out at the sight of her beautiful

body, so smooth and brown and perfect. She stood before him like a chocolate pool and before he could stop himself, he dove in.

When he awoke, Donelle was gone. He quickly dressed and went back out to the party. He was surprised that no one seemed to notice that he had even been gone. Even his grandparents schmoozed on, as if nothing had occurred over the last two hours.

Justin searched for Donelle. She was gone.

That night as Justin lay in his bed, he couldn't sleep. He shared the hotel suite with the drummer, Vince, who was still awake watching television.

He tossed and turned a little longer before he finally gave up and went into the living room.

"Hey, birthday boy," Vince said, with a broad smile coming to his lips. Justin sat across from him on a small footstool.

"I need to talk to somebody," Justin began. Vince clicked off the television with the remote.

"Speak, my child," he said, trying to appear deep and all-knowing. Vince was a Mexican man, about forty. He and Grant were the oldest members of the band.

"It's a . . . about Donelle."

"Did you do her?" he asked.

Justin was caught off guard by his frankness. He felt embarrassed and a little ashamed, stumbling over his words until finally he just nodded. Vince waved a forgiving hand.

"Don't worry about it." He chuckled. He then looked at him with a serious expression showing. "You're clean, right?" he asked.

"Clean?" Justin asked, sounding confused and naive.

"HIV negative, shit like that. You're clean, right?" Vince asked again, as if possibly having a personal stake in Donelle's sex life and whom she shared it with.

"God yes. She was my first," Justin admitted, before thinking. His face was instantly on fire. Vince threw back his head in laughter.

"That girl . . . she's too much. So don't tell me—you love her now, right?" Vince continued to laugh.

Justin was disturbed with the question and even more disturbed with the answer. He shook his head. "That's what bothers me." He smiled boyishly.

Vince grabbed him in a playful headlock. "Don't worry, you don't have to marry her or nothing like that. And you won't even have to sleep with her again until Christmas—unless you want to." He laughed wickedly.

Justin pushed away from the playful grip and laughed too. However, deep inside he wasn't comforted very much. He still had nowhere to place his feelings.

The days that passed were awkward at first. Every time he would try to broach the subject of their encounter with Donelle, she would just smile, furrowing her brow, looking confused, as if she didn't know what he was talking about and then just change the subject. Soon, Justin just didn't try to bring it up anymore and things went back to normal. That is, until they reached Atlanta. She came to his room one night and climbed into his bed. After she left, Justin felt different—hollow inside. He also felt a little out of control. Her body felt so good and yet, his heart felt bad. Soon she began to come to his bed more often, until it was more like a habit to sleep with her. He began to need it—to need her. But he was troubled still with the one question—How could she come to him this way time after time, coming to his bed or calling him to hers, without so much as a hint at commitment? How long would it go on this way?

As the year came to an end, along with the first of their tours, Justin wondered if he would be able to keep up this lifestyle. It was one filled with glamour, nightlife, and Donelle.

What he had left behind, California, haunted him daily. He missed the simple things—Leita and her corny jokes, Margaret and her old eyes, but mostly, he missed Sonnet.

He missed everything about Sonnet. As much as he hated to admit it, sometimes when he touched Donelle in the darkness of his room, he would pretend he was touching Sonnet.

25

The climate there in the valley was treacherous with fog. The Tules made the fog so thick it wasn't uncommon to have less than five feet of visibility until way past ten in the morning. Life all but stopped . . . but not for college students—never for the college students.

It was only November but already the fog was coming in heavily. Sonnet would hang on that fog line for forty-five minutes from that little town of Tulare until she got to Fresno. By the time she would arrive, she would be rattled and nauseated. Sometimes her grandfather would drive her.

"Oh my Gaad, the man is as blind as two bats." Sonnet sighed, flopping down on Margaret's bed, after another treacherous ride home with Grandpa.

Margaret attempted to laugh. The weather had been hard on her and again, she had fallen ill. She was weak from coughing and had to stay home and mostly in bed.

Her weight had dropped tremendously as she could not hold much food down. However, just knowing that she wasn't self-inducing the vomiting made all the difference to Yolanda.

After seeing a therapist, Yolanda had been feeling better

about her life and her daughters' lives. She felt freer to care for Margaret. She could give her all the time she needed. There would be no more threats, no more guilt.

Yolanda had even signed up for a couple of culinary classes at the community college. She had begun working part-time at an elementary school cafeteria, the school she had attended as a child.

Having been born and raised in that town, she at first thought it was going to be difficult seeing all of the faces of people who knew of her past life, her failures, the disappointing life she had chosen, but instead it was almost comforting to be among the familiar. No one there had any thoughts one way or the other about how her life had turned out. And her therapist had helped Yolanda see that even if they had . . . what difference did it make?

"You really are okay," the doctor told her, smiling warmly.

Yolanda just smiled and looked out the window, wanting to believe.

She and the girls had found a small apartment not far from her parents and life was simpler now. They all worked together to take care of the basic needs and life was coming together. Surprisingly enough, Frank was sending money regularly. It was just enough to get by without Yolanda having to work full-time at the school, so she didn't have to quit her classes.

The hardest part of it all for Yolanda was seeing Joseph Brown's family. She had never told them about Sonnet being their grandchild. However, when Mrs. Brown would see them together around town, she would stare, as if she could see a resemblance of some kind in Sonnet to her son. Sonnet did have his eyes and his perfect lips.

Joseph had moved back to Texas many years ago and they didn't see him much, as they had stopped traveling years ago.

"But perhaps he'll come out for Christmas," Joseph's

mother told Yolanda one day in the grocery store. Yolanda tried to hide her excitement, but the smile crept through. Mrs. Brown caught it.

Her mother was noticing her conversation with Mrs. Brown when she informed her of Joseph's possible visit. When Yolanda returned to the checkout line after Mrs. Brown walked away her mother, Mildred, looked around at her.

"Oh, just turn yourself back around, missy," Yolanda said playfully, taking her mother by the shoulders and spinning her back around in the line. She could see her mother's smile, even from behind.

Mildred had always liked Joseph—God knows, better than Frank Patterson.

Mildred was no fool, she'd counted the months; there was no way that nine-pound Sonnet was premature—no way. She knew the baby was Joseph's. Yolanda had changed after she met Joseph; she had become a little more melancholy, like a woman pining, whenever she and Joseph weren't together. It wasn't uncommon to find her daydreaming. She was never that way with Frank. Mildred had suspected that Yolanda and Joseph had become intimate, but Joseph was so polite when he would come calling—she let it go, never even discussing it with her husband. Mildred had so hoped they would marry. But then suddenly, after the prom and supposedly that car accident—which was a bold-faced lie on the part of Frank Patterson—Yolanda changed again, only this time it was intimidation that she wore all the time—letting Frank answer questions all the time, speaking for her, etc. It was obvious that Frank had gained some control over her, which was confirmed when Yolanda came up pregnant within a couple of weeks . . . well, just say this, Mama wasn't no fool. She said nothing though, not even when they married and moved over four hours away. Mildred knew it was so that the Browns would never find out about the baby.

* * *

That evening Margaret could hear the screen door slam from her bed and felt instant relief—Sonnet was home.

Yolanda met Sonnet in the living room with a hot tea.

"Mom, Papa is never driving me to school again, I've had it. The man is a menace on four wheels. I'm going to see if I can just work for the car . . . he'll give it to me, I know he will. His driving has got me so scared, my stomach stayed upset again all day," Sonnet said, rubbing her belly. Yolanda noticed that Sonnet had gained more weight, even over the last week, and all of it was in one area, it seemed. The doctor had told her that after the diet pills were stopped, there would be a rapid weight gain. The doctor assured her of that, and Sonnet was ready for that fact too. However, this was so fast—and so much weight . . .

Sonnet didn't seem to mind much and she had gone back to working out in the gym twice a week. She seemed to be keeping everything in perspective, Yolanda noticed. Both she and Margaret had both seemed to have a handle on food now and everything else going on in their lives, but still something nagged at Yolanda, and she just couldn't quite put her finger on—until today. Maybe it had been seeing Hattie Brown in the grocery store that took her mind in that direction, maybe it was the way Sonnet went at the sauce in the pot with a piece of bread before turning in to Margaret's room. She just dipped into the pot, as if that were normal behavior for her.

Yolanda was studying to get her chef's hat and was cooking a lot more, more than ever. However, the foods were healthy now. There were no more sweets and high-fat foods like before, but dipping in the pots and eating like a refugee . . . that had never been Sonnet's style.

* * *

Sonnet went into Margaret's room. She sat up in the bed ready for conversation, but before they could start, Yolanda called Sonnet back into the kitchen.

It smelled great in the kitchen. Sonnet was sure the people in the next apartment stayed hungry all the time because of it.

"Yes?" she inquired, again dipping another piece of bread into the sauce on the stove.

Yolanda watched her.

"Honey, I've noticed that you are putting on some weight, I mean more weight than I think the doctor said you would," Yolanda began carefully, hoping not to cause any kind of emotional setback for her. Sonnet didn't seem affected by the question in the least. She just nodded and continued to dip the bread. Finally she reached up in the cabinet and pulled down a bowl.

"Yeah, and I haven't had a period either," Sonnet said quickly without looking at her and dipped the ladle in the pot to bring up a serving of rich red goodness.

Suddenly she again felt that nervous quiver in the pit of her stomach. It tickled and made her giggle. She turned to her mother.

"Sonnet, is there something you need to tell me?" Yolanda asked, her voice heavy and showing sadness.

Margaret was both excited and scared for Sonnet that night as they sat up late talking about the coming of a baby.

"I'm not as thrilled as I thought I would be having Wilson's baby," Sonnet admitted.

"Are you gonna tell him?" Margaret asked.

"Hellfire nooo, as Grandma would say." Sonnet laughed.

"I really don't need him making my life any harder by trying to get out of it," she went on to say.

Margaret agreed.

"Is Mom feeling better?" Margaret asked.

Sonnet looked around, toward the door.

"Are you kidding? She about flipped," Sonnet whispered. "Kept talking about life repeating itself. I hope she doesn't go crazy again over this."

Margaret too felt instant concern.

Suddenly Yolanda came into the room. She had been crying. Sonnet immediately jumped up and hugged her mother tight, afraid she was having another bout of deep depression. Yolanda held her back and sat on the bed. She patted the place beside her. Sonnet sat.

"Mama, I'm so sorry . . . I didn't mean to—" Sonnet began, only to have Yolanda shush her.

"I just got off the phone with my mother," Yolanda sniffed, finishing up the good cry she had just had after emptying her heart of all its secrets while talking with her mother.

"Sonnet, I have something to tell you," Yolanda began. "You too, Margaret. I have to tell you girls this and when I'm done, I hope you both don't hate me. I hope . . ." she said, taking a deep breath and then wiping away more tears that had started to come.

26

Leita was very excited when the girls called and told her about the baby. She had just heard from Justin and he was coming out for Christmas with his band. They were going to be performing in Los Angeles and he was going to come see her. Margaret hadn't gotten a letter from him in months. Leita admitted it was the first call she had received from him since his birthday way back in August.

"We're going to come over to see you guys when he comes. He said he wanted to. I was beginning to think he had forgotten us," Leita bubbled. "Oh my God, Sonnet, what will he think?" she said, thinking out loud.

"Think? What do you mean? He won't think anything. He's the one living in New York," Sonnet snipped, showing her jealously before realizing it. "He's probably got a million girls hanging on his big ol' self."

Sonnet and Margaret then giggled at the thought of *big ol' Justin* as a playboy.

Leita looked at the CD cover. There was no more *big ol' Justin*. He had changed, and apparently Margaret and Sonnet didn't know about it.

"Haven't ya'll heard his CD?" Leita asked. "Sonnet, he wrote a song about you on it. It's called 'My Sonnet.'"

"You are so silly, Leita. That is what a sonnet is, a poem, a verse, and besides, I'm sure he didn't write the song, he probably just plays the horn on it. I heard it on the radio. I heard the words . . . they aren't about me," Sonnet went on. "It was really nice though, they're good, especially the woman," she admitted carefully.

"She's very beautiful too," Leita added, looking at the cover.

Donelle's dark eyes could be seen so clearly, even in the picture. They were full of a fire and a passion that Leita knew even Justin had not missed—who could?

"She is?" asked Sonnet, her voice reaching a high pitch.

Margaret noticed.

"Yes, she is. You need to get out more. The CD is in all the record stores," Leita said. Suddenly, noticing Sonnet's silence, she decided she wouldn't say any more about it. Sonnet seeing Justin face-to-face would be just what she deserved for not waiting for his outer beauty to catch up with the inner—that's what Leita thought anyway, looking at the picture of Justin again, shaking her head in disbelief.

They finished their conversation and hung up the phone.

"It will be good to see Justin again, I miss him," Margaret said, sounding bubbly and excited.

Sonnet just feigned disinterest and waddled into the kitchen to get something to eat.

"I think he misses you too. And I know for a fact this song is yours. He told me back in school he had written a song for you. For when you two got married," Margaret called out.

"Married?" Sonnet said out loud, rubbing her large belly. She filled two bowls with the stew and went back in to Margaret, who began eating it without hesitation.

"Would you marry him if he asked you?" Margaret asked,

her mouth full. "I mean fat and all, with all you've been through, if he asked, would you?"

"Justin wouldn't want me—fat and all. I mean, he didn't even want me as a friend anymore. And I don't blame him." Sonnet looked down into her bowl, thinking about the last time she had seen him, how awful she had been to him. "But I'd give anything to have a guy like him back in my life right now," she admitted and then, feeling the baby kick, she giggled. "Well, almost anything." She smiled and patted her stomach; Margaret too patted the little protrusions that appeared on Sonnet's belly. "Yep, fat and all," she added with a grin.

"You know, Sonnet, it's like you were on the road to one another and wham! A big ol' detour sign went up and now look," Margaret said, referring to the baby. She shook her head. "Just like with Mom . . ." she added.

"But, in his last letter, he said, 'tell *everyone* hello,' *everyone*." Margaret winked.

"You're as bad as Leita." Sonnet giggled, thinking about the time, wondering if she would make it to the record store before it closed. The woman's voice was beautiful. As Justin accompanied her on that saxophone of his, it sounded as if they were talking to each other in the song, almost making love to each other through their music. No, Margaret and Leita were wrong; that song was not for her . . . it was for the woman whose voice seduced the music from his horn. Sonnet decided not to go out on the cold night.

Christmas was quickly approaching and so was the end of Sonnet's pregnancy. Yolanda nervously piddled around the apartment. She had hung new curtains and bought three new dresses, as if she were planning a trip and couldn't decide what to wear. She would come into Margaret's room while the girls were visiting there, modeling the dresses for them, one at a time.

"How do I look in this?" she would ask, almost dancing around the room in the dress. Both girls were confused watching the performance but attempted to be helpful anyway. They had never seen her so blissful.

It was finally winter break and Sonnet could get off the road for a couple of weeks. Margaret had started feeling a bit stronger and was up most of the day now. Mildred had come by to spend the evening with them. She had brought Sonnet a quilt for the baby that she had made herself. Margaret quickly wrapped up in it on the sofa.

"Wrong, baby." Mildred laughed, seeing Margaret all bundled up in the blanket—making herself quite at home in it. "Oh, by the way," she led in, sounding very nonchalant, "I saw Hattie Brown today."

Yolanda's eyes darted to Sonnet, who was examining the quilt, unconcerned with their conversation. She then hurried her mother into the kitchen. Mildred's face was twisted in confusion.

"What is wrong with you? Sonnet knows the truth . . . I mean, hell, we all know the truth now—thank you very much," Mildred said, smirking again as her mind mulled over the facts again. Sonnet was Joseph's daughter all right, just like she had always thought.

"Yes, but I didn't tell her he might be coming into town for Christmas." Yolanda wrung her hands nervously.

"You didn't tell her? Oh, Yolanda, when you gonna get straight and just say things the way they are?" Mildred fussed.

"With the baby coming any day, I thought she might get too upset or something."

"Well, I think you're all crazy, but anyway, Hattie and I were talking and she let it slip that Joseph is not married right now," Mildred said.

Yolanda sighed with relief. Mildred rolled her eyes.

"And then wha'd you say, and then wha'd she say?" Yolanda asked eagerly.

"I said, 'Oh, Joseph's not married right now?' And she said, 'No, he's not, Mildred,'" Mildred mocked. "Girl, you sound like you're seventeen again," she said, finally giving way to laughter.

"Be nice if I looked it, Mama," Yolanda said, looking at her reflection in one of her shiny skillets. "It'd be so nice if I was," she added.

Mildred gave her a hug.

"Live life today, Yolanda. You can't change yesterday," Mildred said.

It was Saturday, three days before Christmas. Margaret had never spent a Christmas without her father before and Yolanda thought perhaps she would make contact with Frank—for her sake. Margaret was sitting on the sofa still bundled in the baby's blanket; she had been wrapped up in it for days now. Margaret loved that blanket and didn't plan on giving it up.

"Not for some snot-nose little bum that won't even appreciate it," Margaret argued when Sonnet tried to take it.

"That's his father—now give up the blanket." Sonnet playfully tugged.

Margaret shook her head in refusal.

That night Yolanda moved onto the couch with Margaret and cuddled her. They hadn't cuddled in years. It felt good.

"I was thinking," Yolanda began. She had Margaret's attention now. "I was thinking I'd call Frank," she continued. She didn't look at Margaret but she could tell Margaret was staring at her intently.

"Why?" Margaret asked, with panic building in her voice. "Why would you do that?" She then unwrapped herself from the blanket. "Here . . . here's the blanket. Please don't call Daddy," Margaret pleaded.

Yolanda looked at her.

"Honey, I thought that was what you wanted," Yolanda said.

"Heck no! I'm not well enough for him right now, I may never be well enough for him again. Now you know, he hates me sick, and we all know I'm always sick," Margaret said, sounding almost sarcastic now. Yolanda hugged her tight, wrapping the blanket back around her slender shoulder.

Just then, Sonnet came in the front door. Her face was twisted and she looked dazed. She looked over at her mother and Margaret bundled on the sofa. Yolanda could tell something was wrong. She jumped up, thinking it was time for the baby.

Yolanda panicked. "Sonnet what is it?"

"Mom, something really funny happened in the store just now. There was this man in there and he stopped me and told me to remind you about Christmas dinner." Sonnet looked deep into her mother's eyes. "He said his name was Joseph Brown," she said, letting her words hang in the air.

Yolanda jumped up.

"Oh my gosh, what else happened? Wha'd he say, wha'd you say?" Yolanda asked excitedly, forgetting all about the possibility of Sonnet being in labor.

"Nothing. I just stood there with my mouth gaped open, looking all retarded. I guess because I was staring at him so hard he thought I was crazy . . . oh, and, Mom, he asked me about my baby!" Sonnet's eyes were wide now and filling with tears.

Yolanda reached for her. She was still holding two large bags of deli chicken.

"I just met my father and I was holding deli chicken in the grocery store." Sonnet started crying. "My hair was a mess. I'm as big as a house! Why didn't you tell me he was coming here? That he was here in town?" Sonnet's voice was high pitched, almost a squeal now, as she sniveled.

Just then Margaret noticed the shadowed figure of a man,

coming toward the front door. She couldn't get her mother's or Sonnet's attention to tell them. So she went to the door herself and opened it before the man knocked.

The tall, dark, and handsome Joseph Brown smiled at the frail little girl who looked a lot like Frank Patterson. He glanced in at Yolanda and the girl from the grocery store.

"But I'm not ready to meet him, Mom," Sonnet whined.

Margaret was clearing her throat, loudly, now. Finally, she just yelled out in a loud voice, "Someone is here!" Yolanda and Sonnet turned to the door.

Joseph stepped into the house. Yolanda's grin was bigger than her girls had ever seen or thought her face capable to hold.

Suddenly, Sonnet and Margaret understood everything. In just that instant, they could see love in their mother's eyes for the first time and they understood the lie she had lived for over eighteen years. Her entire face changed right before their eyes.

Yolanda smoothed back her hair and straightened her apron. She had on big thick wool socks and looked a lot more homey than she had planned to, when seeing Joseph again.

Joseph, on the other hand, was very sharp looking with only a bit of gray showing around his temples. He surely was the most handsome older man Margaret had ever seen.

"Hey, Loni, gal," he said to Yolanda as Texas flowed from his lips.

Both Sonnet and Margaret could have sworn at that moment they could see their mother blush.

"Well, Joseph, hello." Yolanda giggled. "I see you've met Sonnet and this is my other daughter, Margaret," she introduced, still a little nervous—fussing with her hair and wringing her hands.

Joseph nodded at Margaret and turned his attention back to Sonnet. He again noticed her stomach and smiled brightly.

"You got a grandbaby on the way, it looks like?" he said

to Yolanda, pointing toward Sonnet, who stood frozen holding the bag of chicken. "I ain't never been blessed that way. See, me and my ex, well, let's just say she wasn't very motherly. We never had children," he said.

"Oh, I see," Yolanda said, trying to control her breathing so her words didn't sound weak or trembling. "What, brings you by?"

"Well, Mama said I should beat it over here and have a talk wit you 'bout some thangs," he began.

Yolanda took a deep breath. She felt almost light-headed now. "Oooh, she did?"

"Yep. Seems your mama and my mama been talkin' and now they say, we need to be talkin'," Joseph repeated himself, only slightly glancing at Sonnet, who still stood frozen, staring at him.

For a second, Margaret started to feel out of place and thought about leaving the room, but this man was all too handsome and this was all too exciting to miss. So she simply reached into the bag of chicken that Sonnet was still holding and took out a leg and a biscuit, sat on the couch, and began to eat, feeling totally entertained. Everyone suddenly turned and looked at her.

"Go on," Margaret said, motioning for the conversation to continue.

Joseph chuckled as he watched her.

"Now that little girl there's got the right idea," Joseph said, taking off his jacket, making himself at home.

"Oh, Joseph, I'm sorry," Yolanda said, taking the bags from Sonnet. "Please stay for dinner. I mean, it's just deli chicken, but you're more than welcome . . . I mean, it's not what I had planned for Christmas dinner but . . ." Yolanda babbled on, leading Joseph into the kitchen.

"You used to be a pretty good cook, if I recollect. Don't think this little dinner here is gonna change Christmas, I can't wait," Joseph said, chuckling as he followed her.

"I'm still a pretty good cook." Yolanda was heard flirting playfully.

"Is that right?" Joseph said, flirting back.

Sonnet sat on the couch next to Margaret, who was working tenaciously on her piece of chicken.

"That's my father," Sonnet finally said. Margaret nodded.

"Yeah, and he's cute, too. I mean, for an older guy," she said between bites.

Just then, Joseph came from the kitchen, stared at the girls sitting on the sofa, and then disappeared back into the kitchen. Within a minute or two he stepped back into the living room a second time and stood with his hands on his hips. He was making Sonnet nervous. This time when he went into the kitchen, Sonnet followed him. Margaret reminded her to bring more chicken back with her when she returned.

When Sonnet entered the kitchen she saw Yolanda at the table. She was crying and Joseph was leaning over her with his cheek to hers.

"It's okay, Loni," he said softly.

"I thought you hated me. I mean, I wanted you too . . . oh, hell, Joseph, I didn't know what I wanted anymore. I just wanted . . ." Yolanda attempted to explain while Joseph shushed her. Finally she looked over at Sonnet and then up at Joseph.

"Frank said he would kill me and you if I ever told you about Sonnet. I was such a fool, I believed him," she admitted now.

The words hit Sonnet like a brick, what a hell her mother had lived through being with Frank Patterson.

"I would have taken you with me if I'd known, Loni. You gotta believe me, I swear to God I would have. To hell with Frank," Joseph said, stroking her hair now, looking over at Sonnet. Yolanda cried even harder now. Without letting go of Yolanda's shoulder, he outstretched his free hand to Sonnet.

"Hi, I'm your daddy," he introduced himself, sounding very matter-of-fact. "And so I guess that little one's my grandbaby too," he said with a grin, pointing at Sonnet's belly.

She nodded and shook his hand.

Joseph was a funny fellow but Sonnet knew she would get used to him. It was obvious he still loved her mother and that was all that was important.

It hadn't taken quite a lifetime to find his way back to her despite the detours and now it looked like the both of them had found their way to true happiness. They would be together . . . as it was meant to be.

Christmas was a full house this year, Joseph Brown and his parents and the girl's grandparents and many new and old friends that Yolanda had from that small town and the life she had lived there before leaving with Frank what seemed like a lifetime ago.

The girls called Leita.

"No, and he didn't even call. I'm very hurt," Leita admitted. "It's not like him to be like that," she added.

"Well, sometimes people get sidetracked," said Sonnet, trying to make her feel better.

"Not Justin, something must have happened," she said determinedly.

27

Christmas for Justin had been spent on the road. The band had played San Francisco and all were tired and cranky. They had been bickering all week. None of the members had seen their families and Justin had missed his connection with Leita in San Jose. He tried to call from the Los Angeles Airport, "Come on, man!" Grant called, causing him to hang up before the call connected.

He sat alone and quiet on the plane now, thinking about San Jose, thinking about home.

Donelle got up from her seat and sat next to him. However, she was the last person he wanted to talk to tonight.

"What do you want?" he asked, his tone hateful.

"You're still mad at me?" she said, smiling sheepishly and with an unearned innocence.

The steward bringing champagne wished them all a merry Christmas. Justin took the flute and drank without speaking.

"I told you Marten was an old friend," Donelle began. Justin glared at her.

"Yeah, well," was all he said.

"You act like you and I are lovers, Justin," she began to explain.

"I want to know what in the hell you call what we are," Justin said, trying to keep his voice down, but failing. Grant noticed the two of them.

"Sex," she answered flatly.

Justin wanted to deny it but he couldn't. He didn't love Donelle any more than she loved him and he knew it. She had been a good sexual teacher and he was grateful to her for sharing her beautiful body with him, but he didn't love her.

But still . . .

It had been more, the humiliation of it all ending the way it did, with him walking in on her and Marten in the bed that way. He had felt more degradation than hurt.

"Besides, if you really loved me, you wouldn't call me other people's names while, uh . . . you know," she remarked coolly, sipping her champagne.

Justin looked at her, suddenly embarrassed. Had his innermost thought come out? Had he actually called her Sonnet by accident while they were having sex?

"What are you talking about?" he asked, looking at her square on now.

She patted his leg softly, and then slipped her hand closer to his sensitive zone. "Every time after we made love, and you slept, I would touch you . . . here," she whispered in his ear, lightly stroking his groin area. He became instantly aroused. "You would moan and say her name." Donelle closed her eyes now. "Sonnet," she purred in mimicry of how he sounded when the words crept from his dreams.

Justin, in his embarrassment, turned quickly to the window.

"Talk about your crowded bed," she said now, returning to a normal volume, all traces of softness gone. "I'll say this," she went on, "getting to her through me is just plain ol' back-ass-ward." She finished up her champagne in one gulp. She then stood to return to her seat.

He looked up at her but could say nothing as she walked away.

There was a knock at the door. Sonnet went to answer it without looking out the window first. She thought it must be her grandfather coming to pick up her grandmother, who had come by for the evening. Sonnet was due any day now and so her grandmother was coming by every day—just in case. Sonnet had also hoped it might be Joseph. He had stayed on awhile longer; he was looking around for a house to buy.

Sonnet stared hard at the tall man in the camel hair overcoat, not recognizing him at first, but then suddenly, when he smiled, she knew it had to be Justin.

But surely, this couldn't be Justin—this beautiful tall man. This tall, *thin* man couldn't be Justin.

In shock, she backed away from the door.

When Justin walked in, Margaret nearly leaped from the sofa. Her squeal brought Yolanda from the kitchen. She too was surprised at Justin's appearance. She immediately thought about Sonnet and the baby.

Life was so very unfair.

Justin hugged Yolanda tight, lifting her off the floor before her thoughts had come back to the now, and she let out a yelp.

"Hey. Mrs. J, got anything sweet baking?" he asked, sounding happy and playful.

"Who is this fine young man?" Mildred asked, admiring Justin. He reminded her of her own husband as a younger man . . . freckles and all.

"This is me and Sonnet's oldest friend, Justin Hamilton," Margaret bubbled, hanging on to his arm after getting her hug in. Justin looked at Sonnet and smiled.

Sonnet's heart melted.

Justin was always smiling when he looked at her—no matter what.

Margaret had talked on and on during dinner, trying to catch Justin up on their lives. She had been more excited than she had been in weeks. It was good to see her that way. However, she had tired herself out and had to go to bed right after the meal. She made Justin promise to stop in her room before he left.

"I'll hunt you down and kill you like a dog if you don't say good-bye to me," Margaret threatened, sounding a little short of breath now, while her mother helped her into bed.

"Yeah, like you can catch me," Justin joked, trying to hide his true feelings about Margaret's health issues.

"Sonnet missed you so bad, Justin," Margaret whispered in his ear when he hugged her. "I didn't though," she added.

"I know you didn't." He laughed, kissing her forehead. "Now you get some rest. I'm not going without saying good-bye," he promised. She smiled, closing her eyes.

Sonnet and Justin sat alone in the kitchen at the table looking at each other. They hadn't said much to one another all evening.

"So, uh, how is Margaret really doing?" he asked.

"She has her up days and down. Her heart's only working at about eighty percent, so she's limited, but you know Margaret . . ." Sonnet smiled, thinking about her sister—tough as nails.

"And your mom?" he asked.

Sonnet rolled her eyes, thinking about her mother and Joseph—and their love affair.

"Crazy, my mother is crazy." Sonnet laughed. Justin's eyes stayed on hers.

"And you, you with someone?" he finally asked.

Sonnet put her hand on her belly.

"No, actually. I'm just pregnant," she answered flatly.

She couldn't decide what she was feeling at that particular moment. She had studied his face all evening. It was the same Justin, all right. Every time he laughed it reminded her of the Justin she had spent her life with. She should have felt so much more comfortable, but instead she was unsure of everything she was feeling and it was becoming quite unsettling.

"Yeah, I kinda noticed." He chuckled.

"You?" she asked.

"No, I'm not pregnant, but thanks for asking," Justin joked, trying not to think about Donelle and the night he had found her with Marten. He tried now to think about what she had told him on the plane. He shook his head, looking more serious now. "Naw, just waiting for you, I guess," he said, looking straight at her.

"Oh, did you like your song?" he went on, quickly changing the subject.

"So, it really was my song, eh? Leita was right." Sonnet smiled, acting as if she hadn't heard his remark about having waited for her.

They sat in silence for a moment.

Sonnet's heart was full of emotion. She couldn't put her finger on just which emotion, but she did know this, she never wanted Justin to leave again, she didn't want to spend her life as her mother had—without the man she truly loved.

Suddenly they began to speak at the same time.

"You go first," Justin offered.

"No, you," she said, hesitating.

"Okay, I will," Justin began, standing up from the table. He began to pace the kitchen and then stopping he looked down at her at the table—puffy and swollen with pregnancy. "You screwed up," Justin said.

Sonnet shook her head and raised her hand. “Wait, I’ll go first,” she said now.

“No, seriously, you ruined your life, our life, and for what?” he asked, flailing his arms.

“Well, maybe certain things are just meant to happen, Justin,” she began, sounding sheepish. Suddenly she thought about the woman on the CD and the life Justin surely had in New York and how he hadn’t written. “Hey, and besides, maybe my life isn’t so ruined. I mean, I’ve found my real father—great guy! Me and Margaret are as close as ever. Oh, and I’ve got my baby to look forward to,” Sonnet defended, while counting her blessings on her fingers.

Justin thought about his life in New York, and some of the choices he had made. He couldn’t say that he had done too much better in the “making all the right choices” department—life on the road, Donelle . . . he could stop there and be tied with Sonnet in the ‘big mistake’ category.

“I’ve always wanted to marry you,” he said suddenly. “I’ve always loved you and—”

Sonnet stopped him. “Justin, if you had you would never have been a part of what you’re doing now. Some things are really meant to be certain ways—trust me. Some detours are for the best, they take you out of the way . . . like, you know, like, taking the scenic route of your life,” she went on, mentally finishing up her conversation with Margaret.

“What are you talking about?” Justin asked, wondering when she had gotten so philosophical.

“No really, look at my mom and Joseph. Even after it all—the lies, me, my da . . . I mean, Frank—even after all of that, they’re still so in love,” Sonnet explained, thinking of her mother’s face and how bright it looked lately.

Justin smiled at what Sonnet had unwittingly implied with her statement.

“So are we still in love?” he asked.

Sonnet felt caught in her own words. When had Justin gotten so smooth?

Sonnet's belly tightened again with a contraction. She'd been having them all evening. At first she just thought they had come with the excitement of Justin showing up, and would go away soon, but as she now felt moisture running down her legs she realized something else was going on. Justin's eyes widened with excitement.

It was late now, and the nurse was giving everyone the evil eye. It had been four hours of hard labor with a smooth birth following. The baby weighed in at eight-five. After another clearing of the throat from Nurse Sandy, everyone slowly began to make their way from Sonnet's room.

"Well, honey, I have to get back to Margaret," Yolanda said, after kissing Sonnet's forehead.

"She's mad as hell that she had to stay home." Joseph chuckled.

"I'll try to get her here tomorrow, though," Yolanda said, yawning and stretching.

Sonnet laughed. Joseph handed Yolanda her coat and scarf. He smiled at Sonnet and then glanced one more time in the basinet at his new granddaughter.

"So what we calling her?" Joseph asked. Sonnet smiled at her father and then looked up at Justin, who stood beside her bed. He had been with her the whole time—assisting, even, in the delivery.

"Justine," she answered, feeling Justin's arm tightening around her shoulder.

Joseph nodded, giving Justin the thumbs-up.

The room emptied except for Justin now. The nurse, thinking he was the father, allowed him a bit more time.

Justin moved over to the basinet, looking the baby over. Her head was full of thick rich dark hair and her skin was a bright red. Justin could already see resemblances of Wilson on her little face. He didn't care though—it didn't matter, it was just another little detour—one of life's scenic routes, no doubt.

"Hello, I'm Justin," he introduced himself. "I'm kinda in love with your mama over there, even though we have a couple of things to work out," he continued, looking over his shoulder at Sonnet, who was drifting in and out of sleep. "You see, I want to ask her to marry me, but I need to be sure she's gonna always love me," he said.

"Always," he heard her say. He turned to her only to see her smiling weakly at him. He went back to her bedside. Their eyes met in a deep moment and then, moving closer to her, he kissed her for the first time.